Cord's eyes were like shattered pieces of glass—cold and clear and completely lifeless.

Georgia was perilously close to tears, but as she lifted her chin, she vowed silently that she would not cry. "It's over, Cord," she said. "I just want to forget this ever happened. I don't want to do anything that will keep reminding me of it, day after day—I just want to get on with my life."

He must have seen the fear and indecision in her eyes, because he gave a quiet grunt of disbelief. "Still running scared, huh, Georgie?" His voice was low and intimate, and his quiet utterance of the name he'd always called her sent shivers down her spine.

Damn you, Cord, she wanted to shout. *You were the one who ran. You were the one who left me behind in this damnable town....*

Dear Reader,

This month it's my pleasure to bring you one of the most-requested books we've ever published: *Loving Evangeline* by Linda Howard. This story features Robert Cannon, first seen in her tremendously popular *Duncan's Bride,* and in Evangeline Shaw he meets a woman who is his perfect match—and then some! Don't miss it!

Don't miss the rest of this month's books, either, or you'll end up regretting it. We've also got *A Very Convenient Marriage* by Dallas Schulze, and the next in Marilyn Pappano's "Southern Knights" miniseries, *Regarding Remy.* And then there's *Surrogate Dad* by Marion Smith Collins, as well as *Not His Wife* by Sally Tyler Hayes and *Georgia on My Mind* by Clara Wimberly. In short, a stellar lineup by some of the best authors going, and they're all yours—courtesy of Silhouette Intimate Moments.

Enjoy!

Leslie Wainger
Senior Editor and Editorial Coordinator

Please address questions and book requests to:
Silhouette Reader Service
U.S.: 3010 Walden Ave., P.O. Box 1325, Buffalo, NY 14269
Canadian: P.O. Box 609, Fort Erie, Ont. L2A 5X3

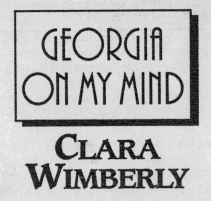

GEORGIA ON MY MIND

CLARA WIMBERLY

Published by Silhouette Books

America's Publisher of Contemporary Romance

SILHOUETTE BOOKS

ISBN 0-373-07612-6

GEORGIA ON MY MIND

Copyright © 1994 by Clara Wimberly

This edition published by arrangement with Harlequin Enterprises B.V.

® and TM are trademarks of Harlequin Enterprises B.V., used under
license. Trademarks indicated with ® are registered in the United States
Patent and Trademark Office, the Canadian Trade Marks Office and in
other countries.

Printed in U.S.A.

Books by Clara Wimberly

Silhouette Intimate Moments

Ryan Blake's Revenge #521
Georgia on My Mind #612

CLARA WIMBERLY

writes her novels in a one-room cabin in the woods, built for her by her husband and two sons. She loves American history and traveling to old settlements and villages, where she says she finds a lot of wonderful ideas and inspiration. "I suppose if I have been influenced by anything, it is the South and the area where I live," Clara says. "In the mountains there are hundreds of quaint stories and unusual characters."

To Sharon, Jan and Susan—
for "girls' night out."
It's good having writers for friends!

Chapter 1

It was bitterly cold at the old city cemetery. And even though the trees on the hill and those that lay below it were full and lush with autumn leaves of orange and yellow, in Georgia Ashley's heart, it seemed as if winter had already come.

In fact, she couldn't imagine that spring would ever come again, or that green grass would ever cover the raw, red Georgia earth on the new grave that she stared at.

Georgia reached down and wiped away a few windblown leaves from the flat bronze marker.

"Bob Ashley," it read. "Born October 22." Today would have been her husband's birthday. If they hadn't been separated when he died, they no doubt would have celebrated, as usual—dinner at the club, dancing, laughing. Too many drinks, too many of Bob's loud stale jokes.

"And I'd have gone home miserable, as usual," Georgia muttered to herself. She wondered if somewhere, somehow, Bob could hear her. And she wished for the thousandth time since his death three months ago that she could ask him what had happened. Why on earth had he ever gotten involved with a woman like Sheila Jamison, the woman everyone said was responsible for his death?

It was still the talk of Farmington, Georgia, her hometown, a small settlement that lay nestled in the foothills of north Georgia's mountain country. And why shouldn't it be?

Murder/suicide was an unusual occurrence here. Georgia couldn't remember it happening in her lifetime.

Everyone in town had looked upon Bob Ashley as the all-American boy. Successful businessman, owner of his own real estate agency, son of one of north Georgia's wealthiest families. Handsome and charming. Even now, after all that had happened, Georgia had to admit that he could be very charming when he chose to be.

They'd married right out of college. He the football star and hometown hero—she the homecoming queen, the sweetheart of the prom.

She wondered what people would think if they knew what their marriage had really been like. If they knew that she hadn't been a virgin on her wedding night, if they knew that she had been in love with someone else.

Georgia shook her head, trying to banish the thoughts and the regrets that always seemed to come when she thought of her marriage... and the reason for it.

It was true—she hadn't loved Bob. Probably never had. But she had become engaged to him, to the best catch in town, as her mother so often told her friends at the club.

She'd always wondered if Bob knew what had happened that summer just before their wedding, when he came home from working in Atlanta. Had he sensed how fragile, how vulnerable she'd been? Had he guessed the reason... that there was someone else? Had he even cared?

Or had he been like everyone else in Farmington—like Georgia herself? Stuck in the traditions, the expectations, of their small-town southern culture. Enchanted with a fairy-tale belief of what happiness should be.

"Probably," she whispered cynically to herself. Now those images had been replaced by reality and something definitely more sinister.

Her husband's murder had happened on a rainy, stormy night three months ago, when the summer heat had lain heavily over the small southern town. When Sheila Jamison had put a gun to Bob Ashley's head, they said, and then killed herself. Bob and Georgia's marriage had been in serious trouble for a year before that. They'd lived in separate bedrooms in their big Victorian home. And that rainy night had put an end forever to any reconciliation of the so-called perfect marriage, and Farmington's own personal and coveted southern tradition of the football hero and his homecoming-queen bride.

Georgia stood perfectly still, her eyes dry against the October wind that gusted across the top of the hill, blowing her short blond hair into a sweeping tumble of curls. She still couldn't cry. All she felt was sadness and a deep wrenching bitterness that her husband and his lover had betrayed her in a way that made her humiliation and grief public... and made everyone wonder, no doubt, how she had failed him and why he had turned to another woman.

The answer to that was why she came, even now, to the grave of a man she hadn't loved. In a southern town like Farmington, tradition, doing what was expected, was everything.

Suddenly there was a movement in the cemetery below that caught Georgia's eye. She held her breath and watched as a sleek, black motorcycle cruised slowly along the winding road, making its way past the dark swaying cedars, through the spray of falling autumn leaves and into the main part of the cemetery.

The rider seemed familiar, so painfully familiar that Georgia became still and breathless. She knew everyone in Farmington and this was not a vehicle she recognized. But the look and the sound of it brought back memories of another time when she was young and carefree. Memories of a man she hadn't seen in ten years.

She could hear the low smooth hum of the engine as the rider pulled the machine to a stop at the foot of the hill where she stood watching. She couldn't seem to drag her eyes away from the vision, or stop her heartbeat from accelerating oddly.

He was dressed in black—black jeans and boots and a long black western coat. Even his helmet had a dark-tinted shield pulled low that hid his face. She watched as he swung one long leg across the seat and banged the kickstand down with a booted foot. She thought there was a familiar anger and impatience in that telling movement and for moments she stood spellbound.

Georgia watched the man pull the helmet from his head and run his fingers through hair that shone blue-black in the morning light. His hair was long, making a dark swath of color against the collar of a white shirt that peeked from beneath his black coat.

Georgia felt her heart stop, then begin again in a tumbling chaotic rhythm. She could feel it beating against her ribs and in her throat, pounding oddly as she tried to catch her breath.

"It can't be," she whispered. Her hand went up to shade her eyes from the glare of light as she stared hard at the man who was now walking rather purposefully toward a grave, one that Georgia recognized only too well—Sheila Jamison's, her husband's lover and murderer.

She'd been told that Cord Jamison had come home three months ago for his sister, Sheila's, funeral. And that he was responsible for the huge pink granite monument that marked her grave and looked so much like something Sheila would have picked herself.

But Georgia had not seen him. She hadn't seen him in ten years, not since the day he rode out of town on a beat-up old motorcycle, much different from the sleek, obviously expensive one he was riding today.

Georgia felt a deep wrenching sob coming up from somewhere deep in her chest. And for a moment, it was as if ten years had simply vanished, leaving the same pain she'd felt that day when Cord rode away from Farmington...away from her.

He'd been the wild boy in town, a long-haired rebel from the wrong side of the tracks. A young man who gained her parents' fierce disapproval when they learned he'd brought her home from a dance, riding on the back of that loud, dangerous motorcycle. Waking the neighbors in their elegant homes along the quietest, wealthiest section of town and incurring her father's wrath because his only daughter had stooped to keeping company with such a person as the notorious Cord Jamison.

"I know you are grown now, Georgia, and of age," her father had told her that next morning at breakfast. "But you are to stay away from that rabble-rouser. The boy is trouble. He's no good. His father was in prison when he died— a sorry worthless excuse for a man, if I ever saw one. And do I have to tell you what his mother is? What that wild, ill-dressed little sister of his is bound to become, too?"

"Horace," Georgia's mother warned quietly, her brown eyes soft with concern as she looked from her husband to her only daughter. Such blunt talk was not in keeping with what Regina Blake considered proper for a southern young lady to hear.

"Stay out of this, Regina." Georgia could see the anger building in her father. He had a terrible temper and in his house there was no room for anyone's opinion except his own. "You have babied and spoiled the girl since she was born. It's no wonder that she has no regard for her position in this town."

"Don't you mean *your* position, Daddy?" Georgia didn't usually defy her father. But she had graduated from college that spring and her being away from home and her graduation had given her a yearning for independence that seemed to cause an argument with him every time they were near.

"You watch the tone of your voice when you speak to me, young lady. This is still my house and I am still your father."

Georgia had lifted her chin in defiance. "You don't know Cord Jamison," she'd declared. "You don't know anything about him."

"I know this," he said, his eyes narrowing dangerously. "I know that you are engaged to Bob Ashley. And by God, you had better not do anything to change that. I will not be disgraced in this town." He walked closer to Georgia, staring hard into her eyes. "Do you hear me? That wedding will go off without a hitch this fall, just the way we've all planned. And if you do anything to spoil that, so help me God..."

"Horace...please." Georgia's mother came forward, as she always did in these situations. Soothing, trying to make peace...taking her husband's arm and pulling him back toward the table. Her dark eyes turned toward her daughter and there was a mixture of sympathy and warning there. "You know he's right, darling," she said in her soft voice. "Cord Jamison is not the young man for you."

They hadn't let her say that Cord Jamison was sweet and tender, that he treated her with a respect and kindness that surprised and touched her. Or that he had rescued her. Swooped into the dimly lighted parking lot of the National Guard Armory just as she was escaping from Bob Ashley's too-ardent, drunken, pawing embrace. Even if they were engaged, it was disgusting and frightening to her when he behaved that way.

My God, how had she ended up marrying him? Marrying the very man that Cord had rescued her from that night?

He'd taken Bob by the collar and jerked him from the car, dragging him across the ground and throwing him up against the hood of the sports car that Bob's parents had given him for graduation.

"Are you all right?" Cord had asked, glancing from the corner of his eyes at Georgia. "Did he hurt you?"

"No," she'd managed to say. "No, he's just drunk. He . . . he didn't hurt me."

"Get your hands off me, Jamison," Bob had growled, trying futilely to untangle himself from the big hands of the man who'd ridden like an avenging angel out of the night and into the parking lot. "This is none of your business."

"No? Well, I just made it my business," he'd said, shaking Bob for emphasis.

Georgia had always been aware of Cord Jamison. At the snack shop across from the courthouse on Saturday nights, at the local football games. And she knew, with a woman's instinct, that he was aware of her. She'd seen him watching her, had even met those blue eyes with a flirtatious smile of her own once or twice.

She had never known where he'd come from that sultry night or how he'd known she was in trouble.

Cord had practically lifted Bob off the ground, holding him by the front of his shirt and shaking him like a small defenseless puppy.

"If you ever hurt her... if you ever treat her like this again, Ashley, you'll have to answer to me. Do you understand?"

Georgia had been shaking, literally trembling from the intensity of Cord Jamison's threats and the pure physical masculinity in his every movement. As she'd stood watching, noting the scuffed boots beneath worn, faded jeans that hugged his muscular thighs and hips, she had been mesmerized. He was an enigma in Farmington, at least to girls like her. He was the rebel with too-long, untamed flowing black hair and dark skin that hinted of long-forgotten Cherokee blood, lost somewhere in his family's past. The boy with startling aqua blue eyes that twinkled and teased and challenged. He was the young man that all their parents had warned them about.

Georgia wasn't the only girl in town who thought he was the hottest, sexiest man she'd ever seen. But she knew he was as forbidden to her as the loud roadside honky-tonks selling illegal whiskey just outside the city limits.

Was that what had drawn her to him that summer? That summer when she'd experimented with her own rebellion and independence? That sense of the forbidden, that hot, elusive curiosity that ran through a young girl's mind and made her spend numerous nights wondering what it would be like to touch those dark muscular arms... kiss his wide, sensuous mouth? Or had she instinctively been trying to prove that her engagement to Bob Ashley was a farce and that she had ideas of her own about the man she wanted?

All those memories came back in a rush as she watched him now in the cemetery below her, noting the way his hand reached out to lightly touch the pink monument. And when he knelt down and brushed away the grass from Sheila's grave, Georgia felt her eyes welling up with tears.

No, it had been more than the forbidden that had attracted her to him, more than sexual curiosity or rebellion against her father and her preplanned, narrow life. She'd recognized the tenderness in him then, the sweet protectiveness and sensitivity that he tried to hide behind his tough facade. She could see it now, even from this distance, in the way he moved, in the quiet slump of his shoulders and low bend of his dark head as he stared down at his sister's grave.

Georgia thought she hated Sheila Jamison for what she'd done. And she could hardly bear the thought of anyone grieving for her or taking her side. But now, Cord's silent grief made it impossible for her to continue hating the woman.

She knew Cord had always loved Sheila despite her reputation and the hard edge that she'd acquired over the years. To him, she was still the little sister who needed his protection, the girl who everyone taunted and called names. And later she was the girl that married men came to, late on Saturday nights or when their wives were in Atlanta on a shopping spree.

Georgia's father had been right about one thing. Sheila had turned out the way he had predicted. Just like her mother.

"Oh, Cord," Georgia whispered, staring at him through dark eyes swimming with tears. "I should have come after you that summer. I should have begged you to take me with you on that wild motorcycle of yours. And I should never have looked back."

The wind whipped the whispered words from her lips and tossed the sound away like the leaves that scattered across the ground. It was as if the wind carried her softly spoken words of regret straight down the hill to the man dressed in black.

For suddenly he stood up, his head coming around sharply as he turned and gazed up the hill toward her. For a moment they were both still, their eyes meeting even across the distance that separated them. Georgia knew he recognized her just as quickly as she had recognized him. It was an instinct, an age-old intuition that swept away time and space. It took Georgia back ten years and she wondered if it did him too.

Georgia stood motionless, unable to move or to stop staring at him. His black coat whipped away from him in the wind, revealing his long legs and lean hips. His hands moved to his hips and for a moment Georgia shivered, thinking he looked dangerous and threatening. She even felt an overwhelming urge to run, to hide from those odd blue eyes and from the look that she knew would inevitably be hidden in their depths.

But she couldn't. She could only stand, watching him, holding her breath and wondering if her heart would ever return to its normal rhythm.

Then in the blink of an eye, he turned and walked away without looking at her again, back to the monstrous black motorcycle. There was an impatience, an anger in his quick movements as he stepped across the seat and stood with his legs spread-eagled across the machine until he'd fastened his helmet in place. Then she heard the smooth purr of the engine and saw him kick fiercely at the support stand.

The shining ebony-and-silver cycle shot away from beneath the trees and down the winding roadway. Georgia felt a small tingle of excitement race along her arms and legs as she watched him. He rode with an abandon as wild as ever, with that fierce freedom that she had always envied.

In the past few months, she'd realized that she had always been afraid of everything. Afraid of speed, afraid of doing the wrong thing, of her family and friends' disapproval. Afraid of the unknown. Somehow she'd thought that if she managed to remain perfectly still, perfectly in control, everything would be all right and nothing could go awry.

How wrong she'd been. Look what her control and fear had gotten her.

And this man, he was a part of all that. He had tempted her that summer and made her long for things she didn't even understand. For some sweet forbidden touch of fire, the hot exhilarating taste of something she knew she might never completely own. There had been an unknown quality about him, the dangerous unapproachable rebel that any sensible, well-bred young woman would stay away from. Most especially, the daughter of Farmington's most prominent citizen.

Quickly she shook her head, trying to banish the thoughts of the raven-haired man dressed in black. Trying not to remember those eyes, how they could go from a hard blue brilliance to a soft stormy tenderness. How they would move from a woman's eyes down to her mouth with such sweet intensity that her insides would melt with longing.

"God," she whispered, feeling her breath coming in quiet little gasps. "Stop this . . . just stop it. He's a man, just like any other man."

But she knew that wasn't true. She'd always known it wasn't true. Cord Jamison was unlike any other man she'd ever known.

Georgia walked to the sleek little red convertible she'd left beneath one of the huge old trees. She grimaced every time she saw the car. She really should get rid of it, she thought.

Not that it wasn't beautiful or that she didn't enjoy driving it.

When it had been delivered to her just weeks after Bob's death, she'd been moved by his generosity. Until she learned that he had bought it for Sheila and that the dealership where he'd ordered it hadn't known quite what to do with it when it came in.

Looking at the car, she thought it did look more like Sheila's kind of car than hers.

"You're too conservative," Bob had often complained. "You've turned into a boring, uptight southern housewife."

Oh, how it had hurt to hear him criticize and complain. She supposed that was when she first began to suspect that he was seeing someone else. When nothing she did could please him.

She slammed the door and glanced into the rearview mirror, studying her eyes briefly before glancing away.

Where was that spirited, bouncing girl with the blond ponytail and a laugh that made people stare? The young carefree cheerleader who had been the most popular girl in town?

Now all she saw in the mirror were sad, hurt brown eyes. Her blond hair, once kept long and sexy the way Bob liked, was cut short and it curled about her face, making her look older, less frivolous. More like a housewife, she guessed.

She did have puppy-dog eyes. Bob had always said so and he had teased her mercilessly about it back in the good days... the happy days. He'd also always teased her about his being able to read her thoughts in those dark expressive eyes.

Just like today, she thought as she recognized that same wistful look, that sadness that seeing Cord Jamison had brought.

Impulsively she reached for the radio, turning the volume up loud, then pressing the button that released the car's ragtop with an electric whirring noise. Driving through town past the courthouse with her radio blaring was a defiant gesture, a silly juvenile one, she'd decided by the time she reached her house. But it had cleared her mind and helped her make a decision.

She was going back to work. She would call Judge Stone at his office at the courthouse this afternoon. He had called often since Bob's death and assured her that her job as his legal assistant was still there, whenever she wanted it.

Well, she wanted it now. She wanted to get on with her life. Seeing Cord Jamison had done that much, at least. She told herself he would probably only be in town for a day or two, nothing to get upset about. He was merely visiting his sister's grave, maybe seeing to the old home place, before he went back to Atlanta and what she had always thought was a fitting job for him as an agent with the Georgia Bureau of Investigation.

What was past was past. Even if both of them wanted to begin again, they couldn't. Now there was more than a father's disapproval between them. There was the murder of her husband and the suicide of his sister—a painful, ironic ending to anything that might ever have been between Georgia Ashley and Cord Jamison.

But that night, despite all her silent protests, she couldn't sleep. And it was Cord's face that haunted her dreams, his hands that she seemed to feel, his eyes that taunted and challenged and made her toss restlessly in the bedroom of her quiet, beautiful, empty house.

By eight o'clock the next morning, she was out of the shower and dressed, ready to go downtown and see Judge Stone. She was glad he came in early, even before most of the offices opened. She didn't think she could bear to sit in this house another moment. There was a restlessness in her this morning, a new determination to get on with her life. And to be happy.

Georgia parked by the sidewalk in front of the old red-brick courthouse. She glanced, as always, with brief appreciation at the lovely gold-domed roof, then at the huge trees and crepe myrtles spaced just so around the gracious lawn. She supposed this was one of the reasons she loved Farmington. The residents here still loved their traditions and kept them well.

Most of the beautiful homes of a century ago still remained, preserved and protected by the families who had passed them proudly from one generation to another. It was a quiet, pleasant town and despite all that had happened here, Georgia could not imagine living anywhere else.

"Georgia! Wait up," she heard from across the street.

She stopped for a moment, glancing at the man who jogged easily across the street toward her. She smiled weakly, for now that she was here, she found her courage quickly deserting her. She had been avoiding everyone, even her family, since Bob's death. And now she knew she would have to face the curiosity, the inevitable questions.

"Mike," she said, taking a deep breath. "How are you?" She glanced at the bright sheriff's badge he wore so proudly on the tan shirt of his uniform and smiled.

"The question is how are *you?*" he asked, coming to stand beside her. His breathing was a little hard, despite his trim, athletic build. "It's good to see you out and about, finally."

She ducked her head, wishing she could avoid the conversation this would inevitably lead to. She'd known Mike Goodwin since kindergarten. His wife had been one of her dearest friends until Bob's death and Georgia's subsequent self-imposed exile from Farmington society.

"Yes . . . well, I thought it was time I got back to work," she said.

"That's wonderful," he said. "Great. Brenda will be pleased to hear it. You haven't exactly kept in touch, you know."

"I know," she said, not quite meeting his eyes. "I'm sorry for that. It's been hard...terribly hard..." Her voice trailed away and she looked up into his face.

"I know it has," he said, touching her arm.

Mike Goodwin was not a classically handsome man, but he always had a way of looking at a woman that made her feel special. There was such warmth and confidence in him. Today the autumn breeze ruffled his straight brown hair, making Georgia wonder how many of Farmington's women longed to brush it out of his eyes.

"Where are you headed?" she asked, turning to walk up the wide sidewalk toward the courthouse. "Do you have court today?"

"Oh, yeah," he said with a grin. "Hell, I have court every day lately. For such a small town, we do seem to have our share of murder and mayhem..." He stopped, his eyes filled with horror and apology. "Oh, God, Georgia . . . I'm sorry. What a stupid, thoughtless thing to say."

She frowned as she felt tears stinging her eyes. Why on earth was she crying now? She'd hardly shed a tear in the last few months. In fact, she'd wished many times that she could. But she'd been numb, stunned with disbelief.

Quickly and impatiently, she wiped the tears away.

"It's all right. For heaven's sake, I don't expect you to avoid using the word when you talk to me. After all, you are the sheriff. I suppose the word *murder* does come up in your conversation from time to time." She really didn't intend to sound so hard and cynical, but she knew she had.

"You know what I mean," he said.

"Yes," she replied with a heavy sigh. "I do know what you mean. Let's just forget it. Please…just treat me the way you always have. I have to get over it sooner or later."

He fell into step beside her, moving up the long sidewalk toward the courthouse.

"Perhaps you should move away from here, hon," he said quietly. "Get away from Farmington for a while. After all, it's going to be a long time before people forget about Bob…before they stop talking about what happened to him and…uh…"

"Sheila," she snapped. "You don't have to be afraid to say her name, Mike."

"I'm sorry," he said, stepping in front of her and blocking her just at the foot of the courthouse steps. "But it's gotten to the point where we hardly know what to say to you anymore. You've rejected our attempts at sympathy. You've locked yourself away in that big old house, refusing to let anyone get close to you. I know Brenda has invited you for supper several times—"

"Yes, she has. Brenda is a sweet, caring friend…and so are you. But this is something I have to work through on my own. It might take me longer—after all, I seem to be a bit slow about some things."

"Georgia," he groaned. "Don't do this to yourself. I hate to see you becoming so bitter and cynical. There's nothing slow about you. No one else in town knew what was going on with Bob and Sheila, either, so don't—"

"Oh, please, Mike…give me a break. Everyone knew it." She turned with an angry jerk and waved her hand toward the red convertible parked at the curb. "Everyone at the dealership knew who he ordered that car for."

"Georgia, honey," he said. "I don't blame you for being angry and resentful. I should have told you…Brenda should have told you. But dammit, we didn't because we didn't want to see you hurt. We thought it was something Bob would get over."

Georgia grunted and moved toward the steps once more.

"Are you going to hold it against us forever, Georgia?" he asked, his voice louder now, his patience seemingly at an end. "That we didn't tell you? Brenda and I want to help you... all your friends do. But we can't do that if you continue to shut us out."

"Well, you must excuse me if I don't know who to trust right now, Mike," she said, not trying to disguise her bitterness. "But it's only been a few months since you came to me in the middle of the night and told me that Bob had been found dead in Sheila Jamison's bed."

"Look, I can't begin to understand what you're feeling, but I—"

"Can't you?" she asked with a cynical little laugh. "Try understanding what it's like being the widow of Bob Ashley—Farmington's all-American hero. The wife who was the last one in town to know who his affair was with. The poor, stupid widow of the man found dead in the arms of the town tramp."

When she swung away from Mike, she came face-to-face with Cord Jamison and from the look in his frosty blue eyes, she knew he had heard every bitter word she'd said.

Chapter 2

"Cord," she gasped, her voice sounding too soft and too breathless.

"How are you, Georgia?" he asked.

His eyes were guarded, suspicious even, and for a moment, Georgia wondered why. Did he, like the rest of Farmington, think less of her because she hadn't been able to keep her wandering husband at home?

Being this close to him, feeling the warmth from his body, catching the scent of the heady after-shave he wore, was almost too much. She had to clasp her hands together to keep from reaching out, from placing her fingers on his chest and holding on to him for support. She actually felt a physical ache shoot through her chest as she looked at him, as her heart and body and soul remembered everything about him.

He'd changed. He was leaner...harder even, and he looked as if he spent a great deal of time in the sun. The darkness of his skin emphasized those incredible eyes, making them seem to blaze down at her. Today they were an odd pale blue, the word *quicksilver* came to mind as she stared up into them.

"I . . . I'm fine," she finally managed to say. "Just fine."

"Are you?" He made no attempt at being discreet as he let his eyes move from her face and tumble of blond hair, down her body, making note of the slender skirt of her black suit that covered a soft, curvaceous body.

She felt herself wanting to brush at the skirt, to tug at the buttons of her jacket or straighten her hair. And for a moment, as she stared at his dark face and sensuous lips, she felt herself transported to another time, to that summer of forbidden desires and wild, unexplainable emotions.

"Yes, I am. Good to see you again. If you'll excuse me, I have an appointment with Judge Stone."

When she walked away from him, she felt her legs trembling weakly, and she could feel the flush of heat on her cheeks. She hadn't even bothered to notice whether Mike Goodwin was coming or not. She was too busy remembering how it had been that summer, how she had wanted Cord with a white-hot passion that went beyond anything she'd ever experienced. Dear Lord, she could feel it even now.

Bob had gone to Atlanta in June that year, to work for his uncle before his and Georgia's planned marriage in the fall. She and Cord had been drawn together since that night at the National Guard Armory. And with Bob's absence, she had openly flirted with danger, teasing herself and Cord at first—testing to see if what she felt could possibly be returned by this sexy, rebellious and perfectly dangerous man. It had been inevitable, their being together—as predestined as the ageless rising and setting of the sun.

She had betrayed her fiancé that long, hot summer. So quickly . . . so easily. And moments ago, as she stared up at Cord Jamison, she had known she was in danger of betraying herself this time.

She'd found herself actually longing to touch the ebony hair that fell in ruffled, wind-lashed layers just below the collar at the back of his blue denim shirt. And here in the morning sunlight, she'd been surprised, moved even, to see touches of gray in his hair where it was cut shorter at the sides.

She was hardly aware that Mike was beside her until he reached out and took her arm, stopping her in the cool marble hallway at the front of the courthouse.

"God, Georgia," he murmured. "What was that all about? You acted as if you were running from the devil himself."

"Nothing," she said. "Just an awkward moment, that's all. I hadn't expected to see Cord Jamison here. I...I didn't know what to say to him."

"I should warn you that you might be seeing a lot more of him."

"Why?" she asked. Little ripples of alarm shot through Georgia's body, all the way to the tips of her fingers.

"He's been asking a lot of questions around town since we closed the case. Seems he's taken a leave of absence from the GBI and plans on being here a while. At least until he gets some answers to his questions."

"Questions? What questions?"

Mike took her arms and turned her so that she was forced to look up at him.

Forced to see the quiet warning in his eyes...and the sympathy.

"It seems Jamison doesn't believe his sister killed herself. In fact, he doesn't think she killed Bob, either." His voice was very quiet, but it seemed to echo in the empty hallway and ring hollowly against the cold marble.

"But...but who does he think did it?"

Mike took a long breath of air and his eyes moved away from her probing gaze for a moment. He shifted restlessly, shrugging his shoulders before he let his eyes swing back to meet hers.

"He's insinuated that you might be the one with the most to gain. That you could even have hired someone. After all, a cheating husband who left a respectable wife for a woman like Sheila Jamison...everyone in town knew the humiliation you felt. If I were looking strictly at the facts and if I didn't know you so well, I'd have to admit that, as a police officer, I might be thinking the same thing."

Georgia felt as if all the blood had drained from her body. She was cold and hot at the same time and she could hear a loud roaring noise in her ears.

Her? Cord actually thought she was capable of doing such a thing? Did he not know her at all? Had he forgotten everything they'd shared...everything he'd ever known about her?

"My God," she whispered, her breath coming in one great rush from her lungs. "I can't believe it."

"Look," Mike said, frowning at her. "I don't want you worrying about this. It'll blow over and Jamison will go back to Atlanta once he sees that it's simply not possible. I've got to get to court. But I want us to finish this conversation, you hear me? Promise you'll come for supper one night soon. Give Brenda a call."

Georgia was still shaking her head, still trying to get Mike's words out of her mind. She felt confused and frightened...and more alone than she'd ever been in her life.

"Yes," she managed to say. "All right."

She hardly knew what she was saying. All she wanted at the moment was to get away, to find a place where she could be alone and think. And more than that, she wanted to

confront Cord and tell him that she could never do what he
suspected her of doing.

She was practically in a state of shock as she moved on to
Judge Stone's chambers and told him she'd be back to work
the following Monday.

"Are you sure you're ready?" he asked.

Georgia had known the judge all her life. He was a friend
of her father's and a very influential man in the state. She
looked at him now, noting the look of concern on his
weathered face. His hair had gotten even grayer than her
father's. In fact, they reminded her of each other, except
that Judge Stone was less intense, more jovial than Horace
Blake.

"Yes, I'm sure," she said. "But I admit, it's not easy, not
when everyone in the courthouse will be staring and wondering ..."

"Well, let them stare," he said, coming around the desk
to put an arm around her shoulders. "You have nothing to
be embarrassed or ashamed about. You were the victim in
this horrible scenario, my dear. You just hold your head up
and look those buzzards straight in the eye when they stare."
His deep southern drawl was soothing to her, just the way
she'd known it would be.

She smiled then and hugged him. She'd have felt im-
mensely better if it hadn't been for Mike's revelation about
Cord Jamison's purpose in Farmington. It kept going
around and around in her head and for the life of her, she
didn't know how he could suspect her of being involved in
anything so horrible as murder.

After leaving the courthouse, Cord Jamison walked casually to where he'd left his bike. With a quick, angry
movement, he kicked the stand away, turned on the switch
and pulled away from the curb. He needed the feel of the

cool autumn breeze on his face, needed to get away from town and all the hypocritical people who stared at him from the corner of their eyes when he walked past them on the street. And most of all, he needed to get away from the image of Georgia Ashley's pale face and sad brown eyes.

She'd changed. But hell, so had he. After all, they weren't kids anymore. He thought Georgia seemed softer, more sophisticated. But he had not expected her to still be so beautiful... as sweetly provocative as she'd been that summer. And dammit, he hadn't expected to see that sad, vulnerable look in her dark eyes.

Cord turned the throttle, pushing the big machine faster through the streets until he was past town and out on a winding country road. He hardly noticed where he was going. He was too intent on remembering Georgia, the look of surprise on her face, the way her suit had clung so invitingly to her softly rounded hips and breasts. He'd always thought she was the most feminine woman he'd ever known, and now she seemed even more so with that haunted look in her eyes.

Did she have anything to do with Bob's and Sheila's deaths? He knew what a temper Georgia could have sometimes and how she liked having her way. She could never stand being on the losing end of anything. Cord knew it must have almost killed her when she learned what was going on between her husband and Sheila. After all, Georgia Ashley was someone, with a capital *S* in the town of Farmington.

"No," he said, shaking his head and taking a deep breath. He didn't want to believe it, or even think about it. Not Georgia.

But she could have hired someone else to do it, his mind warned him. He wanted to reject that idea, too, wanted to forget everything that his trained instincts were telling him.

But he couldn't. Sheila was his sister and he owed her this, at least. What had once been between him and Georgia was in the past . . . long gone, and if he knew what was good for him, that was where he would let it stay.

Before he realized it, the lake was ahead of him, sparkling through the trees that left brilliant autumn reflections in the water. Cord pulled off the road and cruised slowly through a stand of tall pines that murmured softly in the morning breeze. He stopped on a tall grassy bank that overlooked the clear blue water and was a perfect vista for the mountains just beyond.

He didn't bother to get off the bike, but sat with his boots firmly planted on the ground, letting his long legs hold the bike steady. He pulled off his helmet and took a slow shuddering breath of air, running his hand over his face and shaking his head.

What the hell was wrong with him? He'd been gone from Farmington for ten years and he hadn't missed it. He certainly hadn't missed the people who'd looked down their noses at him and his family all his life. He was successful now. He was good at his job and he didn't have to feel ashamed of who he was.

He gritted his teeth as he thought of Georgia's father. A cold-eyed, unfeeling man, as far as Cord was concerned. A man with no regard for anything except his money and his power.

That day ten years ago, he had come to the Jamisons' shabby little house on the west side of town, holding a fistful of money. He had been anything but discreet as he shoved the money toward Cord, who'd stood staring at him as if the older man had lost his mind.

"What do you want?" Cord had asked.

"I know what's been going on between you and my daughter, Jamison. And by God, if you know what's good for you, you'll crank up that mangy cycle you ride and hightail it out of town before—"

"Why would I want to do that?" Cord asked. His eyes moved with curiosity to the thick stack of neatly banded money in Mr. Blake's clenched fist.

"Because it's what Georgia wants. She's going to marry Bob Ashley when he gets home, Jamison. No matter what tawdry little affair you've indulged in with my daughter, she knows where her loyalties lie. In fact, she asked me to give you this...she thought it might make it easier for you to go. Bob will be home soon and she'd prefer not having any embarrassing confrontations."

Cord's eyes narrowed as he looked from Horace Blake's face, down to the bundle of hundred-dollar bills that he held.

"I don't believe you. Georgia wouldn't—"

Mr. Blake laughed then and reached forward, shoving the money hard into Cord's shirt pocket.

"Don't kid yourself, son," he said, insolently patting Cord's pocket. His eyes wandered around the front porch of the Jamison home. There was a sneer of disgust on his face.

"Do you actually think Georgia would give up all she has for this?" Horace Blake waved his hand toward the leaning posts that barely supported the porch, the flaking paint on the sides of the house. Then his eyes traveled over Cord with an amused disdain.

"For you?"

The man was laughing when he turned and left. Cord had stood motionless, stunned by Horace's words and feeling as if he'd just been kicked in the gut. He couldn't believe it was over. Couldn't believe that this bright, wonderful, intangible thing that was between himself and Georgia had ended, just as quickly as it had begun.

Not like this.

But hell, he should have known. If he hadn't kidded himself into believing that her sweet kisses, her soft moans of passion meant something, he might have seen it coming. It was inevitable, wasn't it? The poor boy from the wrong side of the tracks, the beautiful curious debutante just dying to do something wild and reckless before she married.

Her father was the most important man in town. What had Cord expected—her declaration of undying love? It had been a summer fling for her—that was all. One last summer of fun before she married Ashley and settled down for good. Yet in his heart, Cord knew that she could never deny the fire that was between them, that wild, sweet touch of the forbidden that they felt every time they were together.

"But it wasn't enough, was it?" he muttered to himself.

That day, he had looked down at the money and ripped it from his pocket. Then he'd walked inside the house, found an envelope and crammed the money inside. Angrily he had scribbled Horace Blake's name and address across the front.

"To hell with you, Blake," he had muttered. "To hell with all of you."

Shaking himself out of his memories, Cord leaned back on the motorcycle, breathing out a long slow breath of air before he propped the bike up and got off.

He hadn't expected this. Hadn't expected the feelings of bitterness and shame to return so fiercely. Maybe it was Sheila's death that had brought it all back. Maybe once this whole sordid thing was settled, he would be able to go back to Atlanta and back to work and forget about Farmington and Horace Blake's influence and power. Forget about everything, most especially Georgia Ashley.

Cord threw his head back and looked up at the sky. The blue Georgia sky was clear, interrupted in the distance only by the mountains that rose in varying peaks toward the horizon.

How Sheila had loved this place...the lake and the mountains. When they were kids, it had been their only means of escape, their only hope of joy and peace, away from the sordid lives they lived, from the constant stream of men who moved in and out of their mother's bedroom. The lake was freedom to them and it was always available. Here they didn't have to hide and they didn't have to explain themselves to anyone.

And it was where you brought Georgia that first time, his mind whispered.

He shook it off. He had to concentrate on Sheila and why he was here.

What a funny, sad girl his sister had been—hiding her shame and sadness behind a facade of irreverent mischief and bawdy language. He'd known her better than anyone, and despite her problems he had loved her. And if it was the last thing he ever did, he intended to find out who had killed her.

Georgia paced the cool pine floor of her bedroom. It was almost midnight and still she hadn't slept. She had come home from the courthouse, changed her clothes and begun to clean house, even though she knew it was an effort in futility.

Once, she'd had a maid who came in on a regular basis. But now she simply wanted to be left alone. Nothing needed cleaning anyway. But she had to do something.

Not that losing sleep was anything new to her. How many long, torturous nights had she lain awake in this big house, thinking of Bob and the way he'd died? Knowing the whole town pitied her? There were nights when she'd gotten out of bed and driven past Sheila Jamison's house, where it had happened. The small house was like a living thing that whispered to her, a macabre entity, beckoning her to see it, as if by being there she might banish the fear and grief once and for all. It was something she didn't even understand, herself.

But tonight, she had to admit, there was another reason for not sleeping. Cord Jamison actually believed that she'd had something to do with his sister's death.

Suddenly she walked to her closet and pulled out a black jumpsuit. She quickly buttoned the buttons, not bothering with a belt, then brushed her short curls back from her face. She grabbed her purse and keys and went through the house and out to the garage.

She let the car's top down and stuck a disc into the CD player, letting the lively sound of the music and the wind fill her mind and soothe her jangled nerves.

She drove around for almost an hour before she finally had the nerve to turn the car onto Beech Circle. She knew the way by heart. But here in the darkness, she couldn't see that well and she found herself trembling with anxiety.

All she would do was stop for a minute, she told herself. Just pull the car over to the curb on the quiet residential street and take a long look at the house where her husband had died so violently.

There were no lights on in any of the houses, just a security light here and there and the dim streetlights that burned at the end of each block.

She pulled the car to the curb and placed her hands firmly on the steering wheel, holding tightly and willing herself to stay and look.

Georgia sat stiffly, looking straight ahead. She turned off the music and now the sounds of the night could be heard more clearly, the sound of crickets and the intermittent hum of a car passing on the main highway not far away. She shivered and a chill ran quickly along her spine. Her mind felt the terror of that night, the horror of what had happened inside this house. Her fingers moved to reach for the keys in the ignition. She had to close her eyes to fight the panic that threatened to overwhelm her and make her run from her thoughts and from this place.

Suddenly, from nowhere it seemed, a shadow moved along the passenger side of the car. Georgia managed only a small shriek before the car door opened and a man slid into the leather seat beside her.

"You want to tell me exactly what you're doing here?"

She could barely make out Cord's face, but she recognized the deep voice. It sounded cold and hard, and completely ruthless.

"My God, you scared me to death," she gasped.

"Good. At least you have enough sense to be afraid. Did you ever stop to think how dangerous it could be...out here in the middle of the night...alone?"

"I...no. I'm not afraid of the...of the night. As a matter of fact, I often get out and drive around when I can't sleep."

"Do you?"

There was none of the kindness in him that she remembered—none of the sweet tenderness that had once kept her awake at night with longing.

Instead, his voice was filled with a quiet cynicism and suspicion and it made her remember what he suspected her of doing.

"Yes, I do," she snapped. "Is there anything wrong with that? Or is this just your special agent's training kicking in?"

As her eyes adjusted to the darkness, she could see the way the breeze ruffled Cord's black hair. But the night obliterated his silvery eyes, leaving only dark slits beneath his black eyebrows. She'd had no idea he was staying here at Sheila's house. She would have expected him to be at his old home place, if he still owned it. It was obvious he'd come outside on impulse for he wore only jeans and a T-shirt and he was barefoot.

He had come out of the house, crossed the lawn and the street and walked, unnoticed, to her car without making a sound. Georgia felt a shiver at the back of her neck as she realized what a cautious, stealthy man he'd become.

"What did you expect to find here, Georgia?" he asked.

"What do you think? Don't they say the murderer always returns to the scene of the crime?" There was a resentful edge to her sarcasm, but she knew she hadn't managed to disguise the hurt that was there, as well.

Cord's lips quirked in the darkness. So, Mike Goodwin had already told her why he was here. His gaze never left her face and he didn't smile. He was studying her, wondering perhaps if that was exactly what she was doing here.

"How many times have you been here?" he asked.

She could see that he obviously didn't intend to discuss his suspicions with her and she was surprised at how badly that hurt, having him question her as if she were only a stranger, some kind of criminal. As if she'd never known him, never lain in his arms at the lake and watched the stars until the rising sun chased them all away. Never kissed him and held him, or made wild, uninhibited love with him.

She couldn't breathe for the memories . . . and the pain.

"I've been here before," she managed to say. "But this is the first time I've stopped."

He made a low, disdainful sound of disbelief.

"This is me you're talking to, Georgia. Do you really expect me to believe that you've never been here before . . . that you were never curious about where your husband was spending his nights?"

"No...I...I never knew before who... But isn't that the way it always is—the wife is the last person to know?" Her eyes narrowed as she stared at him and tried to see his eyes that were hidden by the shadows from the trees. Occasionally a yellow leaf would drift down from above and land in the car. Neither of them bothered to remove them.

"Damn you, Cord," she whispered. "Why are you doing this?"

"Doing what?" He shrugged his broad shoulders and she could see the muscles flex beneath the soft T-shirt.

"Mike told me what you think . . . that you don't believe Sheila killed herself or Bob . . . that you think I had something to do with it."

"Did you?"

"No!" she said, practically shouting. "How can you even ask me that?" She was so angry that she was practically panting for breath. "Get out of my car. I mean it, Cord. Just get out. I'm going home. I shouldn't have come here. I wouldn't have if I'd known you were staying here."

"What's the rush? Did I touch a nerve?"

She twisted around in the seat, feeling all the frustration of the past months wash over her, feeling all the anger. Her eyes blazed at him and before she realized what was happening, her hand lashed out toward him.

Her arm was immediately seized in a hard, unrelenting grip. Cord pulled her toward him until they were only inches apart. She could feel his breath against her lips, could now see the gleam of light in those pale, cool eyes, and even in her anger, she recognized that familiar spark of electricity that arced between them. She wondered if he felt it, too. Or if he hated her too much to notice.

"Go home, Georgia," he whispered, his voice as cold and cynical as before. He released her hand and pushed her away from him as if he could not bear to touch her. Then, in a

Chapter 3

Georgia hardly slept at all that night. The next morning was Sunday and the street where she lived was quiet. Around eight o'clock, she went into the kitchen to make a pot of coffee. Moments later when she heard the low hum of an engine moving down the street, she knew what it was. She knew *who* it was.

She opened the front door just as Cord was walking up the brick sidewalk. It was a warm morning for fall and he was not wearing the long black coat she'd seen him in before. There in the shelter of the doorway, Georgia's eyes went soft as she noted the way his faded jeans clung to his thighs and lean hips, the way the light blue denim shirt emphasized his broad chest and shoulders.

His long legs brought him quickly to the steps and she thought that, besides his usual confident masculinity, there was an air of purpose about him that morning.

He walked across the wide front porch, coming to a halt just in front of her. In the early-morning light, his eyes were stormy and guarded, an incredible blue-gray that would make any woman catch her breath with interest.

Georgia's first thought was that she must look awful and it usually would have bothered her. But seeing the look on his face, she quickly forgot that she had on the same rumpled jumpsuit that she'd worn last night, or that her hair needed brushing.

He leaned toward her, placing his hand on the door-frame beside her head and staring into her eyes with a quiet purpose.

"I'm going to ask you one question, Georgia. And I want you to tell me the truth, no matter what it is."

She frowned, turning her head to one side as she stared up at him with a look of bewilderment in her brown eyes. For a moment, there was nothing or no one in the world except the two of them. No birds singing in the brilliant trees that surrounded her house, no soft whirring sound of water sprinklers in the neighbors' yards. Nothing except the look in his eyes and the ache in her heart.

"Did you have anything to do with Sheila's death? Did you plan it or pay for it...did you even wish it out loud where anyone could hear you?" He was giving her every chance he could think of.

She started to protest, even put her hand on the door as if to close it in his face. But his hand shot forward, holding the door while he continued staring down at her with such a demanding look that she stopped and stood dead still, staring up at him.

"Just tell me, Georgia," he demanded, his voice deceptively soft. "Dammit, if you did, I'll help you. I'll explain to the authorities how Bob was...the circumstances...I have a friend in Atlanta who is the best lawyer in the South—"

"You'd help me?" she whispered.

"Just tell me the truth. Don't you think you owe me that much after—" He stopped and took a breath of air. For a moment, there was a troubled look in his eyes. But just as quickly as it had appeared, it vanished, replaced by that same steely glint of determination she'd seen when they were at the courthouse.

"I didn't," she murmured. She felt the tears well up in her eyes, but she didn't move her gaze from his. And she didn't bother asking how he could even ask her such a question. She just looked him square in the eye and repeated, "I didn't. I swear to you, I had absolutely nothing to do with Sheila's death, or my husband's."

He straightened and took a long slow breath, letting it out loudly as he leaned his head back and closed his eyes for a brief moment.

When Cord opened his eyes, he stared at her for long silent minutes. He saw the pain etched on Georgia's beautiful face and he wanted to reach out and touch her, just for one moment. Then he shook his head, knowing he could never put himself in that position again. Being hurt by her once was bad enough, being rejected by her was something that had taken years to get over. He knew that a betrayal by this woman was something he wouldn't be able to stand a second time.

"God," he breathed. "I don't know why I should believe you . . . maybe I'm stupid . . . or blind . . . or both, but I do believe you."

Georgia couldn't answer, couldn't say a word. But she smiled tremulously and nodded. She swallowed hard to keep from crying. She couldn't seem to stop nodding as she stepped backward into the house and tried to make her voice respond.

"Come in . . . there's coffee . . . we can talk."

Without a word, he stepped past her into the house, his eyes taking in the cool elegant foyer with its understated designer wallpaper and the expensive mahogany furniture in the sitting room off to the side. He took a paper from his back pocket and handed it to Georgia.

"I have something here I think you should see."

She stood in the hallway, her fingers trembling as she unfolded the piece of paper, and let her eyes scan quickly down the page. She felt a sickening lurch in the pit of her stomach and when she looked up into Cord's eyes again, she couldn't disguise the way she felt.

"An autopsy report?" she whispered, swallowing hard.

"Sheila's," he said, frowning. But seeing the vulnerability on her face, seeing the sickness in her eyes, he wondered if it had been a mistake coming here this way, springing this report on her unannounced. "I assumed you'd already seen Bob's."

"No," she said. Her eyes darted around and she handed the paper back to him. "Uh... could we sit down? The kitchen maybe..."

He followed her down the hallway and off to the side into a wide, spacious kitchen lined with sunlit windows and bright with flowers and shelves filled with antique blue willow china.

Cord noted the way her hand trembled as she poured two cups of coffee. "I guess I assumed that you at least knew the results."

"Yes, basically," she said, shaking her head. She didn't look at him, but sipped her coffee quickly, hoping it would calm her and take away that sick feeling in the pit of her stomach. "It was so horrible...so gruesome that I couldn't bear reading all the details. Besides, there was no point. Mike told me what happened."

"Did Mike tell you that Sheila's gunshot wound was to the right temple?"

Georgia shrugged her shoulders, finally turning to stare at him. The pain in his eyes was evident and she realized that seeing this report was just as hard on him as it was on her. She pushed his coffee in front of him and sat down across from him at the small whitewashed antique table.

"Sheila was left-handed," he explained, seeing her shrug of indifference.

"Oh, I see. That's your basis for thinking it couldn't be a murder/suicide? But...but couldn't she just have used her right hand?"

"She could have. But why would she? Maybe it's nothing, but then maybe it proves what I've believed all along. That it wasn't Sheila who killed Bob or herself. They didn't find any prints on the gun, either. The coroner's explanation was that Sheila was wearing a pair of lacy white gloves."

His voice was gruff and filled with cynicism as he continued. "I don't know about you, but white gloves don't exactly fit the image I had of my sister."

Georgia couldn't quite meet his eyes. She swallowed and stared at the top of the table.

"That was all she was wearing," she said, her voice a mere whisper in the room.

"What?" It was as if Cord was determined to make her repeat all the sordid details of that night. As if he wanted to make her say it out loud.

"I said...it's my understanding that all she was wearing was...a pair of white lacy lady's gloves." She forced herself to look into his eyes, to stare aloofly at him as she repeated the words.

"What are you saying?" he asked, his voice sarcastic and hurtful. "That your husband was in the habit of playing

little sex games ... that he favored the old image we southern men love so well—the demure lady who turns into a
whore in the bedroom? You know the one, don't you?''

Georgia stood up, her movement so violent that her coffee spilled across the table. She could feel her cheeks burning as she stared at him. He knew the details of that night—
he'd known them all along.

''How dare you say that to me.''

He shrugged his shoulders and although there was the
slightest tug of amusement on his lips, his eyes were as cold
and bitter as any she'd ever seen.

''It's nothing personal.''

''What do you want from me, Cord?'' she asked. ''Why
did you come here? I've told you I had nothing to do with
their deaths. Did you come to hurt me? To humiliate me? If
so, you're wasting your time ... someone already beat you
to it.''

She turned to leave the room, but just as quickly she felt
his movement behind her and felt the hard grasp of his hand
on her arm.

He said nothing for a moment as he held her in place.
Both of them were breathing hard and as he stared at her, it
was as if he couldn't quite decide whether to believe her or
not.

''I came to ask you to help me,'' he said finally.

''To help you?'' She jerked away from him, backing off
and watching him with caution. ''Why should I help you?
Why should I have anything to do with you?'' She was so
emotional that she was practically gasping for air.

''Why do you still go to the cemetery, after what he did to
you? Do you still love him?''

''What?'' She shook her head, wishing she could slap that
hard, smug look off his face.

"I saw you at the cemetery, remember? Grieving, obviously. I merely wondered if you still love him." He stepped closer, menacingly close, but Georgia didn't back off again.

"You saw me at the cemetery doing my duty," she snapped, her dark eyes sparkling with fury and resentment. "Just as I've done all my life. And whether I still love my husband or not is really none of your business."

His eyes were like shattered pieces of glass—cold and clear and completely lifeless.

"I thought perhaps you were trying to make some sense out of all this . . . that you might have as many doubts as I do."

She said nothing. She was perilously close to tears, but as she lifted her chin, she vowed silently that she would not cry.

"Personally, I thought Bob Ashley was a first-class jerk," Cord continued. "And Sheila's reputation and behavior wasn't the best in the world." His eyes became still and quiet. "But neither of them deserved this, Georgia. Neither of them."

"It's over," she said. Georgia could feel her insides trembling, could feel perspiration clinging to the back of her neck. "I don't want to help, I just want to forget any of this ever happened. I don't want to do anything that will keep reminding me of it, day after day—I just want to get on with my life."

Cord saw the fear and indecision in her eyes and he gave a quiet grunt of disbelief.

"Still running scared, huh, Georgie?"

His voice was low and intimate and his quiet utterance of the name he used to call her sent shivers down her spine.

You were the one who ran, she wanted to shout. You were the one who left me behind in this damnable town. But she said nothing, only stared at him resentfully.

"What is it that makes you refuse?" he asked. "Hatred...revenge? Did you hate her so much that you don't want to see justice done?"

Damn him. He always knew how to get to her...how to make her feel things she never wanted to feel. How to pull her out of the safety of her warm, secure cocoon and just make her *feel*.

Cord mistook her silence for a yes. Angrily he turned and walked away from her, going to stare out the window with his hands stuck in the back pocket of his jeans before he turned and came back to stare down into her eyes.

"You know there seems to be a consensus in this town about my sister. It's as if the way she conducted her life made her death unworthy of anyone's concern. I see that happening a lot in the city—to poor blacks from the projects, kids in gangs, homeless people—people who don't matter to society. And I understand that's natural in a perverted kind of way—makes all us *normal* people feel safe, I guess."

"I'm not like that. You know—"

"Aren't you?"

She stared at him, feeling guilty, feeling his quiet rage and frustration eating away at her.

"Ask yourself this, Georgia. Why would anyone in this town dismiss Bob Ashley's death that way? Hell, he was one of Farmington's most valued citizens...their hometown boy. Why hasn't there been a proper investigation of his death? They've seen all the facts I have—they must have seen all the things that didn't quite add up."

Cord's gaze wandered from Georgia's troubled brown eyes to her lips, soft and pink and so kissable. How long had it been since she'd smiled...since anyone had seen that hint of a dimple at the corner of her mouth? For a moment, it was all he could do to keep from sweeping her into his arms and kissing away her hurt and her pain. He felt a burning coil of desire flash through him and he wanted to laugh. Here he was, Cord Jamison, so well known for his self-control that his colleagues teasingly called him the iron-man. All it had taken was one softly whispered declaration of her innocence and already he was thinking of carrying her into the bedroom and making hot sweet love to her the way he'd done so many times before.

But she was even more forbidden to him now than she had been then.

"You're right about one thing. I...I've always felt something was not quite right," she said, her voice a whisper.

"What?" He walked to her quickly, taking her chin in his hands and making her look at him.

"I don't know," she managed to say, pulling away from his disturbing hands.

Did he have any idea what his touch still did to her? How her insides trembled just being near him?

"It's as if some little voice always nagged at me, just out of earshot," she whispered. "Something I can never quite hear..."

He took a long deep breath, hands at his hips, and as he looked at her, there was a glint of satisfaction in his eyes.

"I would never have come to you, except you have access to all Bob's papers...his bank accounts, everything."

"I understand."

"It could be dangerous."

"I know." She shivered when she said the words, when she actually acknowledged what she was letting herself in for.

She had courage, Cord had to admit that. He only wished she'd had enough ten years ago and tried to make it work between them.

Hell, he thought. That's over, it's in the past. Get that through your head, Jamison. Or you'll never be able to get anything done while you're here.

"Then I want you to do everything I say," he said. "We're going to proceed very carefully and you're to do everything I tell you."

"All right." Her gaze didn't waver as it met his and he wondered if she had any idea at all what she might be letting herself in for.

"First thing tomorrow morning, I want you to go to the coroner's office and get a copy of Bob's autopsy report. Tell them it's for insurance claims if they ask. You don't have to look at it if you don't want to," he added, seeing the guarded look return to her eyes. "But I need to see it."

"All right," she said, taking a paper towel and cleaning up the spilled coffee and trying to appear calm. She couldn't believe she was doing this. She couldn't believe that someone else might actually have been responsible for Bob's death. And right now, she didn't know how she felt about that possibility.

But there was one thing she was sure about—she was glad Cord was the one asking for her help.

Cord saw how uncomfortable Georgia was with her decision, how troubled. She probably didn't trust him any more than he trusted her. And yet, she seemed perfectly willing to put her life in his hands.

He wished he hadn't had to ask for her help. Hell, maybe he hadn't had to. Maybe he could have found a way to get the information without her. Maybe all he wanted was an excuse to be near her again.

What was it about her brown eyes that got to him? That had always gotten to him? It had been years since he'd allowed himself to think about those eyes . . . that soft feminine body and sweet mouth.

He shook his head and went to get another cup of coffee. He didn't want this. Didn't want a woman in his life—most especially not this woman. He'd told himself for years that it was the dangerous, tenuous quality of his job that kept his relationships with women on a temporary basis. Short, sweet, temporary diversions. Nothing that would ever touch his heart. Nothing that would ever make him long for this particular woman's touch, or that would ever get through the protective shell he'd built around his heart ten years ago.

Stop it, dammit!

Stick to the facts, he told himself. Just like the old "Dragnet" show. Just stick to the facts, solve the case and get out of town.

"What about Bob's personal papers," Cord asked, his voice gruff. "Anything he had on him that night. Do you have them?"

"Yes." Georgia looked at him oddly, wondering at the note of irritation that had crept into his voice, at the impatience in the way he moved. "There were a few things. I'll get them."

Moments later she came back with a small brown envelope and a metal box. Her hands were trembling when she opened the clasp on the envelope and dumped the contents on the kitchen table, spreading everything apart with her fingers. This was actually the first time she'd looked at Bob's personal belongings.

There was a billfold, a comb and handkerchief, a half-used package of antacid tablets. And a key ring with several keys that jangled when Cord picked them up.

"What are the keys for?" he asked.

Georgia reached forward and when her fingers touched his, her gaze flew up, meeting his like a startled doe for only a moment before she looked away.

"This . . . this is the key to his office, these are the house keys, the keys to our cars." Georgia frowned then and pulled the key ring from Cord's fingers, going through them one at a time, as if something puzzled her.

"What is it?"

"I'm not sure," she said, shrugging her shoulders. "I just remember him always having a small red key on here. It was for a safe-deposit box he used for the real estate office."

"A safe-deposit box? Do you have a key to it?"

"No, I never did. It was strictly for his business." She frowned at Cord. "Do you . . . do you think someone took it? That it had anything to do with—"

"I don't know," he said. "But it's something we need to look into. All right," he said, nodding to the things on the table. "Go on."

"That's all," she said, opening the metal box. "These are deeds, insurance and business papers." She picked up Bob's billfold. "There could be something in here."

He nodded solemnly, indicating she should be the one to look through her husband's billfold.

Slowly Georgia pulled out a few papers, a car registration, driver's license, insurance cards. She laid them aside and glanced through the pictures Bob carried. She took a deep breath and felt it catch in her throat as she saw one of her and another of her and Bob together. Happier times, she thought. Suddenly her eyes darkened as she unfolded a piece of paper and a picture fell out.

Picking it up, Georgia saw Sheila Jamison's cloud of black hair, her perky animated face and brilliant arrogant smile. She was wearing long sparkling earrings that hung almost to her shoulders.

Georgia slid the pictures across the table toward Cord. "Maybe you'd like to have this," she said.

Cord took his sister's picture, staring down at it for a few moments before slipping it into his shirt pocket. It was the picture of a woman who had lived too hard...too fast. A woman consumed with her face and body. But Cord, better than anyone, knew the reasons for that. Sheila had been looking for love all her life and the way she lived was the only way she knew how to find it. But no matter how she'd lived, she'd been his sister and he loved her and mourned her loss. When he looked at the picture, he obviously didn't see the same thing that Georgia saw.

He looked into her eyes then and he recognized the pain. He wanted to tell her that her husband was a fool. That his betrayal had nothing to do with her beauty or her worth. It was Bob's problem, dammit, not hers.

But Bob was the one she'd chosen—and Cord couldn't let himself forget that.

He put his coffee cup down.

"I have to go," he said. "We'll talk about all this tomorrow, after you get the report." He turned, and without looking back at Georgia, began to walk toward the front of the house.

"But..." She stood up to follow, then slowly sank back into the chair. She heard the front door slam and she couldn't understand why his going left her feeling so alone, so bereft. She was used to being alone.

Georgia sat for a long time in the kitchen, long after the low humming sound of Cord's motorcycle had drifted away into the distance. She felt oddly restless and troubled by what lay ahead for her, not knowing who was involved in Bob's death, or why. But for the first time since it had happened, she felt hopeful and not quite so useless.

By the time evening came, she felt pleasantly exhausted and thought perhaps she might be able to sleep. She took a long, leisurely shower and washed her hair, toweling it almost dry until it lay in shining curls around her face. She pulled on a soft pink satin nightshirt that fell a little above her knees. She was just getting into bed when the phone beside her bed rang.

"Hello?"

There was no answer at first, but the line was open and she thought she heard a noise. She held her breath and sat very still, holding the phone tightly against her ear.

"Hello?" she repeated. "Is anyone there?"

When there was no answer, she felt quick jangles of alarm race down her arms. Then she heard his voice, soft and breathless, the one word he said blurred and so quiet she could barely make it out.

"Georgia..."

"Cord, is that you?"

"Do...do you have the house's security alarm on?" He was breathing heavily, as if he'd been running, or as if the effort of speaking exhausted him.

Georgia frowned and gripped the phone tighter. She could feel tingles of fear shoot through every inch of her body.

"Cord...what's wrong? What—"

"Just answer me," he said with a soft grunt. "Do you?"

"Yes I do. But—"

"Good...that's good."

He was fairly gasping for breath. "Turn...turn all your outside lights on, too..." He stopped and all she heard was a soft moan.

"Cord! Cord...what's happening? What's wrong?"

"Nothing," he grunted. "Just a small...welcoming committee...waiting for me when I got..." Another soft grunt. Then curses that sounded very far away and very quiet. "...home."

"You're hurt. I knew something was wrong. I'll call Mike. I'll be right over."

"No! No...don't...don't call anyone and I want you to stay...right where you are and...do as I say." There was another long pause as he seemed to be trying to catch his breath.

"Do you have a gun? God," he murmured softly, his voice catching with pain.

"Where are you hurt? Please tell me. Do you need a doctor? Should I—"

"No...no doctor. I don't know who I can trust right now. No doctor...no police. And you're not to come here. If these...thugs know I've talked to you...they might put two and two together...if they can count that far." His attempt at humor brought another soft groan.

"Listen to me, Cord," she said, trying to sound sensible. "I can't just sit here while you're—"

"Dammit, Georgia," he said, cursing softly beneath his breath. "Just...do it... That was the deal—all right? Just do as I say."

She heard a loud click, then the endless hum of the dial tone.

Chapter 4

"Cord? Cord!"

What had they done to him? He could be shot, for all she knew . . . bleeding to death at this very moment. Her heart was thudding against her chest as all the possibilities raced through her mind, tormenting her with every imaginable horror.

"Oh, God," she said. Every nerve in her body warned her to stay put as Cord had ordered. To curl up tightly in the bed and pull the covers over her head until morning. He was the trained agent—he knew what to do.

But even as she was feeling the fright and the self-protecting emotions, she was swinging her bare legs over the side of the bed. She didn't bother changing clothes, but pulled a long lightweight coat from the closet. She didn't bother changing from her house slippers, but just grabbed the car keys, resetting the house alarm system and turning on lights as she went out, running as fast as she could to the car.

The house on Beech Circle was dark when she arrived. She parked across the street the way she had the last time. As she stared at the house, she felt her heart skittering wildly in her chest, felt her mouth go dry with fear.

This was where it had happened. This was the house that had brought so much morbid curiosity and caused her so many sleepless nights. And now, if she wanted to help Cord, she knew she had to go in.

It was one of the hardest things she'd ever forced herself to do.

By the time she reached the door, she'd forgotten her fear, even forgotten where she was. All she could think of was Cord, lying wounded somewhere inside, perhaps even dying. The front door of the small house stood open and the interior was pitch-black except for one small shaft of light that came from the back of the house and fell across a hallway.

"Cord?" Her voice was a croak, raspy and barely intelligible. She cleared her throat, holding her hands together to stop their trembling.

"Cord?" Please, answer me, she was saying to herself. Please be all right. "Cord, are you here?"

She heard a noise from one of the bedrooms, then a soft groan and she headed in that direction. She felt as if each step were in slow motion, as if she were in a nightmare. She felt blood roaring in her ears, so loudly she could barely hear. But she forced herself to take that last step past the hallway into the darkened bedroom.

"Cord?" she whispered.

"Dammit, Georgia, what are you doing here?"

She heard his muttered curse from out of the darkness. Quickly she raked her hand along the wall until she found the switch that flooded the small bedroom with light.

She gasped when she saw Cord sitting on the floor, his back propped against a bed. The phone still sat on the floor beside him. In his hand was a Smith & Wesson, which he slowly lowered to the floor when she came into the room.

Georgia ran across the room and dropped to her knees beside him, her hands reaching out instinctively to touch him. His face was battered and bruised, but his silver-blue eyes were alert and clear as he stared at her with something between amusement and anger in their depths.

"Dammit . . . don't you ever listen?" he gasped.

"You aren't shot or . . . or anything like that, are you?" Her hands moved quickly over his body, searching for any serious bleeding.

" . . . told you not to come here. I told you to lock your doors and—"

"Well, I'm here now and there's no need to discuss it any further." She couldn't explain her emotions. She felt angry . . . more furious than she thought she'd ever felt in her life. She thought if the men who'd done this were here, she could kill them herself. "How could you do this?" she said, blaming him for her pain, needing to blame someone. Her words were clipped, and angry tears stung her eyes as she continued to check him for wounds.

"I didn't exactly plan it," he said wryly.

Cord saw her anger. And he saw the tears. And for the life of him, he couldn't explain how it affected him, or why such a warm rush of emotion swept over him. He shouldn't have involved her in this. She shouldn't be here like this in the middle of the night, still dressed in her soft nightgown, tears in her eyes, obviously frightened out of her wits. All he could think was that he should never have told her anything.

"I'm going to lock the front door and get some water and towels. I'll be right back."

As she left, she heard his sign of exasperation, but he made no other protest.

Georgia locked the front door and saw the splintered lock on the door at the back. Quickly she dragged a chair across the kitchen, positioning it under the doorknob. She turned on every light in the house, even the outside lights. Then she hurried to the small bathroom and gathered some towels, rummaging through the medicine cabinet for antiseptic and bandages. Before going to the bedroom, she ran back out to the tiny living room, where she'd seen a small bar when she'd turned on the lights.

She grabbed a decanter of bourbon and a small glass and hurried into the bedroom. It frightened her that Cord was still on the floor for she knew his stubbornness and his pride. If he'd been able, he would have dragged himself to his feet by now.

"Let me call a doctor," she said, placing all her supplies on the floor as she knelt beside him.

"No." He reached forward and took the decanter with his right hand. His left hand was wrapped around his rib cage and he kept his movements small. He drank one glass of the amber liquid straight down, then poured another.

"My Lord," Georgia whispered. "Don't you want some water or—"

He gazed at her wryly, then tossed the contents of the second glass down his throat.

"You shouldn't have come here." His voice was raw from the effects of the bourbon.

"What was I supposed to do, let you die? Just go to bed and say, ho-hum ... I'll think about this tomorrow?"

"I'm not going to die," he said, his mouth quirking to one side.

"Well, I didn't know that. You sounded terrible on the phone. And I must say, you don't look much better in person."

"Gee, thanks," he muttered.

She ignored his grunted protests as she cleaned his face with cool water and applied ointment to the scrapes and bruises. The worst cut was at the corner of his mouth…his very sensual, very disturbing mouth. Before she was finished, she found her own breathing had grown a little shaky. And it didn't help that all the while she worked, he watched her steadily, his silvery eyes moving over her face and down to the open coat where the outline of her breasts could be seen clearly beneath her nightshirt.

Cord was glad he wasn't standing, glad she couldn't know the effects of her nearness on his body. But for the life of him, he couldn't make himself pull away from her soft little hands, away from the feathery light touches that were causing the blood to pound hotly through his veins.

He could feel the effects of the bourbon begin to take hold, feel the warmth spread from his belly and down his legs. He couldn't take his gaze away from the woman in front of him, or ignore the way her beautiful pink mouth pursed thoughtfully while she cleaned the blood from his face. There was a slight wrinkle between her eyebrows as she worked. And her hair was still damp—a feathering of soft blond curls that framed her flushed face. She smelled of soap and shampoo and when she touched his mouth, her lashes suddenly lifted and those expressive brown eyes looked straight into his own.

She looked like a startled, frightened kitten as she stared into his eyes. He found himself wanting to reach for her, wanting to hold her and tell her everything would be all right. He wanted to kiss that soft sexy little mouth until she begged him to make love to her.

Georgia looked away from his eyes.

"Who did this to you?"

"Just some *good ole boys,* as they say in these parts."

"Must have been pretty *big* good ole boys," she said tersely. "You certainly look capable of taking care of yourself, in most circumstances."

"Didn't notice their size," he said. "I was too busy trying to get up off the floor."

"This is not funny, Cord," she said, her eyes going back to his face. "Were they here waiting? Did they catch you off guard?"

"Yeah, right," he said. His voice was sarcastic and hard, but she thought he hadn't managed to hide that little hint of embarrassment. His manly ego had been bruised as well as his handsome face, it seemed.

"It could happen to anyone," she said softly, sitting back on her heels and looking at him.

"It didn't happen to anyone," he said. "It happened to me, dammit..." He moved restlessly, grunting at the pain in his ribs.

"Here, let me look at those ribs. Do you think they're broken?"

"No," he said, moving away from her, away from her cool disturbing hands. "I'm all right. Just let me get up." He grunted again as he managed to come to his feet, bringing the liquor decanter with him. This time he took a drink straight from the bottle.

"Will you stop being so stubborn?" she said. "I'm going to look at your ribs, and that's all there is to it. And if I think they might be broken, I'm going to take you to the hospital."

He started to protest, but the pain in his side made it almost impossible to speak and breathe at the same time. For a moment he swayed, reaching out for Georgia as he did. He felt her hands at his waist, felt her pulling his denim shirt from the waistband of his jeans and he groaned.

"Sorry," she said. She stepped back, running her hands lightly over his ribs and probing at the bruised areas.

Cord was fascinated by the way her eyes softened as she examined his cuts and bruises. By the way her pink tongue darted between her lips as she worked. Hell, fascinated was hardly the word for what he felt when he looked at her.

She was still sexy as hell and yet there was a sweet vulnerability to her that hadn't been there before. Perhaps it was his need to take care of a woman. Maybe it was the contrast of her softness to his firmness. He didn't know. All he knew was that no other woman had ever done it for him quite like she had.

The very one he shouldn't want and couldn't have.

He staggered and gave a quiet groan as he tried to steady himself.

Georgia's hands stopped their movements and she lifted her chin, staring into his face with a puzzled expression.

"Cord Jamison," she whispered. "I do believe you're drunk."

"I sincerely hope so," he whispered, grinning crookedly at her.

"Have you eaten anything?"

"No...unless you count beer as one of the major food groups."

"Well," she said, nodding, "I'm beginning to see. You'd obviously had a few before you came home. That's why they took you by surprise and why the bourbon has taken effect so quickly."

"You sound like a teacher...and a little damned smug," he muttered, swaying.

"I don't mean to sound smug. There's nothing wrong with going out for a beer. It's just that when you came home—"

"Never let your guard down," he muttered. "One of the first things they teach you is never let down your damned guard."

"I don't think your ribs are broken," Georgia said, still exploring the smooth textures of his dark skin. Seeing a bruise she'd missed, she moved her hands lower, slipping her fingers just beneath the waistband of his jeans.

She heard his quick gasp for air and felt his hand clamp around her wrist. Slowly he pushed her away and inched himself straight, setting the bottle down on a table near the bed.

"That's enough for tonight, Nurse," he said sarcastically, his voice a husky whisper of protest.

"We need to get out of here, Cord. The men who did this could come back. Why do you think they came? Do you think it has anything to do with all the questions you've been asking around town?"

"Yeah," he muttered. "That's exactly what I think. But all they've done is confirm my suspicions. They're probably too dumb to know it...they're probably just doing someone else's dirty work. But they've made a major mistake...*major.*"

Georgia shivered, hearing the resolve in his voice, seeing the glitter of determination in his silvery eyes. Cord Jamison had grown into a very dangerous man since leaving Farmington. She'd hate to be on the opposite side of those impenetrable eyes when he was mad.

Seeing him stagger, Georgia put her arms around his waist. He was a tall man and despite his trim, muscular build, he was heavy. He was no longer the boy she used to know, but a man now, trained by hard work and physical exertion. She imagined that in his job it was a necessity. But all she could think of at the moment was how good he felt, how completely hard and masculine. They swayed together and Georgia placed her back against the doorframe for support.

With a soft grunt, Cord leaned against her, every inch of his hard body pressing against her softer one. He muttered something and pushed his fingers into her hair, holding her head still as he stared at her eyes, her mouth.

Georgia waited breathlessly, expectant and still. And she tried to tell herself all the reasons this shouldn't be happening—he was hurt; she was afraid.

"Cord, you're drunk," she whispered. "And you're hurt."

"Hell," he grunted. "I'm not that drunk."

Cord thought he'd never wanted anything in the world more than he wanted to taste her lips. She was so soft against his body, so warm and deliciously sweet. The hunger he felt practically ripped through him, startling and disturbing in its intensity. Even his being hurt couldn't stop it. He thought he could be dying and he would still want this woman. He had to force himself to pull away from her, and force himself to stand alone and watch her scramble away from him.

He stepped away from the doorway so she could get through without touching him and then he smiled.

"Go home, Georgia. You don't have to stay here and play nursemaid ..."

"I'm not leaving," she said, her lips clamping together stubbornly.

She'd managed to surprise him with that answer. He'd have thought the one thing she wanted at this moment was to get away from him. The quicker the better.

"So what are you going to do? Stay here and protect me?" he asked wryly with a soft sound of humor. "I don't need a mother or a baby-sitter."

"That's exactly what I'm going to do," she said, ignoring his sarcasm.

"In this house?"

Georgia froze. She stood dead still, feeling the hair at the back of her neck stand on end. Her lips parted and her eyes grew wide with alarm. She could feel the trembling begin from her toes and rush like wildfire up to her head.

"Oh, my God," she whispered. "I forgot. I completely forgot where I was." She glanced around at the bedroom as if seeing it for the first time. "Is this where—"

"No," he said quickly. He immediately regretted reminding here of what had happened in this house. He'd only intended to make her leave. But now the frightened haunted look in her eyes made him feel like a louse. "No, that room is closed off."

Georgia turned, her eyes going to the other side of the hallway where the bedroom door was closed. She shivered then and swallowed hard against the sick feeling that rose in her throat.

"I'm sorry," he said. "I shouldn't have—"

"No," she said quickly. "It's all right. I think I've needed to come here since...since it happened. Tonight with you...it isn't so bad." She stopped and stared into his eyes. "Will you come home with me?" she asked.

She saw the look in his eyes, the heat that turned his silver gaze to a dark disturbing blue. She felt the flush on her cheeks and she looked away.

"I don't think that's such a good idea...do you?" he asked.

She knew what he meant. And she knew what he wanted. The same thing she wanted. But she also knew it was too soon . . . too frightening to be experiencing all the explosive emotions she was feeling tonight.

"We're both adults," she said with a stubborn little lift of her chin. "Surely we can manage to stay in the same house for one night until we figure out how much trouble we're in and what we're going to do about it."

He smiled then, his look amused and wry, his eyes wary if not entirely clear of the desire he was feeling. He was in trouble all right. Big trouble. And it had absolutely nothing to do with the hoodlums that were trying to run him out of town.

"Hell," he said with a cool look. "What's one night?"

Chapter 5

Cord hadn't said a word since she helped settle him into the car. Georgia glanced at him from time to time on the short ride to her house, and each time, he was staring straight ahead...his gaze in the dashboard lights thoughtful and brooding.

When she parked in the garage and hit the switch to lower the door, she thought she heard his sigh of resignation and she knew he didn't want to be there. She knew all too well how he hated depending on anyone.

Before she could get out of the car and go around to help him, he had managed with an impatient groan to open his door and stand up. She thought he couldn't possibly imagine how it made her feel, seeing him with his pistol drawn, moving cautiously along the wall toward her back door. She stood transfixed as she watched him peek in, then reach his hand back toward her.

"Toss the keys here."

She did as he asked and stood beside her car, waiting and feeling little tingles of apprehension race along her arms and up the back of her neck.

She was surprised, after he unlocked the door, when he reached his hand toward her again.

"You'll have to come with me while I check out the house. I can't leave you here alone."

"I'll be fine—" she began.

Only his eyes moved toward her, riveting her to the spot where she stood.

"You don't have a pistol," he snapped. "You don't even have your car keys," he said, dangling her keys in the air. His voice was neither kind nor patient.

Finally Georgia sighed and walked up the steps to take his hand, still outstretched toward her. He pulled her around behind him, still holding her hand as they went into the kitchen and cautiously proceeded through the house. She was glad she had left all the lights on.

Once he had checked all the rooms downstairs and the front door, he turned toward her and handed her the car keys.

"I'm going to check the rooms upstairs. Stay close to the back door, have the keys ready. If you hear anything, you take the car and get out of here. Do you understand me?"

"Cord, don't you think—"

"I *don't* think," he whispered, his voice and eyes hard and wary. "If you take time to think, it's too late. Now go on. Do as I say."

She rolled her eyes in exasperation. She knew he only meant to protect her in case someone really was waiting upstairs. So she did as he asked.

Cord's steps were quiet as he moved from room to room upstairs. Up here, no lights had been left on except in one room at the far end of the hallway. Slowly he made his way through each bedroom, flicking on lights, checking closets. He didn't intend to be taken by surprise again.

When he came to the last room, the one with the light on, he held his breath as he opened the door. He stepped inside, walking quickly across the cream-colored carpet to check all the doors and windows. Once he was satisfied that the room was secure, he turned slowly, allowing himself a moment to study the bedroom that he knew had to be Georgia's.

It was as neat as the other rooms. Yet it was more lived-in . . . warmer and more feminine. And there was the sweet, lingering scent of perfume—her perfume.

That familiar fragrance brought everything back to Cord with a hard jolt to the pit of his stomach—memories he once thought he'd banished forever. He closed his eyes, remembering. Warm summer nights and the pungent scent of the lake, brown eyes looking up into his with such sweet trust, soft moans of pleasure . . . and the tantalizing fragrance of this same perfume.

"Hell," he said, opening his eyes quickly and forcing himself to move out of the disturbing room. But he couldn't keep his eyes from wandering toward the bed that dominated the room—the delicately scrolled white wrought-iron bed—so completely feminine, so breathtakingly Georgia.

He swallowed hard and took a deep breath, forgetting his ribs until the movement sent pain shooting through his side. He gasped and bent over, steadying himself until the pain subsided, then backing out of the room and closing the door.

To Georgia downstairs, the waiting seemed interminable. She was aware of even the smallest sounds—the ticking of the kitchen clock on the wall, the quiet hum of the refrigerator. And when the ice maker suddenly dumped ice out inside the freezer, Georgia jumped and felt her heart begin to accelerate.

She didn't know when Cord came back downstairs. She didn't hear him at all until she looked up and saw him standing in the doorway across the room from her.

She jumped again and closed her eyes for a moment, as her hand moved upward to clutch at her heart.

"Good Lord, you scared me," she whispered. "Is everything all right? Has anyone—"

"The house is clear. Windows and doors are all secure—no sign of tampering. You can reset your alarm now."

She thought he sounded so impersonal and so calm. So professional. As if she were only an acquaintance and he an officer of the law doing his job.

After she set the alarm, she turned back to him, hardly knowing what to say. He was really here, really standing across her kitchen looking at her, and now that he was, after all the years of wondering what she would do, what she would say, she found herself practically speechless.

"Would...would you like some coffee?" she managed to say.

"Yeah, that sounds good." He took off his shoulder holster and placed it and his pistol on the kitchen cabinet.

Georgia noted how stiff he was and how slowly he moved because of his bruised ribs, and for a moment, she wanted to go to him and offer her help. But she knew instinctively that he wouldn't welcome it.

"Does the gun bother you?" he asked, nodding toward his holster. "You never used to like guns."

"No...no," she stammered, not looking at him. "It doesn't bother me." Actually it made her feel safer. *His presence* made her feel safe.

It was the first time he'd made reference to what used to be and she didn't want him to know how it made her knees feel weak and rubbery.

Georgia busied herself in the kitchen while the coffee perked. There was only the silence of the night surrounding them, the quiet ticking of the clock, the distant barking of a dog and the house's familiar night sounds.

She didn't sit at the table with him until she placed a cup of coffee before him.

"Those men tonight," she began. "The ones who attacked you. Did they say anything? A warning or—"

"They told me I didn't belong here." His eyes as he looked at her were frosty, a clear aqua blue beneath the bright kitchen lights. " . . . any more than Sheila had. But hell, I knew that."

Georgia frowned and bit her lip. He'd never felt welcome in Farmington, even though he'd grown up here just as she had. It had been one of the things she couldn't understand about him when they were younger. She had loved Farmington—of course, she would love it—she had been well cared for, welcomed and loved by everyone in town. She was a Blake. It had only been in the past few years that she had come to see exactly what Cord meant when he said he hated the small-town condescension and its self-imposed caste system.

Now, because of Sheila, she supposed he had even more reason to hate it.

"Is that all?" she asked.

"Isn't that enough?"

"Cord," she said with a sigh, "I'm on your side."

"Are you?"

She stood up from the table and walked to the cabinet, keeping her back to him and holding on to the sink to still her trembling hands. He made her feel so defensive, so frustrated. Why couldn't he just say what he meant? And why couldn't she simply offer him her sympathy and her support?

"Whether you believe it or not, I do understand how you feel," she said, forcing herself to turn and face those wary blue eyes.

"Oh," he said, leaning back in his chair with a smug look on his handsome face. "Do you now? Why don't you tell me how it is I feel."

She went quickly to the table, sitting and leaning toward him, looking intently into his eyes and wanting more than anything in the world for him to know that she did understand.

"A long time ago, I'll admit, I probably *didn't* understand. But I was young and naive—I saw the entire world through this rosy optimistic glow. But I do know how you feel. I've seen the snobbery, the difference that's made in this town between people like my father and—" She stopped, staring at him and seeing the slow sarcastic smile that came to his lips.

"And people like me?"

"Why do you still see yourself that way? You're a respected, intelligent man—you've proven yourself. No one can deny that."

"Maybe you're right," he said, his eyes still cold and emotionless. "Maybe I have. But the question is, why did I have to prove myself? I'd think that would be unnecessary to anyone who knew me."

When his lashes flickered upward quickly, revealing those stormy blue eyes, Georgia felt a tremble course through her entire body. There was something in his eyes...a mistrust, some long-hidden pain that she couldn't quite understand. All she could do was stare at him, drowning, remembering...as lost as she'd ever been when he was near.

She stood up suddenly, almost turning over her coffee in the process. "I...I have to get to bed or I'll never make it to work on time." She glanced back at him and saw that he was still watching her.

"You can take any of the bedrooms upstairs," she said. "Mine is the one at the end of the hall."

She didn't have to tell him that, he thought, staring hard at her. He'd already discovered that for himself.

"Tomorrow I'd like to look through Bob's bank statements, if you don't mind. I have a hunch I'd like to check out."

"Of course," she said, trying to remain as impersonal as he was. "What hunch?"

"I want to check deposit dates for the past year against Sheila's. A few months before she died, she wrote to me—a bubbly, excited letter telling me about a money-making scheme that she was onto. She said that if things worked out, she wouldn't have to ask me for money ever again. At the time, I thought little of it—she was always trying to hit it big with one crazy scheme or another. But when her personal effects were finally released to me, I discovered that she had almost fifty thousand dollars in her bank account—a fortune for someone like my sister. She never had that much money in her life...never had a prospect of making such money. I want to know where it came from. And I want to know if Bob gave it to her, or if, perhaps, he was receiving payments, too."

"What do you suspect...drugs?"

"Maybe."

Seeing the defensive look return to his eyes, Georgia didn't bother telling him that she disagreed about drugs being involved. Bob might have drank too much, but she had never known him to take drugs, or even to show an interest in them. And he certainly hadn't needed the money, not from something as risky as drug dealing.

"I'll leave his bank statements on the desk in the study," she said. "Feel free to stay here tomorrow as long as you wish. There's pain medication in the bathroom upstairs if you need it." She ignored the glitter of amusement that came to his eyes and turned and left the kitchen.

She couldn't sleep. How could she sleep with Cord Jamison just down the hall? With the memories that he'd resurrected by his return, burning in her mind? There had been many nights when she'd lain in bed, thinking of him, bringing him back to her, if only for a time, if only in her thoughts. Even after she was married, before Bob had moved into another bedroom, she had lain beside her husband and wished Cord Jamison back to her. She'd used those visions, those memories, to soothe her heart, to console herself whenever she felt lost and alone, when she wanted to cry out to the night with anguish at what a waste her life was and how defeated she felt in her shell of a marriage.

God, he had been her imaginary savior those nights, just as surely as he had been that summer night so long ago. And now he was here, so close and yet so very far away. And she thought that the memories were not real anymore, and could never be brought back. The cold look in his silver-blue eyes made that much perfectly clear.

It was well past midnight when she finally drifted off into a restless sleep.

The visions came quickly, it seemed. Fragmented images and shadows at first. Then the voices, whispery and eerie, forcing her to listen against her will.

Her dreams were all mixed up—shadow pictures of Bob, images of Sheila, laughing . . . taunting Georgia with her insolent, brazen beauty and her easy, thoughtless conquests.

Georgia wanted to wake up. She tried hard to open her eyes, but the dreams only became more real and vivid. She saw Cord then—tall and strong, imposing in his masculinity, his eyes tender as he held out his hand to her.

"Cord," she whispered, moving toward him. She reached out for his hand, wanting more than anything to feel the warmth of his skin, to feel his strong arms enfold her and pull her against the length of his muscled body. The sight of him, looking at her that way, waiting expectantly with such love in his eyes, made her feel good. Made her feel wanted and loved for the first time in years. Was it any wonder she felt such impatience to go to him?

But she couldn't seem to get closer. Every time she reached out, he moved farther away. Now there was hurt in his eyes, as if she had failed him, as if he wanted to keep her at arm's length.

"Go back," she heard him say.

And then she saw them. Two shadowy figures, moving out of the darkness behind Cord, coming toward him in crouched, menacing positions, their faces blank and terrifying.

"Cord!" she screamed, trying to warn him.

He didn't seem to hear her, but continued waiting, hand outstretched, his eyes pleading.

"No," she cried again as she saw the men moving closer to Cord.

They were going to kill him. Right before her eyes, they intended to kill him and take away her last hope of ever holding him again. And she couldn't bear it. The thought of never seeing him, never holding him or kissing him was more than she could stand. She screamed out one last time, hoping against hope that he would hear her and turn and save himself.

"Cord!" The name rang through her mind again and again. Was it her voice, repeating it? Or was it an echo?

"Georgia," she heard someone whisper.

She opened her eyes and he was there. Strong and solid. Warm. Real.

Georgia was barely awake and she forgot everything except the dream, everything except the feeling of despair she'd felt when she thought she might lose him.

"Oh, Cord," she gasped, throwing her arms around his neck, pushing her face against his throat, shuddering as she breathed in the scent of him and felt his strong arms hesitate, then move around her. She was holding on to him for dear life. "Oh, Cord, I thought they were going to kill you...I thought—"

"Shh," he whispered against her ear. "It was only a bad dream. I'm here. Everything is all right."

How long had it been since he'd held her this way and reassured her...so tenderly...so sweetly? An eternity, it seemed.

Cord had known from the first moment he'd walked into this house that it was a mistake staying here. Every time he looked into Georgia's soft brown eyes, he knew that. Every time he felt the sexual tension between them, reaching out, pulling at him, making him remember, making him feel, he knew it.

Dear God, but he wanted her. After all that had happened, he still wanted her as hotly as ever. And he knew she felt the same way.

When she turned her head and he felt her breath on his cheek, he moved by pure instinct, forgetting his cut lip and taking her mouth quickly, desperately. Before he let himself think about the consequences.

Georgia welcomed his hard, almost bruising kiss. It had been so long. No one had ever made her feel this way, had ever made her feel such wild, uncontrollable longings.

When his hands moved along her body, she drew him down from a sitting position, forgetting his injuries until she heard his quiet groan. She pulled her mouth away from his, looking up into his eyes in the dimly-lit room. She meant to ask if he was in pain, but there was no time before he was kissing her again. And she was lost.

Her memories and her dreams could not compare to this, to the reality of his touch.

Cord felt her body beneath his, warm and soft and pliable beneath her silky nightgown. He wanted to push the material out of the way and take her then and there. Wanted more than anything to make love to her, hear her soft cries of pleasure. He shuddered as he felt her small hands moving lightly down his body. Impatient, wanting hands that had always been able to make him do anything.

Suddenly he pulled away from her, taking her wrists and dragging them upward until he held them pinned over her head.

"Do you have any idea what you're doing to me?" he asked, his voice gruff and breathless.

"I know. Oh . . . I know."

It had happened so quickly. He hadn't been asleep when he'd heard her cries and rushed in to find her thrashing on the bed in the frightening throes of a nightmare. He hadn't had time to think—to even hear the warnings of his own mind.

Knowing he shouldn't, as he held her arms with one hand, he let the other trail down her bare shoulders, move slowly downward to cup her soft full breast. When she gasped and closed her eyes, he bent to kiss her open mouth, her little moan of pleasure driving him out of his mind.

Holding her, kissing her, brought memories of all those nights. Those hot, forbidden nights by the lake. Knowing she didn't belong to him had made it even more exciting at first. But he thought he had loved her from the very beginning...perhaps even before he knew her. And he had been certain that she loved him, too.

Until her father came with the money. Until that fall when he'd seen the newspaper clipping that Sheila sent—the picture of Georgia gazing up at her bridegroom with that same look of trust in her eyes.

It was that image that finally caused Cord to pull away from Georgia. He heard her murmur of protest and saw her eyes open wide as she stared up at him with a questioning look.

For a moment he was frozen there above her, gazing into her eyes, trying to fight the rush of desire that urged him to go on, to ignore his conscience and take her the way she wanted to be taken. The way they both wanted it.

He told himself it didn't matter. That he could make love to her here and now, satisfy the craving he had for her that never seemed to go away. Forget the past and just let it happen. It was what he wanted...it was *all* he wanted.

The muscles in his arms were trembling from holding himself away, from waiting for the fulfillment that was so near. For a moment his eyes moved away from her, to the lacy, feminine bedroom as he tried to reason between his body and his brain.

With a deep breath, he pulled away from her, releasing her arms and sitting on the edge of the bed.

"This isn't right," he whispered hoarsely, pushing his hand impatiently through his hair.

Georgia sat up in the bed, her brown eyes pained and uncertain.

"Why?" she asked. "Why isn't it? I want you to...I..."

"Don't," he growled, standing up and moving away from her. "Don't even say it."

"Cord..."

Her soft, troubled eyes tempted him to a level that was almost more than he could endure. Her sweetly scented skin, aglow beneath the dim lights, made him want to lose himself in her.

She was his one weakness. And that weakness in himself angered him and brought back all the pain, all the bitterness he'd held against her memory all these years.

"Do you really think I'm going to make love to you here? In Bob Ashley's home? In his bed?" His voice was harsh, filled with a bitter ugliness that he couldn't stop.

Georgia thought she had never seen such a look in anyone's eyes. It was as if he hated her. She felt completely defenseless against it...devastated.

She watched in disbelief as he turned and stalked out of her bedroom, the light turning his dark skin a warm, honey color. She wanted to leap from the bed and run to place her hands against his muscled back.

Instead, she pulled the lace-trimmed sheet up beneath her chin, taking the edge of it in her teeth and closing her eyes against the onslaught of pain she felt at his leaving.

She had made a fool of herself. He probably thought she had faked the entire thing, pretending to have a bad dream just so he would come to her rescue.

But he couldn't deny he wanted her, just as badly as she wanted him. His kisses were wild, the kisses of a man filled with an almost uncontrollable hunger. She had felt his body against hers, hard and ready, and she had reveled in the fact that he still felt the same, that she still had the power to make him feel that way.

Was it the bedroom that had made him turn away...this house? She'd always known he resented Bob and everything he represented in Farmington. Should she go to him . . . tell him that this was her bedroom and hers alone? That no one had ever slept in this bed except her?

That she had never loved Bob?

She couldn't understand why he didn't know that his resentment was unnecessary. It wasn't as if she had chosen Bob over Cord. *He* had been the one to leave her that summer. If anything, she should be the one holding back, the one refusing to become involved again.

"Then why, Cord?" she whispered, her troubled gaze moving toward the closed door. "Why?"

She didn't sleep for hours. And she knew that Cord didn't, either. She could hear him well into the early hours of the morning, moving around in the room next to hers, the floor in the old Victorian house creaking beneath his footsteps as he paced.

When she finally slept, it was from sheer exhaustion. She went to sleep half sitting, half lying against the pillows in her bed, waking the next morning with a stiff neck and a dull headache.

She thought she heard the sound of the shower down the hall, but after she emerged from a quick bath, she heard nothing and she wondered if she had imagined it. If Cord was as exhausted as she, he was probably still in bed.

It wasn't until she came down the stairs, dressed and ready for work, that she smelled the coffee and heard the sound of someone in the kitchen.

A muscle quivered nervously in the pit of her stomach as she stepped through the kitchen doorway and saw Cord standing at the window, his back toward the door.

He was dressed in faded jeans and a soft blue corduroy shirt neatly tucked in at the waist. His shoulders were broad and powerful-looking, and Georgia held her breath for a moment as she let her eyes have their fill before he realized she was there. She even imagined walking to him, putting her arms around his trim waist and resting her head against his back, breathing in the freshly-showered scent of him.

"Good morning," she said finally, feeling shaken, feeling her knees begin to tremble as she watched him.

He turned slowly, his gaze coming quickly to her as he took in every inch of her body. For a moment, his eyes were unguarded and filled with a quiet longing.

"I made coffee. I hope you don't mind."

"Of course I don't," she said, trying to ignore the way his eyes changed as she walked into the room. "How are you doing?" She noted the bruise on his jaw.

"I'm fine."

He had become wary again, his eyes closed and unreadable. As if they hadn't kissed. As if he hadn't lain in her bed and held her so tightly that it took her breath away just thinking about it.

As if they hadn't almost made love.

"I . . . I wasn't sure you'd still be here," she said, pouring a cup of coffee with trembling hands.

"I intend to go over Bob's statements . . . remember?"

"Yes," she said, still shaken by his presence and all the emotions he made her feel. "Yes, of course I remember. I'll get them before I go to work."

He didn't say a word as she left the kitchen and went to the study. Silently she cursed her cold, trembling fingers as she found Bob's papers and placed them neatly on top of the huge old desk that dominated the study.

When she came back to the kitchen, Cord was pushing his arms into a soft leather bomber jacket.

"I'll drive you to work."

"No," she said quickly. She looked straight into his eyes. "That won't be necessary. I'll be fine."

"I insist. Besides, I need a car today. That is, if you don't mind."

"Oh . . . no. Of course I don't mind. But there's another car. Bob's—"

His look stopped her words. That and his softly muttered curse.

Of course he wouldn't want to drive Bob's car. What was she thinking?

Without another word, she took her car keys from the hook near the door and handed them to him, careful that their hands did not actually touch. Then she got her purse and moved past him.

There was a heavy air of tension in the car as Cord drove silently through the leaf-littered streets toward the courthouse. And although Georgia glanced at him from time to time out of the corner of her eye, she said nothing.

He was so different this morning. So cold and distant that she could almost imagine last night had never happened.

When he stopped at the curb in front of the courthouse, Georgia was aware of the looks of curiosity from passersby. Several of the women who worked in the various county offices even stooped down, peering into the car with blatant disregard for her privacy. Georgia saw their eyes widen, saw their looks of speculation when they recognized the driver, and she wanted to laugh.

She got out of the car and turned to close the door.

"You won't forget the autopsy report," Cord reminded quietly. "And try to find out about the key to the safe-deposit box."

"I won't forget. I haven't forgotten anything," she added. She gazed into his eyes for a moment before closing the car door and turning to walk away.

"Dammit," Cord muttered. He gripped the steering wheel so tightly that he could feel the ache all the way to his shoulders and down along the bruising at his side.

He watched Georgia walk away, couldn't force himself not to watch as she moved briskly up the steps toward the courthouse. Her hips beneath the staid, neatly-fitted black skirt were tantalizing. He doubted that she even realized how provocative her walk was, or what the slight swing of her curvaceous hips and the purposeful stride of her beautiful legs did to a man.

He was still cursing softly as he put the red sports car in gear and wheeled it away from the curb.

Chapter 6

Georgia didn't know how she made it through that day. All she could think about was Cord, and the look in his eyes last night when he'd walked out of her room. And as much as her mind was filled with him, her heart was consumed with a bittersweet, undeniable longing that she didn't quite know how to handle.

She was the only one working in Judge Stone's office and of course he had made her feel very welcome. But other women in the courthouse, some of whom had looked into the car so curiously that morning, made a point of welcoming her back, as well.

She knew part of it was out of genuine friendship. And although no one actually mentioned Cord's name, she knew that part of their interest was also simply blatant curiosity.

With everyone knowing that Cord had brought her to work, she realized it was only a matter of time before her parents learned that he was back, too. And that he had stayed at her house last night. She supposed she should tell them before they found out from someone else. At least she could explain the circumstances before they jumped to their own obvious conclusions.

She was thankful that she had something to do at lunch, forcing her to turn down the invitations from her curious co-workers. She wasn't in the mood to answer their questions, certainly not to discuss Cord Jamison with them.

She went to the coroner's office first and when she told the secretary what she wanted, she was surprised when the young woman went into another office and came back with the county coroner behind her.

"Dr. Stamps," Georgia said, a bit taken aback. "I really didn't mean to bother you. All I need is a copy of Bob's autopsy report." She smiled at the timid-looking doctor, whose eyes were almost obscured behind thick wire-rimmed glasses.

"Quite all right," he said. The doctor had an unusually deep voice that sounded slightly incongruous coming from such a frail-looking man. "Quite all right." He turned to one of the file cabinets, although Georgia didn't understand why the secretary couldn't have done that just as well.

"If you don't mind my asking…what exactly do you need it for?" the doctor asked, glancing at her over his shoulder.

"Oh, just insurance claims," she said, remembering Cord's warning.

"Well, I'm not convinced you really need to see it. So disturbing and all," he said with a concerned smile. Still, he continued to shuffle through the files. "My, I'm having a hard time finding it. Why don't I just make a copy of it when I find it and send it to the insurance company for you. You don't want to have to bother with this."

She glanced at him for a moment, then at his secretary, who couldn't quite seem to meet Georgia's eyes.

"I don't have the address with me, and I really don't want to put it off any longer," Georgia said, hoping her explanation sounded calm and reasonable. She told herself there was no need to be suspicious. She had known Dr. Stamps all her life and she was sure he was genuinely concerned for her welfare. "I don't mind waiting while you look," she added.

"Well," he said with a shake of his head, "let's see."

"There it is, Dr. Stamps," the secretary said, reaching over his shoulder into the file cabinet. "You just passed it."

"So I did," he said, chuckling. "So I did." He turned back to Georgia, the paper in his hand. "Are you sure, now? You can call tomorrow if you like...give us the address. We'll be more than happy to—"

"I'm sure," Georgia said, feeling suddenly impatient and jittery.

Silently the doctor gave the paper to his secretary and she went to the copy machine.

"I hear you went back to work today," he said.

"Yes, I did," Georgia said, glancing past him at the secretary. She didn't wonder how he knew. Farmington was a small town. Everyone knew everyone else's business here.

"You look tired," he said. "I hope you're not pushing it, going back to Judge Stone so soon."

Georgia took a deep breath, trying to remain calm and to be polite.

"It's been over three months," she said. "I hardly think that's too soon. I probably should have gone back before now."

He nodded, and for a moment Georgia felt guilty. She didn't mean to be impatient or short with him. She was just tired of everyone prying into her business and trying to run her life for her.

She wondered what he would think, what all of them would think, if they knew the real reason she looked so tired today.

She took the report, not bothering to look at it, and folding it, stuck it down inside her purse. Then she left the office and headed down the street to Bob's office to see if they had an extra key to his safe-deposit box. She hadn't cleaned out his office yet—everyone told her there was no hurry. After all, she still owned the business and could do with his office as she pleased.

There were only two women in the office that day and both of them seemed genuinely happy to see Georgia. They were sweetly solicitous, going immediately to unlock Bob's office when Georgia told them what she was looking for.

"He didn't leave an extra key with me," Mrs. Ramsey said, shaking her head. She was the office secretary and had been there since Bob first opened the real-estate office eight years ago. "But then he probably wouldn't have for his personal box. If there is an extra, it will be in his office."

Georgia felt her heart skip a beat as she stepped into the quiet, airless office. It was the first time she'd been there since Bob's death. Quickly she pushed her anxieties away and began to rummage through his desk.

"Have you decided what to do about the office?" Mrs. Ramsey asked from the doorway. "I hope you don't intend closing it. Jobs are hard to find nowadays."

"I don't know," Georgia said, barely glancing toward Mrs. Ramsey. "I really haven't decided yet. But don't worry," she said, smiling at the older woman. "If I do decide to sell, I'll make sure you and Trisha have a job." She glanced into the other room and saw Trisha's smile of relief.

She sighed, turning around in the room and looking at the row of keys that hung on the wall behind the desk. Surely

Bob hadn't put an extra set of safe-deposit box keys with the real-estate office's house listings. She flipped through the keys just in case, but there was no small red key there, either.

"Well," she said. "Maybe he didn't have an extra key. Maybe I'll just have to ask the bank about it."

"Sorry," Mrs. Ramsey said, shrugging her shoulders.

Georgia glanced at her watch. "I hate to run, but I'm going to be late," she said.

"Not that the judge would mind," Mrs. Ramsey said.

"I know," Georgia said. "But I don't like to take advantage of his kindness."

"Well, you take care now, hon," the woman said. "And come back anytime. We leave Mr. Ashley's door locked, you know, so no one will bother any of his things. I know you haven't felt up to clearing out in there. But there's no hurry—it's not like we need the space."

"I'll do that real soon," Georgia said, knowing that Mrs. Ramsey was only being polite and that she'd probably like to put Bob's office to better use.

Back at work, as five o'clock grew nearer, Georgia found herself becoming more and more nervous. She told herself it was because she hadn't had time to eat lunch, that she'd grabbed only crackers and a soft drink from the concession stand downstairs and that she'd had too many cups of coffee during the long afternoon.

But she knew deep inside that it was the prospect of seeing Cord again.

When she walked outside and saw the red convertible sitting at the curb, she felt her heart begin to accelerate. Gold-and-orange leaves drifted like snowflakes around her as she walked toward the car.

It was a warm autumn afternoon and Cord had the car's top down. Georgia could see the glint of his black hair in the waning afternoon sunlight.

She walked quickly to the car, opened the door and slid in, meeting his eyes before he turned away and started the engine.

She ignored the looks of everyone passing by them on the sidewalk.

Let them look and wonder. Let them all gossip and speculate to their heart's content. She didn't care what they thought. Only that he was here with her, close enough to touch.

"Did you get the report?" he asked.

She reached into her purse and handed the folded report to him. Cord's eyes were watchful as he took it and slid it into his shirt pocket.

"Have you looked at it?"

"No," she said, her voice quiet as she turned her head to gaze at the colors on the distant mountains.

"I'm sorry if this is difficult for you," he said quietly.

She turned to look at him, noting the way his eyes made quick observances as he drove. She let her gaze linger on his strong jaw and mouth before he turned and caught her watching him. Still, she didn't look away. At the moment she simply didn't care if he knew how she felt. Didn't care if he saw the wanting in her eyes.

She saw the muscles in the side of his face flex as he turned his eyes back toward the road.

"How about you?" she asked. "How's your side?"

"It's fine," he said, his voice curt and dismissive.

"How did your hunch turn out?"

"Better than I expected, actually," he said as he turned into her drive. "I'll show you when we get inside."

In the house, she followed him to the study and saw that there were papers scattered across the top of the desk.

Cord flipped on the light and moved to the desk. Across the upper portion were papers unfamiliar to her—Sheila's bank statements—and lined up beneath them were Bob's. Certain numbers on the pages were circled in red.

Georgia leaned closer, glancing from the bottom row of papers and up to the top row to make comparisons.

She couldn't believe what she saw.

"You see," Cord said, standing very close behind her and pointing at the papers with a pencil. "These deposits here and here are identical, both in date and amounts. A couple of others have the same amounts, but the dates vary by a day or two. But I don't think that's significant—Sheila's deposits were made before Bob's and that could mean only that she was more eager than him or that he was busy or out of town."

"I can't believe this," Georgia said, turning to look at him. "What do you think it means exactly?"

"I'm not sure where they were getting the money. But I'm positive these deposits are not coincidental. Once I began to find the similarities, I knew it was what I'd been looking for. I could feel it."

There was such quiet determination in his voice that Georgia didn't doubt him for a moment. And she couldn't doubt the figures, or the feeling she got when she saw them. It was like Cord said—that feeling of being onto something important.

"What do we do now?"

"I'm not sure. What about the safe-deposit box key? Did you find a duplicate in his office?"

"No... nothing. But I think he has a receipt here somewhere," she said, bending to open one of the desk drawers. "It would have the box number on it."

Cord's gaze rested on the back of Georgia's head, noting the way the shining blond curls lay tousled and windblown. It was all he could do to keep from reaching out and touching that mass of gold. And when she stooped down to open a bottom drawer, he felt his stomach muscles tighten as he let his eyes absorb the vision of her rounded hips and the tantalizing glimpse of stocking-covered thighs where her skirt slid upward with her movements.

He took a deep breath and deliberately turned away.

"Ah," she said. "I knew it. Here it is."

He turned back to see her holding up the receipt. There was a sparkle in her brown eyes, like a child who'd found the prize Easter egg.

"Number ninety-eight." She waved the paper toward him, her eyes serious and determined. "Tomorrow I'll take this to the bank and explain that the key is lost. It's my father's bank, so I'm sure there will be no questions asked."

Cord's lips quirked to one side and his lashes slowly lowered, closing off his emotions. The mention of her father seemed to always have that effect on him. Georgia wondered why he disliked her father so much. She could understand if Cord had ever known what Horace Blake really thought about him. But she'd purposely kept her father's disapproval from Cord, because she hadn't wanted him to be hurt.

Before she had time to say anything, the phone on the desk rang. Georgia picked it up immediately, without a conscious thought.

"Yes, hello..."

"Georgia, for heaven's sake." It was her mother's voice and there was definite agitation in the soft southern lilt. "Have you completely lost your senses? Letting that...that man actually stay in your house. I heard he even drove you to work this morning. That he was driving *your* car, for pity's sake. Your father is going to have a conniption when he hears about this.''

Georgia made a quiet huffing sound and rolled her eyes toward the ceiling. She shifted her weight onto one leg, her hips to one side as she held the phone between her shoulder and ear and crossed her arms.

Cord watched her steadily, making no attempt to leave the room or to pretend he didn't hear the agitated voice on the other end of the phone, and didn't know what was happening.

"Georgia? Do you hear me?" her mother said, her voice rising with exasperation. "Well . . . is it true?"

"Yes, Mother, as a matter of fact, it is. Cord Jamison did spend the night here, in the guest room."

Cord leaned back against the desk, crossing his arms over his chest. His chin came up and he gazed straight into Georgia's eyes, smiling when he saw the flush of color rush to her cheeks.

Georgia clamped her lips together and her eyes grew dark and filled with frustration.

"Mother, I don't have time—''

"Well, you just take time, young lady. This is serious. Do you have any idea what everyone in town will say . . . what they will think?"

"I don't care what they think," Georgia said through clenched teeth, trying desperately to ignore Cord's self-satisfied smile.

For a moment Georgia considered telling her mother the circumstances of Cord's presence. About how he had been hurt, how she had insisted on his coming here. But she didn't, merely because she was sick of the interference, not only from her parents, but from everyone in town.

"You know, Georgia, as soon as your father finds out, he'll be right over there to talk to you."

"No," Georgia said quickly. "No, Mother—I don't want him over here. This is no one's business but mine."

"Well, I declare," her mother huffed in exasperation. Georgia could practically hear her gasp on the phone before she spoke again. "He's there, isn't he? He's right there with you, listening to this conversation. Oh, Georgia, sweetheart—this is not wise. You know that man is pure trouble. You know how he took advantage of your innocence, how he left you. Oh, honey, I don't ever want to see you hurt that way again—"

"Mother," Georgia said quietly. "Mother, listen to me. It's not the same...all right?" She glanced at Cord, feeling as if he could actually hear her mother's side of the conversation, too.

"I'm a grown woman now. It's not the same." She pulled her gaze away from Cord's riveting blue eyes. "Please...do me a favor—if Daddy doesn't know yet, don't tell him tonight. I've had a very long day and the last thing I need is a visit from him."

"He'll be extremely angry with me if he finds out that I knew and didn't tell him."

"Then don't let him find out, Mother." Georgia said impatiently. She was quickly losing all composure because of the conversation, especially with Cord watching her. She didn't understand why her mother felt she had to tell her husband everything she knew. "I'll talk to him about it tomorrow."

"You promise?"

"Yes, I promise," Georgia said, taking a long slow breath. "Good night." She hung up the phone, not even waiting to see if her mother said anything else.

When she turned to Cord, he was still watching her. His quicksilver gaze hadn't left her face for a moment. She frowned at him, feeling childish and defensive, feeling the need to run from those quiet, intelligent eyes.

"What?" she snapped.

He shrugged his powerful shoulders and continued gazing steadily at her in a way that made Georgia want to scream.

"What's not the same?" he asked, his voice deep and deceptively quiet.

She didn't intend to play games with him. Not now...not with all the emotion that surged between them every time they were near.

"You and me," she whispered, looking into his eyes.

"Ah," he said, leaning his head back, but still not moving from his position against the desk. "You and me. And what did your mother say?"

"What do you mean what did she say?" she asked, moving restlessly around the room, adjusting a lamp shade, moving decorative objects only the slightest bit.

"Does she approve...disapprove?"

"You know very well she disapproves," she said, frowning at him.

"Why? Because of who I am...who I *used* to be," he corrected as she opened her mouth to object. "Why didn't you just tell her the truth? That there's nothing between us anymore. That what we had was merely a summer infatuation. Or was that what you meant when you said you were a grown woman now?"

"You know it isn't. You know—"

"I don't know anything," he said, pushing himself away from the desk and lowering his hands to his hips. "When it comes to understanding you, Georgia, I don't know a damned thing."

"Cord—"

Just then the doorbell rang at the front of the house.

Georgia frowned and shook her head. She wanted to tell Cord that what he'd said wasn't true. Not for her, anyway. What was between them that summer was anything but an infatuation. And he knew it. Damn him, he knew it. He hadn't forgotten.

How could he even say such a thing, after last night? What she didn't understand was why he was still so bitter about the town and about her.

The doorbell rang again, more persistently this time.

"Oh, hell," Georgia muttered, turning to stride angrily out into the wide hall and toward the front door.

She groaned when she saw Mike Goodwin through the window, standing on the front porch with his sheriff's hat in his hands. This was all she needed—more advice, more interference from someone who had no idea what was going on with her.

She was aware of Cord behind her, stopping at the doorway to the study and leaning his broad shoulder against the wall.

Georgia attempted a smile as she opened the door, but she didn't step aside or indicate that Mike should come inside.

"Mike," she said brightly. "Is anything wrong? What are you doing here?"

Mike moved his head, looking around her. She knew he saw Cord standing in the hallway. She could see the disapproval on his boyish face.

"Nothing's wrong," Mike said. "I just wanted to come by and see if you were all right." Again he glanced at Cord. "May I come in?"

Georgia frowned and glanced over her shoulder at Cord. She knew Cord wouldn't want Mike to see all the papers spread across the desk in the study. But she needn't have worried. Cord reached behind him and quietly closed the door.

"Of course." Georgia smoothed her skirt and with a wave of her hand motioned him into the living room across the hall from the study. "I...I just got home from work and...you know Cord Jamison, don't you?"

Mike stepped forward, offering his hand. "Sure do. How you doin', Jamison?"

Cord nodded, but he said nothing as he reached out to shake Mike's hand.

The three of them went into the living room and Georgia sat restlessly on the edge of the dark green and gold-striped taffeta settee. Mike sat across from her, looking out of place against the formality of the elegant room. He held his hat brim in his hands, twisting the hat around and around as he glanced from Georgia to Cord, who was standing with his elbow propped against the mantel of the marble fireplace.

There was a moment of awkward silence before Mike spoke.

"Dr. Stamps said you asked for a copy of Bob's autopsy report today."

"Yes, I did." Georgia wouldn't let herself glance at Cord. She didn't want anything she said or did to give them away.

"I could have done that for you, Georgia. There was no need for you to trouble yourself about any of this sordid mess."

She felt rather than saw Cord stiffen.

"He was my husband, Mike. Besides, I'm not helpless. I just want all this settled and to get on with my life."

Mike glanced toward Cord then and his dark eyes held little friendliness.

"I thought it *was* settled," Mike said. "Until Jamison here came back asking questions, stirring up trouble where there is none."

Georgia's eyes widened as she saw the animosity between the two men surface. She slid forward until she was almost off the edge of the couch. She wanted to say something, to try to control the situation before it got completely out of hand. But seeing Cord's clenched teeth and rigid jaw, she forced herself to remain silent.

"Maybe there's something you're afraid I'll find," Cord said in a quiet, deadly tone.

"What does that mean?" Mike asked, coming slowly to his feet.

"It means, maybe there's something you're afraid I'll find," Cord drawled sarcastically, not moving from where he stood.

"Hell, no. I'm satisfied with the results of the investigation. It was a murder/suicide, whether you choose to believe that or not. There's nothing else to find out. Bob Ashley was a friend of mine—don't you think I'd do everything I could if I thought something was not right about what we found?"

"I don't know," Cord said. "Would you?"

Mike took a step forward, but he had to look up into Cord's face. Mike Goodwin was a masculine man, certainly no weakling. But standing in front of Cord, he looked slender and decidedly outmanned.

"You listen to me, Jamison," he snarled. "Georgia is well thought of in this town. We're not about to stand by and see her hurt again by the likes of you—"

"Mike," Georgia warned, finally coming to her feet.

Cord's lids lifted slowly, his gaze touching Georgia coolly for just a moment before he turned his attention back to the sheriff.

"Again?" Cord said. "I don't know what you're talking about. What was between Georgia and myself is in the past. I'm here to find out what happened to my sister. It's only logical that I would talk to Georgia, considering her husband's involvement."

"You just remember what I said," Mike warned, shaking his finger toward Cord. "Georgia doesn't need anyone stirring up such nonsense. Use your brains, man, and your training. Go back to Atlanta where you belong."

"Funny," Cord drawled. "Those are almost the same words a couple of redneck thugs used when they jumped me the other night."

Mike stared at him a moment, then shook his head. He placed his hat on his head and turned to go. "I don't know what that's supposed to mean. But maybe you should take their advice. And if you've had a problem since you came back, why didn't you report it to the law?"

"I think I can handle it myself," Cord said, a quiet look of scorn across his face.

"Mike, please," Georgia said, taking his arm and moving with him toward the hallway. "I don't want any trouble. I'm fine. There's no reason for you or anyone else in town to worry about me." She glanced back at Cord, at the hard glint of distrust in his eyes. "I'm perfectly safe with Cord."

But she didn't feel safe. She felt completely beyond her league and out of control where he was concerned. He was as fierce as some ancient warrior. And sometimes just as frightening.

She walked Mike to the door, assuring him again that everything was all right. When she walked into the living room, Cord was at the window, watching Mike get into his patrol car.

"I don't know why you felt it necessary to insult him," she said. "Mike could help you if you'd only ask."

Cord grunted and turned to frown at her as if she'd lost her mind.

"Help me? God, you don't get it, do you? Hasn't it occurred to you that he's just a tad overcautious where you're concerned? Or that he might have some reason not to want you to see the autopsy report or to be involved with me and my investigation?"

"His concern for me is personal," she said, stung by his words and not wanting to admit that he might be right.

"Oh, it's personal all right. His personal hide would be my guess."

"This is ridiculous. Surely you don't suspect Mike Goodwin of being involved. For heaven's sake, Cord—he was one of Bob's best friends. And if the rumors are true, a few years ago, before he was married, Mike was even involved with Sheila. He—"

"When?" he snapped. "How long ago?" He came across the room, taking her arm and pulling her toward him. She felt as if she were being interrogated.

"I don't know," she said, trying to pull away. But his hard fingers held her tight as his eyes blazed down at her.

"Before he married Brenda. But you're wrong, Cord. This time you've let your resentment lead you in the wrong direction. Mike could not possibly have had anything to do with Bob's and Sheila's deaths. Never."

"Never say never," he said, his eyes glittering.

Suddenly the anger and the bitterness between them changed. Changed quickly to another, more intimate emotion—one that was always there when they touched. She could feel it and she could see in his eyes that he felt it, too.

"Let me go," she whispered.

"Why? Why should I?"

"Because," she said, her voice a soft plea. "I don't want it to be this way between us. I don't want—"

"How do you want it to be between us, Georgia? Like this?" He pulled her closer, his hands moving over her, touching her intimately and causing a small quiet groan to escape past her lips.

Only moments ago, there had been anger in his movements, that brisk efficient anger that never seemed to leave
him. Sometimes he looked at her with such hostility that she
found it hard to imagine his sweet, seductive lovemaking of
so long ago.

But now . . . now he was that way again. The fire in him,
banked to a soft gentle ember, his fury moving away from
them quickly, like a storm on a hot summer night.

He bent his head, touching her lips so softly that she
leaned toward him, moving into his kiss, into his embrace
with a quiet sigh of surrender. When he felt that surrender,
he swept her up, hard against him, moving his hands down
her waist and to the soft swell of her hips as he held her
tight.

Her arms went around his neck, holding on, urging him
with her softness and her hungry kisses to make love to her.
To put an end to the longing, the impatient tension that was
between them.

She heard his quiet groan, felt his lips trail away from her
mouth to the soft curve of her neck. She yielded to his every
movement, giving . . . encouraging, wanting him more than
she'd ever wanted anything in her life.

Then just as suddenly as it began, he pulled away, looking down at her, the fire still smoldering in his eyes.

"Is that how you wanted it to be?"

"Yes," she whispered. "Yes," she repeated, reaching for
his mouth again.

"But it was a lie," he said, his words hissing quietly in the
room. "All the sweetness, all the soft caresses . . . the lovemaking . . . God, especially that. It was all lies. I thought
you'd be able to admit it by now."

"Cord, what are you saying? And why?" she asked,
frowning and reaching for him as he pulled away. "Why are
you being this way?"

He turned from her, grabbing his leather jacket from a nearby chair and moving toward the front door.

"I swore when I left Farmington that summer that I'd never come back," he said, his voice shaking with anger. "And I swore I'd never live my life again based on a lie. You're tempting as hell, sweetheart, but I don't usually make the same mistakes twice."

He slammed the front door and Georgia went to the window. Her legs felt heavy and weighted and the soft sweet coil of desire deep inside her still pulled at her, still made her feel languid with heat and want.

She watched as he strode down the walkway and into the street, walking with long-legged strides as if the devil himself were behind him.

"Cord," she whispered, touching the windowpane. Hot tears rolled from her eyes and down her cheeks, but she barely noticed. She couldn't feel it for the terrible, burning ache in her heart.

Chapter 7

Even a quiet, warm bath didn't help Georgia relax. She was too restless, too troubled to sit still for very long.

Later, dressed in warm pajamas, sitting in the kitchen, she ate a bowl of soup. But she couldn't help going to the window often to look out at the darkened streets. She held her breath at every sound, at every passing car. She even considered calling Sheila's house to see if Cord was there.

"He'd hate that," she muttered as she paced the floor.

Would he ever come back? Did he intend calling off his investigation, after Mike's visit this afternoon? And if he did continue with it, would he still include her?

She didn't know. His actions, his lingering bitterness, left her completely baffled and confused.

By ten o'clock, she was exhausted and emotionally drained. She fell into bed, only to waken several times during the long night. Once, she even tiptoed next door and peeked into the dark guest bedroom, hoping that Cord had come back.

By morning, she was angry as well as worried.

"To hell with this," she muttered as she made coffee. "And to hell with you, Cord Jamison."

But even as she said it, she knew she didn't mean it. She had terrifying visions of him lying in the street somewhere, the victim of those same thugs who had attacked him before. She envisioned him lying on the floor of the bedroom in Sheila's house, hurt and unable to call for help.

She knew there was nothing she could do, so as she dressed for work, she made a bargain with herself. If she had not heard from Cord by the end of the day, she would go looking for him, whether he liked it or not.

She used her lunch break that day to go to the bank. She went immediately to the office lettered Henry Jarvis—Bank President. Henry was not only a business associate of her father's, he was also his oldest and closest friend. As Georgia's godfather, he was practically a member of the family.

"Georgia, honey," he said, coming from behind his desk with outstretched arms. His look was kind as he took Georgia's hands and bent forward to place a kiss on her cheek. "It's wonderful to see you, darlin'. But you are lookin' a little tired."

Lord, was everyone in Farmington going to tell her how tired she looked?

"I know," she murmured. "I haven't been sleeping very well."

"You need to come to the club Saturday night," he said. "Visit with your old friends, dance a little, have a good meal. Who knows, there might even be an eligible bachelor or two lurking in the crowd somewhere."

She made a soft murmur of protest and pulled away from the older man's grip. "Oh, I don't know, Uncle Henry. I'm not sure I'm quite ready for that."

"You're not . . . seeing someone, are you?" Something in the tone of his voice, in the way he held his breath as he waited for her reply, rang a little bell in Georgia's head.

Her chin came up and she looked into his eyes.

"Do you mean Cord Jamison?" she asked stiffly.

"Well," he said with an embarrassed little laugh. "I had heard—"

"I don't know why everyone in this town is so concerned with my business," she said, moving away from him. "I am not *seeing* Cord Jamison, not the way you mean. Or any-one else, for that matter. Oh, Lord, does my father know about this already? I asked Mother not to say anything un-til I'd had a chance to talk to him myself."

"He knows," Henry Jarvis said with an understanding nod. "And I imagine he heard it, not from your mother, but from someone here in the bank when he came in earlier. It's all anyone's talking about this morning."

Georgia glanced through the open door and saw several of the women clustered around a desk. They were watching her intently and when they saw her staring at them, they turned and scattered.

"Sometimes I understand why Cord hates this town so much," she said beneath her breath.

"What's that, darlin'?"

"Nothing . . . nothing. Uncle Henry, I came to ask you a favor." She took the receipt for the payment of the bank box from her purse and handed it to him. "Bob's key to his safe-deposit box seems to have disappeared. I wondered if you could open the box for me and—"

The look on his face stopped her. He was frowning as he shook his head. And he was looking at her with just the ti-niest hint of pity, as if she'd quite lost her mind.

"Well, I'd be happy to do that for you, of course, but..."

"But what?"

"Georgia, honey... the officers confiscated the contents of that box the day after Bob's death. Didn't they tell you? My guess would be that's where the key is, too."

Georgia felt a ripple of disbelief race all the way through her body. She stared at Henry Jarvis, unable for a moment to comprehend exactly what he was saying.

"But... but Mike never mentioned..." She took a deep breath to steady herself. "The investigation has been completed—why haven't they returned it to me?"

The man before her shrugged and shook his head.

"Well, they should have, I agree. I don't know why. But you know how the police are—all the red tape and formalities."

"Yes," she said, feeling confused. Wishing Cord were here to tell her what to do next. "I'm sure that's it. Well, I have to get back to work." She moved forward and stood up on tiptoe to kiss his cheek. "Give Aunt Sally my love."

"I will. And you call me anytime, sugar, if you feel up to dinner at the club. Sal and I will be glad to come by and pick you up."

"Thanks. I will."

She hurried toward the courthouse, thankful that the sheriff's office was on her way and that she had a few more minutes left on her lunch break. As she walked, she glanced across the street and behind her.

"Cord, where are you, dammit?" she murmured. "I need you."

The young officer at the desk in the sheriff's office smiled at Georgia. When she told him what she wanted, he turned to a computer, gazing intently at the blue screen for a moment before turning back to Georgia.

"Sorry, Mrs. Ashley," he said. "I don't see it listed anywhere. I think you'll have to see Sheriff Goodwin about it."

"Fine," she said in exasperation. "Is he here?"

"No, ma'am. He's out on a call. Old man Mosely out in Three Acres trailer park is drunk again...on a shootin' rampage," he said with a wry grin.

"Will you be sure and tell him that I came by?" she said, feeling the impatience beginning to build inside her chest. "And tell him what I want?"

"Sure 'nuff."

Georgia tried to lose herself in work for the rest of the day. But she found herself glancing at the clock, thinking about the deal she'd made with herself not to look for Cord until after five. But where was he? And what on earth was he doing?

Once, in midafternoon, she almost lost her resolve. She heard the ominous blare of sirens in the city streets and she very nearly jumped out of her chair. She went to the window and even though she felt a bit of relief that the siren belonged to a fire truck instead of an ambulance, there was still a troubling little fear that nagged at her.

She watched silently as the red truck raced along the narrow, crowded streets and out of sight.

About an hour later, Mike Goodwin walked through the door.

Georgia stood up. She could feel her heart pounding. It seemed now that every time she saw Mike, she expected some kind of bad news.

"Is everything all right?" she asked.

"Sure," he said, looking at her oddly. "Fine."

"I came by your office today," she said, breathing a quiet sigh of relief.

"I know. That's why I'm here." He took off his hat and stood in front of her desk.

"What's wrong?"

"Well, nothing really," he said. "Just a minor embarrassment, I hope."

"Embarrassment?"

"Yeah. To be honest, I think we've lost the contents of Bob's safe-deposit box. And I feel I owe you an apology. The investigation was done by both the city and the county, but the confiscated personal items belonging to the victims is my office's responsibility. I guess we blew it."

Georgia stared at him. He certainly looked sincere, standing there in his neat uniform, with his hat in his hands. Had she been around Cord so long that she was beginning to be as distrustful as he was?

"Lost," she murmured.

"I'm sorry, Georgia. I've told everyone to turn the entire building upside down till it's found." His smile was sweet and a little sheepish. "Was there anything in particular that you were looking for?"

Suddenly the office seemed very quiet. Georgia could almost hear the beating of her own heart.

"No," she said, forcing herself to smile innocently. "Nothing really. It's just that I think it's time to get all his papers in order. I need to clean out his office . . . things like that."

Mike nodded. "Mrs. Ramsey said you were thinking about selling the real-estate office."

She couldn't help laughing. News sure traveled fast in this town. "I told her I hadn't decided yet."

"Oh," he said, grinning. He started to go, then turned back, his eyes more serious now. "I'm sorry about that little run-in yesterday with Jamison. It's your home and we shouldn't have aired our differences there."

"It's all right," she said. She didn't want to discuss Cord with him.

"By the way, I guess you've heard that he's had another bit of bad luck today."

Georgia thought her heart might actually jump out of her chest.

"No, I haven't heard," she said quickly. "What's happened? He's not hurt? He's not—"

"No, no," he said, frowning as if he disapproved of her obvious concern. "I just saw him. He's fine. Sheila Jamison's house caught fire. In fact, it's probably still burning."

Georgia gasped as she stared at Mike with wide, disbelieving eyes.

"Fire...?"

"Afraid so."

"My God."

"You know Jamison better than anyone in this town. You don't think *he'd* do something like that, do you? Insurance or—"

"Burn his sister's house? Of course not," she snapped. "Not in a million years. Despite what you and the rest of this town seem to think, Cord Jamison is an honorable man...he's an officer of the law for the state of Georgia, for heaven's sake. He'd never do anything like that."

"Yeah, well..." Mike's lips twisted to one side, but he said nothing.

Don't say it, Georgia wanted to shout. Don't say that Cord behaved in less than an honorable manner ten years ago when he left without even a goodbye.

As if Mike could see the warning in her eyes, he said nothing. Then he turned and with a wave of his hat, went out the door.

"You take care now, Georgia. I'll let you know if the stuff from the safe-deposit box turns up."

Georgia began to put her desk in order, silently cursing her trembling fingers. It was not yet five o'clock, but she didn't care. She was leaving. The judge was gone for the rest of the day and she could not keep her promise to herself any longer. She had to find Cord.

She didn't have to look far.

As soon as she pulled the car into her driveway, she saw the big black motorcycle. Then she saw Cord, sitting on her front steps, his arms draped casually across his knees.

She parked the car in the driveway and jumped out, running across the leaf-covered yard toward him. She was conscious of the sound of crunching leaves beneath her feet, of the pungent, earthy smell that her footsteps stirred to life. Every sound, every smell seemed to have become more real and vital as she moved toward him.

"Where have you been?" she asked, her voice breathless, her eyes filled with worry. "I was worried sick about you. Mike said there was a fire."

He stood up, looking tall and imposing as he towered above her on the steps. Now that she was closer, she could see smudges of black on his face and hands. His jacket lay on the porch where he'd been sitting and it, too, showed evidence of the fire.

"Are you all right?" she asked, standing very still and staring up at him. "You weren't in the house? You weren't—"

"No, I wasn't in the house. And I'm fine." He reached down for his jacket, then walked down the steps, taking her arm and pulling her with him back toward the driveway. "Let's go inside," he said, looking around suspiciously.

Georgia thought it was his voice more than his actions that caused a tingle of alarm to race along her spine. She found herself scanning the thick row of hedges that separated her house from her neighbor's, gazing anxiously at a man who was walking down the street, until she realized that it was only a neighbor taking his dog for a stroll.

She glanced at Cord from the corner of her eye. Did he have any idea how badly she needed to touch him? How much she wanted to hold on to him for a moment and feel the strength of his body, the reassurance of his strong hands? She had not realized this would be so hard for her or that she would need him so much.

He stood watching as she started the car and moved it into the garage. Then he followed her in and waited as she closed and locked the door.

Inside the house, he insisted on checking every room, even though the security alarm was still set.

While she waited, she made coffee and took sliced turkey and cheese out of the refrigerator for sandwiches. Cord looked so tired—his eyes red-rimmed and weary. She had felt her nurturing instincts come to life when she saw the fatigue in those blue eyes and caught the acrid scent of smoke that still clung to his clothes. There was a sadness in his eyes today that tore at her heart and made her want to hold him and comfort him.

When he came back into the kitchen, she had the sandwiches almost made and the bowls of soup in the microwave. He washed his hands at the sink and with a heavy sigh went to sit at the table.

"What happened?" she asked as she placed the food before him. "Coffee? Or do you still prefer milk with your soup?"

"Milk if you have it," he said. For a moment his eyes were warm and filled with an amiable look that was familiar. "Coffee later," he added.

She poured his glass of milk and slid into her chair, not bothering to eat, but leaning forward, anxious to hear what he had to say.

"I went to the house last night to get the bike, but I spent the night somewhere else," he said, glancing away from her.

"When I came back this afternoon, the house was on fire. I think every fire truck within twenty miles was there."

"Was it a total loss? What about your clothes...all your—"

"Yeah, total—it burned to the ground. The fire was so hot that nothing the firemen did could stop it. I didn't have much inside—what clothes I brought were in the saddle-bags on the bike."

"I'm sorry," she whispered.

"Eat," he said, glancing pointedly at her food. "You look as tired as I feel."

She picked up her spoon, dutifully shoveling a bit of soup into her mouth.

"I...I was worried. When you didn't come home..." She stopped, realizing what she'd said and feeling a rush of heat in her cheeks. "When you didn't come back last night, I was afraid—"

"You don't have to worry about me, Georgia," he said. "I'm perfectly capable of taking care of myself. I've been on my own all my life."

Why did she feel guilty every time he said something like that? As if she were responsible for his being alone.

"Do you think someone burned the house as a warning? Maybe those same men?"

"I definitely think it was arson. I spoke with the fire investigator and even though he said it was too early to tell, I think he suspects arson, too. Just a feeling I got. But I think it wasn't done so much as a warning—maybe to make sure there is absolutely no evidence left for me to find."

"Oh, Cord. This scares me."

He nodded as he gazed into her brown eyes and saw the fear for himself. This was not what he wanted. He had never intended to make her afraid or put her in danger. But he hadn't expected Sheila to be mixed up in something so big.

Whatever it was, Cord was certain there was a lot of money involved.

"I went to the bank today," Georgia said.

His head came up and there was a glint of surprise in his eyes.

"Did you think I would just quit?" she asked, seeing that look. Her voice held a bit of resentment, her brown eyes a little spark of defiance. "Did you think I'd give up when you weren't here to help me?"

It was what she'd felt like doing. But she didn't tell him that.

"The thought crossed my mind," he said, looking into her eyes.

He seemed different today. Not quite so angry or so distant, and as he continued to look at Georgia, she had the feeling there was something else he wanted to say.

"I should never have involved you in this," he said, pushing his soup bowl aside and leaning back in the chair. He shook his head and rubbed his hand along his unshaven jaw. His eyes were troubled and stormy.

"It's too late," she said. "I *am* involved and it was my decision to be."

He nodded and took a deep breath, seeming to come to a decision with it.

"What did you find out at the bank?"

"You're not going to believe this," she said breathlessly, leaning forward eagerly.

He grunted. "Try me," he said with a wry twist of his lips.

"The law confiscated the contents of the safe-deposit box the morning after the murders. And they haven't returned it." She was pleased when Cord leaned forward, placing his elbows on the table and seeming to hang on her every word. "That was what Mike came by to tell me when he mentioned the fire. He said they had misplaced the box and can't find it.''

"Why doesn't that surprise me," he answered, his words soft and thoughtful.

"I know you don't trust Mike and that you don't like him very much. But surely you don't suspect—"

"At this point, I suspect everyone in this town. Maybe you should, too."

"Not Mike . . . not—"

"What's so special about the good sheriff?" he asked with a hint of his old sarcasm. "They hadn't made him a saint last time I heard."

"He was Bob's friend. He—"

"Yeah, I know. You've told me." He stood up, going to the window and standing thoughtfully for a moment. "You still have all those old loyalties, Georgia. You're still blinded by this town."

"You talk as if the town were real . . . as if it has a heart and a soul."

"Not a heart," he said quietly, turning to meet her eyes.

"Is there anything wrong with being loyal to friends? Is there anything wrong with seeing good in people?"

"I guess not," he said, his voice cool. "As long as you can be realistic in the bargain."

"I am," she said.

His lids lowered, closing away his eyes from her, shuttering the doubts that she knew she would see in their blue depths.

"The problem is, what are we going to do now," she said, wanting to change the subject.

"I'm going to go over the bank statements one more time. And I really haven't had a chance to study the autopsy reports. You go on to bed—you look—"

"I know, I look tired," she said with an exasperated sigh.

"I'll reset the security alarm when I leave."

"But you can't..." She didn't want him to know how desperately she wanted him to stay. "You know you're welcome to stay here, Cord."

"I think I've caused you enough trouble as it is." His eyes met hers with the impact of a freight train.

"I don't care what everyone says, Cord," she whispered. "I don't care what they think or—"

"Maybe you should."

"I'm a grown woman, perfectly capable of making my own decisions," she snapped, finally losing all patience. "You're not the only one who's lived on your own. I was alone long before Bob died." There was only the softest catch in her voice as she said those last words.

Cord couldn't help the way he felt when he looked in those big brown eyes. He had cautioned himself all night and all day today about her, about the way the sight of her affected him, the way the scent of her perfume lingered in his mind. The way he forgot every resolve, lost all control when he was with her. It made him imagine what it would be like to make love to her again.

Just once. Just for old time's sake. To see if the flame was still as bright, the heights as high.

When he was away from her, he felt strong and confident, certain that he had all the control in the world. But when he looked into those eyes...

"I want you to stay," she whispered. Her eyes sparkled and there was just the slightest tremble of her chin when she spoke. "Please...I...I feel safe when you're here."

"Lord," he muttered beneath his breath.

Why did she have to look at him that way? And why on God's green earth was he letting her get under his skin again?

"All right," he growled. "But I promise you, there will be no repeat of what happened the other night in your room."

"You don't have to—"

"I do," he said through clenched teeth. "Believe me, I do." He turned then, pushing back his chair so violently that it almost turned over. "I have to get to work. Since I have the bike back, I won't need your car tomorrow. So...I'll see you."

Georgia sat at the kitchen long after he'd left the room, feeling stunned and hurt, as confused as ever when he was near. He intended to shun her in her own home, it seemed.

She took a long deep breath, feeling angry, feeling just the way she did when her father tried to tell her what to do. Well, this time she wasn't going to stand for it. If Cord thought he was going to ignore her and push her out of his life so easily, he just didn't know her quite as well as he seemed to think he did.

Just then, as if thinking about her father brought him to her, she heard the sound of a car engine outside, pulling into her driveway. She knew it was her father's car—she recognized the smooth quiet purr of the engine and the muffled thud of the heavy door.

"Oh, no," she whispered, hurrying through the house to the front entryway. This was all she needed tonight, a visit and the inevitable lecture from her father.

Her father wasn't a big man, no more than five-nine in his prime. But as Georgia opened the door and stood looking up at him, he seemed, as usual, like a giant.

"Hello, Daddy."

"Is that all you have to say? Aren't you going to invite me in?"

With a heavy sigh, Georgia opened the door wider and stepped aside. Her father, still dressed in his business suit,

moved past her in a faint wave of expensive after-shave and
with all the elegant bearing of a nobleman.

"You know what I came to speak to you about," he said,
turning to face her in the foyer.

"About Cord Jamison, no doubt. It seems to be all anyone in this town wants to talk about."

Georgia heard her father give a low mutter of disapproval. When she turned around, she saw Cord standing at
the door of the study. He and her father stared at each other,
neither of them speaking or smiling.

"So... it's true," her father said, his voice accusatory.

"It's true that Cord is staying here, if that's what you
mean," she replied.

"Jamison, you're making a big mistake coming back
here," Horace Blake said.

"Believe me, I don't like being here any more than you
like having me here. And just as soon as I find out who
killed my sister, I'll be out of this snotty little burg so fast
it'll make your head spin. Sir," he added sarcastically.

"Find out who killed your sister? That's ridiculous. She
committed suicide." He turned to Georgia, his eyes blaz-
ing. And just as he'd done as a child, he made her feel useless and inadequate. "This man's sister murdered your
husband, Georgia. And now you let him in your house?
What's come over you?"

"Daddy, I don't want to hear this. I'm not a little girl
anymore—I'm thirty-two years old, I support myself, I have
my own home, and I don't have to—"

"Don't you speak to me in that tone of voice, girl."

"Just say what you came to say, Mr. Blake," Cord said,
his voice quietly menacing. "It seems to me that if you're
really concerned for your daughter's welfare and peace of
mind, you'd want to find out who murdered her husband as
much as she does."

"This is nonsense...total nonsense. Everyone knows who murdered Bob—your sister! Now I want you out of this house, Jamison. Right now! I want you out of this town and I don't want you interfering in Georgia's life anymore."

"No, Daddy," Georgia said, stepping forward and facing him with her chin lifted defiantly. "This isn't about what *you* want anymore. The truth is, I asked Cord to stay. I want him to stay...here with me."

"By God," her father whispered, his eyes expressing horror. His face was crimson and for a moment Georgia had a frightening vision of him keeling over, of her being the one responsible for his death.

"Please leave, Daddy," she said, feeling the sting of tears in her eyes.

She had never defied her father this way before. Oh, she had argued and she had done as she pleased many times without his knowing it. But she had never openly challenged him. She wasn't prepared for the look of total disbelief in his eyes, or the sadness that suddenly changed him into an old man.

Horace Blake looked from Georgia to Cord and back to Georgia again.

"You never learn, do you? He'll take what he wants, just like before, and he'll break your heart again," he said, keeping his voice low. "He'll be gone, riding out of town on that trashy machine of his. And you know where you'll be? You'll be sitting here in this house, alone. Do you hear me? Alone, Georgia." Her father turned and stalked toward the door, turning for one last word.

But Georgia beat him to it.

"I'll get a cat!" she said, clamping her lips together and brushing the angry, defiant tears from her eyes. "Or I might even take in boarders!"

Her father's mouth flew open and he seemed completely astonished.

"You have lost your mind, girl," he said. "You have completely lost your mind."

"Good night, Daddy," she said, going to the door and staring at him with brazen insolence.

Horace Blake turned to glare at Cord one last time before marching out the door.

Georgia bit her lip and took a deep shuddering breath of air. She leaned against the closed door, willing herself not to cry.

Cord saw her shoulders begin to tremble. She had surprised him tonight. Everything about her since he'd come home had surprised him. Her sweet concern, the pain and empathy he often saw in her eyes, the way she seemed to isolate herself from the people she'd grown up with. Horace Blake had been right about one thing. His daughter was already alone... and lonely.

"Georgia," Cord said quietly as he walked up behind her. He didn't trust himself to touch her. "I'm sorry."

"No," she said, whirling around. "Don't you be sorry. You have nothing to be sorry about, Cord Jamison. Nothing to feel ashamed or guilty about. My father and these... these people here, they are the ones who should be sorry. For the way they treated you all your life. And for the way they let Sheila go without giving a damn, just because she wasn't one of them. You were right," she whispered as tears streamed down her face. "You were right."

She turned and ran up the steps, not bothering to look back.

Cord watched her. He could remember thinking more than once that he'd like to see her suffer. That he'd like to see her pay for all the sleepless nights she'd caused him. But seeing the tears in those soft brown eyes made him realize that wasn't what he wanted at all. He never wanted her to be hurt. Not now...not ever.

Cord felt a little ache in his heart as he watched her race up the stairs, as he acknowledged the genuine grief and despair she was feeling. She loved her father and it had taken a lot of courage to defy him tonight. Cord's eyes were wide with surprise. It had been a long time since anyone had gotten close enough to make him feel that little ache.

A damned long time.

Chapter 8

For once Georgia went straight to sleep, despite Cord's presence in the house. She was hurt and confused and completely exhausted by all that had happened in the past few days. She used sleep that night the way she always had, as an escape.

She woke around midnight with a pounding headache, which she blamed on the crying and the tension. She knew she'd never be able to go back to sleep until the pain subsided. Finally, with a sigh, she dragged herself out of bed into the bathroom and rummaged through the medicine cabinet.

"Damn," she muttered, finding the aspirin bottle empty.

Quickly she slipped a soft white robe around her shoulders and went to the doorway, peeking out into the hallway to see if Cord's door was closed.

It was and the hallway was dark. She tiptoed to the light switch and turned the dimmer on low, leaving only enough light to see to get to the bathroom next to Cord's room.

It seemed cold in the house and as she approached the door, she drew her robe tighter around her shoulders.

Suddenly the bathroom door opened and Georgia stopped, stunned as she found herself staring into Cord's face.

His black hair was wet and shining, his chest bare and gleaming in the dim light. He wore nothing except a large white towel, which was wrapped around his hips.

"Oh...I'm sorry, I didn't..." She tried to avert her eyes, tried not to sound as breathless as she felt. "I was just looking for some aspirin."

"You don't have to explain," he said, drawing in his breath at the sight of her. He thought she looked like a small ethereal angel, standing there with the lights playing against her hair and pale skin. "It *is* your house."

Georgia wondered if he had any idea what the sight of him did to her senses. Any idea how she longed to move into his arms, let her fingers touch the dark, sleek skin of his chest and flat corded stomach. For a moment she swayed toward him, wanting him, wishing things could be different between them . . . longing for things beyond her control.

He was looking at her so intently, his blue eyes studying her, waiting, it seemed, for her to make a move. But she thought there was no more welcome in that look than there had been before.

"Sorry," she said quietly, lowering her gaze from his and moving around him. "I don't want to keep you standing here in the hall—you must be cold."

She felt his hand on her arm, holding her, then slowly turning her around to face him.

"I'm not cold," he said, his voice husky. "Believe me, I'm not cold."

Georgia didn't know how it happened but suddenly she was in his arms, holding him, feeling her robe fall away to the floor in a soft mound at her feet.

Cord's mouth took hers with a sweet, hungry savagery. It was the kiss of a man long past the limits of his control.

Georgia breathed in the heady masculine scent of him, shuddering as she gave herself over to the sensuality of his kiss, his touch... gave in finally to the pleasure and the longing that had been her constant tormentors since he'd come back.

She felt his body against hers, hard with desire. She moved herself even closer, letting her arms snake around his neck, tangling her fingers in the damp strands of his hair and sighing as she opened her mouth beneath his.

She could feel his heart pounding, beating just as erratically as her own. And she thought that if he didn't take her into his bedroom and make love to her, she might actually die from wanting him.

"Georgia," he whispered, finally pulling away with a hoarse gasp. His eyes were dark, hot with desire as he stared down at her.

All Cord wanted at that moment was to make love to her. To finally let it happen and experience all the fulfillment he had been denied for ten long years. But in that moment he knew it was more than just a physical need he felt for Georgia—in her arms and her kisses was home—sweet sanctuary that he had been seeking all his life.

But even as he felt the desire for her rip through his entire body, Cord remembered her father's words earlier and he remembered that summer day so long ago when Georgia had closed him out and all the light had gone so suddenly and unexpectedly from his life.

He took a long deep shuddering breath. His hands on her arms held her away as he leaned against the wall and closed his eyes, trying to gain some measure of composure.

"Cord," Georgia whispered, her word a quiet plea. She couldn't believe he was pulling away from her again. Not after this...not after his hot breathtaking kisses and the hunger that neither of them could deny. "Don't push me away again. I want you and I know that you want me." She reached forward to touch him. His eyes flew open as his hand shot forward to grasp her wrist. Still, he allowed her to touch the skin of his chest, as if he couldn't help himself. But as she looked into his eyes, she saw his determination and knew that she still had not gotten past those barriers that he used against her.

"We have to talk," he said, his breath ragged. "I don't understand you, Georgia. But this time, I intend to find out exactly what it is you want before—"

"I want you," she whispered, leaning toward him with a wild urgency that shook him. "As simple as that. Don't you...?"

"Yes, dammit," he said through clenched teeth. "I want you more than I've ever wanted anything. Does that answer your question?" His hand tightened around her arm, shaking her, then pushing her gently away.

"That much hasn't changed, not in all the years I've been gone, not even when I saw your wedding picture and knew that you belonged to someone else. And not now...I imagine it will be this way for the rest of my life."

"Then why, Cord?" she asked, trying desperately to see into his eyes and to understand. "Why do you keep pushing me away? What is it you want from me?"

"God," he whispered, raking his hand through his wet hair. "I want it all—can't you understand? I want more than you've ever been willing to give."

"That's not true," she whispered, bewildered by his statement. There was a time when she would have given him anything...done anything. Hadn't he always known that? Didn't he know it now?

"Look," he said, pulling his gaze away from her soft, pleading eyes. He bent to retrieve her robe, draping it with rough, impersonal movements around her shoulders. Yet he couldn't resist taking the lapels over her breasts and using the robe as leverage to pull her toward him for one last lingering kiss. "Get dressed. I can't think straight when you're like this."

"Neither can I," she said quietly, letting her look move down his chest but making no effort to touch him.

She saw the chill that raced along his skin, saw the muscles in his chest quiver. Her eyelids flickered open and she met his look with something akin to awe. She saw and felt her own power. In that moment she knew that all she had to do was touch him, kiss him and all his denials, all his doubts, would be forgotten. She would have what she wanted.

But she realized that wasn't how she wanted it to be. He was right. They had always fallen so easily into each other's arms...*too* easily. When they were young, there had been no need for talk—just the sweet hot pleasure of lovemaking, of satisfying their need whenever they wished, wherever they wanted.

And that pleasure was still there. Thank God, it was still there in every beat of their hearts, in every look and every touch.

But she found that now she wanted more. She wanted to hear what he had to say. She wanted there to be more between them than sex. Georgia wanted to know everything about him—what he liked, what he dreamed of and most of all what he wanted from her.

And in that sweet, breathtaking moment of realization, she thought that whatever he asked could never be more than she was willing to give him.

Slowly she pushed her arms into the sleeves of her robe, her eyes never moving from his.

"I'll go down and make coffee while you get dressed," she said.

There was a tiny flicker of light in the depths of his beautiful blue eyes as he looked at her. Then he nodded and turned to go into his bedroom.

Georgia stood for a moment, letting her breathing slow, willing her heart to stop pounding. Finally she made her feet move, going into the bathroom to find the aspirin.

She stared into the mirror above the sink as she drank the water and swallowed the tablets. Her eyes looked huge, her skin pale. Slowly she smiled wistfully, staring at her image as if she'd never seen herself before, thinking of Cord and the way he made her feel. She thought she could see it in her eyes, that desire, that desperate need she felt whenever he was near.

How could anything keep them apart any longer after tonight?

Downstairs in the kitchen moments later, Georgia turned from getting cups when she heard Cord's footsteps behind her.

He wore a pair of soft jeans and a blue flannel shirt that almost exactly matched the color of his eyes. He padded across the kitchen, nothing on his feet except socks.

Georgia felt a bit of disappointment as her gaze moved quickly over him. It was a shame to cover up that body, she thought. But she knew Cord was not a pajama-and-robe kind of guy. For him it always seemed to be all or nothing.

His eyes were determined, though, and serious. Georgia had hardly set the coffee on the table before he spoke.

"What did your father mean tonight—that I would take what I wanted and break your heart again?" His silvery gaze never left her face.

Georgia blushed, despite her resolve to be cool.

"You know what he meant," she said, sliding into her chair across the table from where he sat.

"No...I don't."

She sighed. If he wanted to play this game, she supposed she would have to go along with it—at least until she found out why he was so bitter.

"When you left that summer, Cord...without a word, it didn't take a rocket scientist to see that I was hurt. Of course my father would notice. He and my mother both—"

"Wait...wait. I don't get this." He hadn't touched his coffee, but sat with his hands around the cup, as if he needed something to hold on to.

"What don't you get, Cord?" she asked, unable to keep the irritation from her voice. "You don't get that I was hurt? Did you think I wouldn't notice that you were gone...or that you didn't bother saying goodbye...that I'd just bounce back, find another man as if—"

"Didn't you?"

Georgia wasn't sure what hurt more—his accusation or the look in his eyes when he said it.

She said nothing. How could she defend herself against those words? How could she ever make him understand why she'd married Bob when she wasn't even sure anymore herself?

"You were the one who wanted me to go," he said.

"Me? What are you talking about?"

"Georgia, don't play games, baby." The sarcasm was back, the cold look of fury in his eyes. "Dammit, can't you admit it, even now? Can't you say it once and for all? That I was good enough for a summer fling, but when it came time for marriage, you wanted me out of town...out of sight, so you could marry Daddy's choice?''

"Cord," she said, frowning and shaking her head, "I never wanted you to go...I swear, I have no idea what you mean."

Suddenly there was a sick feeling in the pit of her stomach as she stared into those steely blue eyes. She saw the hurt and she knew he wasn't lying about any of it.

"I'm talking about the money, Georgia. Or does money mean so little to you that you've forgotten? How much did you send, baby? Was I worth a lot...or a little? I've always wondered about that, but you see I was too sick at heart to count it."

He was leaning back in his chair, one hand hooked through a belt loop in his jeans. His eyes were wary and accusing. But despite his attempt at nonchalance, she could see that even now, he was hurt. It took everything he had to get this out. And she was beginning to understand exactly what had happened and why he had left her.

"My father," she whispered, knowing. She reached her hand across the table, meaning to touch him, to reassure him.

He stood up, pushing the chair back so suddenly with his legs that it toppled over with a crash.

"You're damned right," he growled. *"Your father."* He practically spat the words at her.

Cord walked around the table, putting his hands beneath her arms and lifting her up until she was standing, hands clinging to his soft flannel shirt for support. The heels of his hands were warm and firm against the sides of her breasts. She couldn't breath, couldn't say a word.

"How much, Georgia?" he growled. "How damned much was I worth?"

He jerked her against him, grinding his mouth against hers in a kiss that was more punishment than desire.

"Ten thousand?" he asked, pulling away, his eyes glittering down at her. "Fifteen?" He shook her then, until the tears in her eyes spilled over and ran down her cheeks.

"He came to you and offered you money," she whispered, understanding at last. "To... to leave Farmington. Oh, my God... Cord..."

Georgia reached up then, touching his cheek, letting her hand linger as she looked into his eyes. Tears ran freely down her face as she realized what her father had done all those years ago, and as she knew finally why Cord had left.

She felt numb with disbelief.

"What did you do?" she asked, her voice soft and filled with an aching sympathy. "Throw it back in his face?"

Cord was frowning at her. He shook his head as if he could not believe what he saw in her brown eyes, what he felt in his gut to be the truth.

She hadn't known.

"Close," he growled, stepping away from her and from her disturbingly sweet touch. "I mailed it back to him... just before I left town with every penny I had and two changes of clothes strapped to the back of that old Harley."

"I never knew," she whispered. "I swear to you by everything I hold dear, Cord... I never knew."

It was everything Cord wanted to hear. The scenario he had imagined over and over in his mind on those long first nights away from Georgia and the sweet warmth of her body.

But now that she was saying it, he felt only a cold, dull ache in the pit of his stomach. He didn't know what he was supposed to feel, what he was supposed to believe. But he had not expected to be standing in her kitchen, listening to her, seeing that look in her eyes, having her touch him, and still feel lifeless and numb.

Cord turned away from her, walking to the sink and staring out the window into the darkness.

"What did he say?" she asked.

"That you wanted me to leave. That you realized you could never love someone like me. And that you intended to marry Bob Ashley in the fall as if nothing had ever happened."

"And you believed him?"

"You married him, didn't you?" he said, turning with harsh, angry eyes to stare at her.

Georgia frowned and looked away. How could he ever understand her confusion that summer? And after what she did, how could she ever expect him to believe that she had never stopped loving him?

"I wouldn't have ... God, I shouldn't have," she said. "But I thought—"

"You thought, hey ... since old Cord's out of the picture, might as well marry the one that brung ya, huh?"

"Don't," she whispered. "Don't keep holding on to this bitterness, Cord. We can get past it ... can't we? Tonight, upstairs in the hallway, we—"

"We what?" he snapped. "Almost made love? Almost gave in to what's always been there between us? And then what, Georgia? Then what?"

"I want to start over. Now that this is all out in the open, I want—"

"Hell," he said, raking his hands through his hair. He walked across the room and took his jacket from a brass hook. As he thrust his arms into the sleeves of the leather jacket, he looked into her eyes.

Georgia thought she had never seen such sadness and defeat as she saw now, staring back at her.

"I'm not so sure I can do that," he said, clenching his jaw as he looked at her. "It'd be kind of like rebreaking a fracture that's healed, wouldn't it? Why would any sane man want to put himself through that?" He walked toward the door.

"Where are you going?" she asked, not following but standing very still in the middle of the room. Her heart was breaking and he wasn't even going to give her a chance to explain.

"Anywhere," he muttered. "To a roadhouse...a whore...riding, I don't know."

He slammed the door, causing the pictures on the kitchen wall to rattle. Then after the muffled roar of the motorcycle engine died away, the house was silent except for one quiet little sob that escaped Georgia's lips before she sank into the kitchen chair and laid her head on the table.

Finally Georgia went back to bed. She felt sick at heart and Cord's bitter accusations would not leave her as she lay staring into the darkness. Every sense in her body was attuned to the sound of a motorcycle as she waited, her muscles tense.

As she lay there listening, she thought of what her father had done. It didn't surprise her, except that Cord had believed the story Horace Blake told. Her father was renowned for his manipulative skills and his lack of compunction at using them. There was nothing he wouldn't do to get what he wanted.

Georgia gritted her teeth together, thinking of all the anguish her father's maneuvers had caused her. And although she knew she couldn't blame him completely for her disastrous marriage, she knew that he had played a part in it.

But she had been the one to say yes. The one to walk down the aisle dressed in an expensive French gown and pretend at the country club reception that she was happy. She'd known that very day that it was a mistake.

Then why? Why had she married him?

"I was afraid," she whispered into the darkness.

Afraid of being rejected by her father and her friends. Afraid of being alone. Scared to live without Cord and needing someone's reassurance that she could survive.

She had been a little girl in so many ways.

"But not anymore," she said, sighing, thinking of all that had happened in her life the past few years.

Georgia had had to grow up, despite herself. And it had been a hard awakening.

When her alarm went off at seven, Georgia felt she had just fallen asleep. With a groan, she dragged herself out of bed, her mind immediately going to Cord and wondering where he was and what he was doing.

Later, as she was backing out of the driveway, she heard the sound she'd been listening for all night. The low drone of a motorcycle engine.

When she saw him, she thought her heart might actually stop, and she could not keep the look of relief from her face when he stopped beside her car.

The electric hum of the car window sounded loud and grating in the morning quiet.

Cord took off his black helmet and shook his head, running his fingers through his hair. When he turned to look at Georgia, his eyes were weary and red. He looked awful and she knew he'd spent the same kind of night as she had.

Knowing she probably shouldn't, Georgia stepped out of the car and went to him. Ignoring the look of warning surprise in his eyes, she reached out to touch his face. His beginning growth of beard felt rough and scratchy beneath her fingers. When her hand moved to his mouth, Cord took her wrist, but he made no effort to push her away.

Georgia thought there was even a hint of apology in those blue eyes.

"You asked why I married Bob," she said quietly. "That's something I've asked myself for ten years. And I thought about it all night, after you left."

He waited, his gaze never leaving her face.

"I think . . . I think I was afraid," she said, looking at the ground self-consciously. She could barely stand to look into his eyes when she spoke of this subject. No one in the world knew how ashamed she was that she'd made the wrong choice. That she'd been too weak to make it on her own.

"What were you afraid of?" he asked. For once, his voice was patient and if he was not exactly sympathetic, there was no trace of bitterness in his tone, either.

"I know you might not believe this, but even at twenty-two, I wasn't exactly worldly."

"I know," he said quietly. "I remember."

She had been innocent, protected from the world by her father and by the quiet, peaceful life of Farmington.

"When you left . . ." She had to stop. She looked up toward the blue morning sky and bit her lips to stop their trembling. She wanted to do this right. She took a deep breath of the cool morning air. "When you left, I was destroyed," she said, gazing into his eyes. "I thought I would die . . . that I couldn't go back to the way it had been before. It was just the way everyone said it would be . . . worse even."

Surprisingly, Cord reached out and touched her face, his eyes warm and tender as he waited patiently for her to finish.

"How did everyone say it would be?"

"That you could never love a girl like me. That Cord Jamison was a wild, free spirit . . . a man who wasn't about to be tied down to one girl and one town. That you had a different girl every summer and that summer I just happened to be the one."

He shook his head slowly, still looking into her eyes.

"Didn't you know?" he asked, frowning. "Couldn't you tell that it was real . . . that what I felt for you was real?"

"No," she whispered. "Oh, Cord, you have to understand how I grew up. I couldn't imagine anyone would ever love me except for the fact that I was a Blake—Horace Blake's daughter. And so I tried to be the perfect daughter—I always did everything to please my father. I thought he knew everything, that he would never tell me anything that wasn't right. And so, when all he'd said about you seemed to come true, I fell back into the same old patterns. It was easy and safe. And I cared about Bob—I won't lie to you and tell you that I didn't. He was good to me at first— we had a nice quiet pleasant life for a time. But I didn't love him, Cord. Never. It could never have been the same."

Cord withdrew his hand from her cheek and rubbed his eyes. He sat for a moment, astride the big motorcycle, staring down at the ground. When he lifted his head and met her eyes again, there was a quiet resignation in those blue depths.

"I won't ask you about him again," he said, his voice steady and quiet.

Georgia wanted to throw herself in his arms. She wanted more than anything to tell him that she had never stopped loving him, that she loved him still. And she wanted to go into the house with him and make sweet passionate love all day.

But she knew him, even after all their years apart. She knew that he needed time to resolve this in his mind. And she could only hope that in time, he might be ready to love her again.

"Will you be here when I get home?" she asked.

"Yeah," he said. This time there was the slightest hint of a smile in his eyes. "I'll be here."

Chapter 9

Georgia could hardly wait to get home from work. She even thought about calling several times during the day, but then she would remind herself of Cord's pride and independence—his need to work things out on his own terms—and she would hang up the phone and sit staring at it for long minutes.

She was hurrying along the sidewalk and toward her car at five o'clock when she almost ran into Mike Goodwin.

"Whoa," he said, laughing. "Where you goin' in such an all-fired hurry."

"Nowhere," she said with a shrug. "Home."

"Brenda said she came by to see you at lunch, but you were already gone—out on your own, someone told her. What's wrong, Georgia, you don't associate with any of the courthouse gang anymore?"

She couldn't lie to Mike. He knew her too well.

"It's not the same now," she said, looking into his eyes. "We...we don't seem to have anything in common...

nothing to talk about except what's happened to me.''

"Well, I can understand that," he said. "But Brenda was a little concerned . . . we just hope you're not behaving this way because of Cord Jamison."

"Why?" she asked, her eyes suddenly snapping to life. "What do you have against Cord? You and Brenda hardly know him."

"See how defensive you are," he said with a knowing shake of his head.

"Mike," she said, lifting her hands like a shield in front of her. "Really, I'm tired. I don't want to discuss this right now."

She could see the irritation in Mike's eyes as she started to turn away, and she was surprised. He was one of the most easygoing people she knew.

"You listen to me," he said, stepping close and taking her by the arm. "That man is just looking for trouble. This is some kind of a vendetta he has against Farmington and against people like your daddy. He has a chip on his shoulder a mile wide and if he's not careful, it's going to get him in real big trouble."

"Is that a threat?" she asked, her eyes growing wide. She was staring at Mike as if she didn't know him at all.

"No threat," he said, his look serious. He lifted his hand and shook his finger in front of her face. "If you really care about him, Georgia, you'll convince him to go back to Atlanta and keep his nose out of Farmington and things that don't concern him."

"I would say that his sister's death *does* concern him," she said, not backing away.

"It's over and done, for heaven's sake," he snapped. "Why can't he just let it rest? Nothing can bring them back.

Both of you just forget about it, Georgia, and get on with your lives. Preferably yours *without* Cord Jamison."

"*Forget* about it?" she asked, her voice incredulous as she stared into his unyielding eyes.

When he turned and walked away, Georgia shivered. She had never seen Mike Goodwin behave that way and she had known him all her life. Suddenly all she wanted was to see Cord and touch him and make sure that he was all right.

He opened the back door as soon as she stepped out of the car. There was an impatience in his movements and she saw that in his hand he held several papers.

"What is it?" she said, going into the kitchen and putting aside her purse. "Have you found something important?"

He still looked tired, and although he had changed clothes, he hadn't shaved yet. She thought the dark stubble of a beard made him look mysterious and even sexier than usual. Georgia stepped closer, gazing at the papers he held and not ashamed to use any excuse to be near him.

"Did you study the autopsy reports? Were there similarities?"

"No similarities. But there were marks on Bob's wrists," Cord said, his eyes glittering dangerously. "Bruises not unlike handcuffs would make."

"But what . . . what explanations were there for that? He wasn't tied or handcuffed when they found him—I know that much for a fact."

"The medical examiner's explanation was similar to the one he used for Sheila's gloves—participation in sexual fantasies . . . games, as he put it."

Georgia frowned and looked away. "It could be true."

"It could be, yes. But I don't think you believe it applies here any more than I do."

Seeing the look in her eyes, Cord pointed to the papers on the desk.

"Look . . . let's change the subject. I've spent practically all day going through these bank statements. And this time I took all of Sheila's receipts for the period and added them up. I couldn't reconcile her deposits with Bob's before, but doing it this way, her expenditures add up to almost exactly the same amount as his. But she wasn't the most responsible, organized person in the world. And of course it's speculative and would never stand up in court."

"I'm convinced they're the same, too," she said. "But you're right, we'd never be able to convince a jury, especially suggesting someone like Bob did something illegal. He could have gotten the money legitimately from any number of business associates."

Cord shook his head and tossed the papers on the kitchen table.

"I've reached a dead end. We've gone through Bob's papers—Sheila's house is gone, the contents of his safe-deposit box are missing." He was pacing the floor, rubbing his jaw. "There is one thing . . ."

"What?" she asked, her voice breathless.

"Last night I think I saw the thugs who jumped me. I followed them out on old Highway 4 to Queenie's Roadhouse."

"You followed them? Oh, Cord, you shouldn't—"

"It's my job," he said with a patient grin. "You don't think I'm so inept at it that I'd let them see me, do you?"

"No, I don't think that. But what if they had? What if—"

"They didn't. And tonight when I visit the roadhouse, even if they see me, they won't recognize me." He rubbed his new beard for emphasis.

"Tonight? You're going back to Queenie's tonight? Then I'm going with you."

"Oh, no," he said, shaking his head and walking away with his hands on his hips. "No way, lady, are you going out there."

"And why not?" she demanded.

He stopped dead still, then walked to her, taking her by the shoulders and turning her all the way around. As she turned, his gaze raked over her from head to toe, taking in the long colorful print skirt and coordinated sweater, the patterned cream-colored hose and very expensive shoes.

"Why not?" he asked with a mocking grunt of disdain. "Just look at you. You'd stand out like a fluffy little kitten in a lion's den. My God, you're a walking advertisement for Liz Claiborne."

She made a huffing noise of exasperation and lifted her chin.

"I'm not a kitten," she snapped. "And for goodness' sake, I hadn't intended to wear these clothes. I'm perfectly aware that I wouldn't fit in at Queenie's in this outfit. I'll wear jeans and—"

"Those cute little designer things I saw you in the other day? Uh-uh," he said, shaking his head. "I don't think so."

"I always wanted to see what it was like inside Queenie's. You'd never take me before..."

"And I'm not taking you now," he said with a determined look.

"Cord, I'm going," she said stubbornly. "I have as much at stake here as you do. You can't just drag me into this case, then push me aside when it suits you. Besides, you won't be noticed as much if you're with a woman."

"Dammit, Georgie..." He gritted his teeth and shook his head at her again. But she could see a gleam of appreciation in those blue eyes and she thought he was weakening.

"Yes," she said with a pleading look in her dark eyes. "Say yes, Cord."

"Only if I dress you," he said finally with a heavy sigh. Then he smiled, his blue eyes twinkling at her. "In a manner of speaking."

"It's a deal," she said. "I'll wear whatever you say."

"I doubt if you have anything in your closet that I would pick."

"You never know," she said sarcastically. "I might surprise you."

"I doubt it."

Moments later they were in her bedroom. Cord stood in the middle of the room as Georgia pulled various pieces of clothing out of the large walk-in closet.

"Levi's," she said, shaking the practically new jeans at him with a self-satisfied look.

"Nope," he said, shaking his head. "Too new...too clean."

"Too clean?" she said, making a face. "You didn't tell me I had to be dirty."

He laughed and crossed his arms over his chest, nodding patiently at her.

"What else?" he asked.

"How about this?" she asked enthusiastically, pulling out a bright red jumpsuit.

Cord's eyes lit up for a moment as he glanced from the slash of red that she had draped across her arm and then back to her. His eyes wandered slowly down her body.

"I always did like you in red," he said, his voice soft for a moment and unguarded. He cleared his throat and shook his head. "But no." Suddenly he stepped toward her, his stomach just brushing against her breasts as he moved into the closet.

"Here, let me look," he said.

Georgia suddenly had a vision of both of them falling together into the closet, closing the door and imprisoning themselves in the small dark place. Closing out the world, shutting out any doubts and giving in to the temptation that both of them were feeling.

When she shook herself out of the fantasy, Cord was holding up a pair of shiny black satin pants. There was a decided look of satisfaction in his eyes.

"No," she said, shaking her head. Bob had bought her those—she'd supposed in one of those moments when he wanted her to be something or someone other than who she was. She'd always hated them and she'd never worn them.

"It's not leather," Cord was saying. "But in the dim lights, it'll at least look the part."

"I'm not wearing that," she protested. She watched in exasperation while he pulled out a long-sleeved black turtleneck sweater.

"Expensive," he said with a soft whistle. "But I doubt anyone at Queenie's will notice." He pushed the sweater into her arms while he turned and rummaged through the clothes.

"Cord," she protested again.

"What?" he asked, standing in the closet, frowning at her. With the growth of beard on his face, she thought he looked imposing, to say the least. "Do you want to go or not?"

"Yes, I want to go, but—"

"Then this is what you're wearing."

"God, you're just as bossy and overbearing as ever," she snapped.

"And you're just as stubborn and willful."

They stood staring at each other for a few moments before Cord's features softened and he took one step toward her.

"Georgia," he said, his voice low. "We can't take any chance of those men knowing who you are. If I thought we couldn't pull this off, I wouldn't let you go. But to do that, you have to do exactly as I say. You have to trust me."

She took a long shuddering breath as she looked into those blue eyes.

"I do," she whispered. "But..."

He said nothing, only lifted his eyebrows as he stood waiting.

"Oh, all right," she said. "I'll do it. Can I at least eat supper before we go? Or do I have to survive for the rest of the night on pretzels and beer?"

"You may eat dinner," he said, smiling.

Georgia shook her head at him. But finally she smiled back. When he looked at her that way, with that mischievous little-boy look, she thought she might possibly do just about anything he demanded.

Even now, being this close, looking into his eyes, she could feel her knees trembling. Feel the warm languid heat in the pit of her stomach.

As Cord followed Georgia out of the bedroom and downstairs, he thought she was without a doubt the sexiest, most feminine, most beguiling woman he'd ever met.

And he'd known a few.

He wasn't at all sure that letting her go with him to Queenie's tonight was the most practical thing he'd ever done in his life. But at least, he told himself, she would be where he could keep an eye on her.

Last night after he'd stormed out of her house and away from those pleading brown eyes, he had decided that he wanted to believe her. Despite the anger and the bitterness that he had wrapped around himself like a shield for ten years, he wanted more than anything to believe her. There had been an honesty in her voice and in her eyes when she talked about what her father had done and about her relationship with her husband. Cord knew he might risk being the biggest fool in Gordon County for letting himself trust her again. Yet where she was concerned, he couldn't seem to help himself, any more than he could stop the world from spinning.

After supper, Georgia went upstairs to dress. It was well past nine o'clock when she stepped from her bedroom and headed downstairs to meet Cord in the kitchen. She had listened to his command that she apply enough makeup to make her look hard and worldly. Against her better judgment she'd done just that—arching her light eyebrows with dark pencil, applying a heavy layer of rosy blusher to her cheeks until she thought she looked more like a clown than an experienced woman of the world. The final touch was a deep red lipstick that she usually wore beneath lip gloss. Tonight she applied it full strength, then sat back and looked at herself with dismay.

She looked like a hooker.

She ran her hands down the sleek black satin pants that fit like a glove from her waist to her ankles. There was no more than a millimeter of space between her bare skin and the slinky material. The expensive black sweater was tucked in at the waist, emphasizing her round breasts and making her blond hair seem bright and brassy. She wobbled for a moment on the black stiletto heels, then walked with her head up, testing her balance and an exaggerated swing of her hips.

She hesitated only a moment before stepping into the brightly-lit kitchen.

Cord turned. His eyes changed into a warm, silvery blue color as his gaze raked her from head to foot.

She was supposed to look cheap, dammit. Not sexy as hell and breathtaking, to boot. On Georgia, even the bold black outfit and the overdone makeup looked good.

Damned good.

When he managed to get his breath again, he nodded.

"It'll do," he said, trying to sound as if the sight of her hadn't hit him like a sledgehammer.

"Do I look tacky enough for Queenie's?" she asked.

Cord thought her soft southern voice sounded strange, combined with the look she had tonight. It was an angel's voice in a temptress's body.

"Tacky?" he said, unable to keep his eyes from wandering over her again. "Well, tacky isn't exactly the word I'd use."

"I look awful," she said, misinterpreting his words. "That's good."

She stared at Cord, noticing his own clothes. Actually he didn't look much different than he usually did, except for the beard. But tonight there was a red bandanna tied around his upper thigh. She couldn't help noticing how her eyes were drawn automatically to the scarf or how it emphasized his muscular thighs and narrow hips.

God, but he was gorgeous. Hard and dangerous-looking and completely gorgeous.

Letting her eyes move upward, she shivered, seeing the wide leather scabbard attached to his belt. She knew without asking that it held a deadly-looking knife. And she sensed Cord wasn't wearing it merely for looks; no doubt he knew how to use it if he had to.

"Does the knife bother you?" he asked quietly, seeing her look.

"No," she said quickly. "I agreed that you would be in charge tonight. Whatever you say is fine with me."

"You'll need a jacket," he said. "It'll be cold on the bike."

He reached for his leather jacket while Georgia nodded and stepped out toward the hallway to find herself a coat.

When she came back, Cord nodded his approval at the scruffy, faded blue denim jacket she wore. It looked just offbeat enough with the sleek black pants and high heels to be authentic.

"My gardening jacket," she said with a self-conscious little laugh.

"It's a good touch. Ready?"

She took a deep breath of air and nodded.

"Ready."

Cord was right—it was cold riding out on the open highway. At first, she had put her arms around his waist, leaning back away from him so that nothing else touched. But as the wind whistled past them, Georgia scooted forward, happy for an excuse to wrap her arms around him and cuddle up against his broad, muscled back.

When he felt her move closer, Cord reached one hand back, slipping his fingers around the outside of her knee and with an intimate movement sliding her closer to him. Georgia couldn't help sighing as she snuggled against him. She heard him mutter something but the words were immediately whipped away by the wind and hurled into the darkness that surrounded them.

Traffic became lighter as they drove farther away from town and nearer to the roadhouse. As they approached Queenie's, Georgia could see dim yellow lights stretched out from the corners of the long low building that sat well back off the main road. Colored neon signs flashed silently against the rough cedar siding and as Cord pulled into the parking lot, they could hear the rockabilly beat pounding rhythmically from inside.

The parking lot was crowded and several couples went into the building as Cord brought the motorcycle to a complete stop in the shadows at one end of the juke joint.

Georgia slid off the bike before Cord turned the engine off. She watched him remove his helmet and position it over the front light. She handed him her own helmet and ran her fingers through her blond curls as he got off the bike and turned to her.

"I don't want you out of my sight in there," he said quietly. "And I want you to do exactly as I say. Don't talk to anyone—if these roughnecks hear you, they're going to know right away that you're not a biker's woman."

"But I can—"

"Not a word," he said, brushing his fingers across her lips.

When Cord put his arm around her, pulling her up close, Georgia felt a little thrill in her chest. Until she realized that this, too, was just for show. After all, they had to look the part.

He held her tight against him, her hips pressed against his leg. They walked to the front door and stopped before a burly-looking man whose bald head glimmered beneath the neon lights.

"Hey, dude," he muttered as he watched Cord pull out a roll of money from his jeans pocket. "What's happenin'?"

"Nothin' much," Cord said. He looked down at Georgia and pulled her tighter against him. For a moment, Georgia thought he might actually kiss her. "Just lookin' for a quiet spot where me and my lady can do a little relaxin'— a little dancin'. Know what I mean?" Cord patted his jacket pocket where the outline of a bottle was clearly visible.

"Oh, yeah," the man said, staring at Georgia with a glint in his eye. "I gotcha," he said with a wink. "Queenie's is the place, all right. Law won't bother you none here."

The man grinned at Georgia, then nodded as Cord pulled her with him into the dark smoky interior of the honky-tonk.

This was the kind of place that had always been forbidden to Georgia and her friends. It was dark and primitive—filled with loud, uninhibited laughter and music that was so deafening she could feel it vibrating through her entire body.

Cord didn't have to remind her to stay close. She clung to his jacket as he guided her through the crowded tables toward the back of the room. Georgia was aware of the looks directed their way and for a moment her heart skittered frightfully.

What if she gave them away? What if someone recognized her?

As they sat at a table, Georgia glanced back toward the crowd and saw that no one was looking now. Perhaps they had just been curious.

"Looks as if you made quite an impression," Cord said, bending close.

Her gaze flew to his eyes, wondering for a minute what he meant.

"You don't think they recognized me, do you?" she asked. "You don't think—"

"Sweetheart, I don't think any of them got past the black pants." His blue eyes twinkled when he moved his head as if to look at her beneath the table.

"Oh," she said, closing her eyes with a relieved sigh. "Thank goodness."

When she opened her eyes, Cord was watching her. His eyes had turned serious and now his gaze scanned her face, moving to her lips.

She wondered what would have happened if the waitress hadn't chosen that particular moment to walk to their table. The brash-looking redhead couldn't seem to resist putting her hand on Cord's broad shoulder.

"What can I get for ya, sweetie?"

"I brought my own," he said, placing the bottle on the table. "But I think I'll take a little house bourbon and cola, just so I can watch you walk to the bar and back." Cord grinned as he flirted outrageously with the older-looking woman. He hesitated a moment before turning to Georgia. "And a light beer for my lady."

"You got it, sweet thang," the waitress said, wiggling her hips as she walked away.

As they waited for their drinks, Cord's eyes scanned the crowd. Georgia thought he looked rather like a hawk searching for prey. His eyes were hard and impenetrable, so different than they were when they looked at her.

Suddenly he turned to her, putting his hand to her face, entangling his fingers in her hair and pulling her forward for a kiss that took her breath away. His mouth was warm, his touch sweet and soft.

She was gasping for air when he pulled away and she felt a little twinge of disappointment when she saw his gaze move to two men who were walking past their table. She heard one of them laugh.

"Are they the ones?" she asked after the men disappeared down a dark narrow hallway.

"Yeah, that's them," he said.

The waitress came and brought their drinks. Cord tossed several bills on her tray, then reached across the table toward Georgia.

"Dance, baby?"

Georgia knew it wasn't a question, but a command and that his endearment was for the waitress's benefit. His hand clasped around her wrist, pulling her up with him before she could say a word.

He held her against him on the crowded dance floor. Colored lights flickered and blinked above them, muted and foggy through the smoke that hung over the dancers. The music had a heavy beat, and after a while it was all Georgia could hear. It was a loud, thumping rhythmic beat that reached down into her chest and seemed to match the steady march of her heart. It made her feel hot with its sensual, primitive tempo. Georgia clung to Cord, looking up into his handsome face.

But he was looking elsewhere. She knew he was scanning the crowd for the two men they'd seen earlier.

She snuggled against him, resting her head against his chest and closing her eyes as they moved slowly in time with the music. She didn't care that he was preoccupied. All that mattered was that she was in his arms, held tightly against his strong body, feeling his thighs brush against hers, breathing in the sexy scent of cologne that he wore that made her heart ache with the remembrance of long hot summer nights.

When the music ended, Cord put his arm around her waist as they walked back to their table. They sat down, and he took a long drink of his bourbon and gazed across the table at her.

"You don't have to drink the beer," he said.

"No, its all right," she said, taking a sip from the frosty brown bottle just to prove that it didn't bother her. "We could hardly have asked for a wine spritzer," she said, smiling into his eyes.

"Or Perrier," he agreed with a quiet smile. "Look, I'm going to the bar, see what I can find out about those two guys we saw. Will you be all right?"

"Sure I will," she said. "I'll just sit here quietly and sip my beer." She lifted the bottle in a little salute.

"I imagine you'll be besieged with dance requests as soon as I leave. Tell them no." His eyes were steady and serious and she knew he meant it. What she didn't know and didn't ask was why he said it.

"All right," she said softly.

"I won't be gone long."

Georgia watched him walk away, enjoying the confident way he walked, the fit of his soft faded jeans against narrow hips and muscular thighs. His black hair gleamed beneath the dim lights and his shoulders in the leather jacket were broad and powerful-looking.

Georgia sighed, taking another sip of her beer. Lord, but he was as sexy as ever. She could see the other women in the club eyeing him as he walked past and for a moment she felt an unexpected twinge of jealousy. It made her feel hot, made her chest tighten with anger and frustration. She wanted to jump up and tell them to keep their looks to themselves.

Finally she laughed softly at herself and shook her head.

"Careful, girl," she murmured. "He doesn't belong to you anymore."

But he had, dammit. At one time he had, and Georgia found that more than anything, she wanted it to be that way again.

At last she saw him coming back through the crowd. He didn't look pleased. Then Georgia saw their waitress following behind him.

When he sat down, the waitress leaned across his shoulder, placing another glass of bourbon and cola before him.

"I know you didn't order it, shug," the redhead said. "But this one's on me."

"Thanks." Cord nodded his appreciation and finished his first drink. The waitress waited as he picked up the fresh one and took a long swallow.

"I heard you askin' about those two men," she said in a voice so low that Georgia could barely hear.

"Your bartender didn't seem anxious to tell me anything."

"He's afraid," she said, pretending to rummage in her apron for change. "They're rough, them two. They're from across the mountain, near Coaltown. Gary Soames and Jeff Watson. Both of 'em spent time at Leavenworth. Not much they ain't done at one time or another."

Cord reached out and put his arm around the waitress, pretending to be flirting with her. Both of them laughed.

"Would the word *arson* happen to be in their vocabulary?" he asked beneath his breath.

"Oh, yeah," she said. Her eyes were wide with fright, and Georgia realized how much courage it took for her to tell Cord what she knew. "That and a lot more."

"Like what?"

"I better go," she said, glancing around. "But next time I bring you a drink, I'll tell you what I can."

Cord nodded and took another swallow of his drink, gazing toward Georgia over the rim of the glass.

Cord reached for her hand again, pulling her out toward the dance floor as the band began to play a slow, plaintive song.

Georgia didn't know if it was the music or the effects of the bourbon... or if it was merely a pretense. But this time Cord's attention was for her alone.

He held her tight, taking her arms and placing them up around his neck. Then his hands moved down her back to her waist, and lower to her hips. He looked down into her eyes and in the smoky light, she thought she saw a hint of the old Cord. The wild impetuous man who would make her want him with one kiss, one look from those quicksilver blue eyes. The dark-haired forbidden rebel she had never been able to forget. Had never been able to resist.

And still couldn't.

After the dance ended and they returned to the table, the waitress reappeared, placing a cold beer in front of Georgia and leaning toward Cord again.

"They're not much more'n thugs for hire," she said. "They'll do just about anything for money. Burnin' cars for insurance, terrorizin' people, burglary, drugs."

"Murder?" Cord asked.

She straightened then and there was genuine fear in her eyes.

"Oh, Lord," she said. "I...I don't know about that."

"Do you know anybody they've ever done work for?"

"Sure," she said. "Mostly bigwigs in Farmington—the money people. Who are you, anyway? You ain't with the feds or anything, are you? Look, honey, I got kids to support. I don't want my name to ever come up in conversation about those two."

"It won't," Cord said. "I promise." He leaned back and reached into his pocket, taking out two twenty-dollar bills and stuffing them into her apron. "I appreciate your help."

"Sure 'nuff, sugar," she said, grinning at him again. "Anytime I can do anything else, you just ask for little old Michelle. And next time, honey, leave the blonde at home." She winked at Georgia and grinned. "Nothin' personal, shug."

Georgia gritted her teeth as the redhead sauntered away, swinging her hips provocatively. She was seething as Cord watched the woman, obviously enjoying the flirtation.

"I wonder what she'd think if I kicked her cute little butt...*shug*," Georgia fumed.

Cord looked surprised. Then he grinned.

"You think you could?"

"Oh, I could," she said, her brown eyes sparking fire.

Cord leaned his head back and laughed out loud. It was the first time she'd heard him laugh that way since his return to Farmington.

"Come on," he said. "Let's have one more dance before we go."

The band was playing an old song. A slow, provocative rendition of "Georgia on My Mind." As Cord pulled her into his arms, he murmured against her hair.

"They must be playing this one especially for you."

"Actually, I was named Georgia because of this song. Mother said it was her and Dad's favorite."

"Somehow I can't picture your father making a decision based on his emotions," Cord said.

"Me, neither," she said with a nervous laugh.

Georgia closed her eyes, letting the music reach into her soul, letting the husky voice of the singer on stage whisper the words to her heart.

"Just an old sweet song, with Georgia on my mind..."

She didn't know if he remembered, but she and Cord had danced to the song before. One sweet balmy night beneath the whispering pine trees on the bank overlooking the lake. The music had hummed from an old portable radio out into the darkness, blending softly with the wind and the lap of the water. It was the first time they had made love, the first night Cord had taught her what being a woman was all about.

Georgia looked up into his eyes and she knew he remembered it, too. And that he was feeling all the emotions, all the sweet memories that she felt.

She seemed to melt against him, feeling as if his warmth invaded her skin, feeling the hardness of him against her softer body. Letting go of all the pain, all the regrets that had been between them the past few days.

When the music ended, they still stood in the middle of the dance floor. He continued to hold her and slowly he bent to kiss her, touching the soft moistness of her lips with his tongue.

Cord could feel Georgia shudder, then move closer, encircling his neck with her arms as she returned his kiss. His hands moved to her hips and he pulled her tighter against him, remembering the feel of her, his body remembering everything about her and the way he'd held her this way so many times before. The way his desire for her always began in the pit of his stomach and wound its way quickly through his veins like a hot, liquid flame.

He pulled away with a soft groan and took a deep breath.

"We'd better get out of here," he murmured, kissing her upturned mouth again.

Without a word, she took his hand and followed as he led her through the crowd and toward the front door.

Chapter 10

It began to rain when they left the club and lightning flickered in the dark skies to the south. Georgia felt the raindrops against her face. She felt so hot that she thought the rain might actually sizzle where it hit her skin.

In the dimly-lit area where Cord had left his bike, he turned to her, pulling her into his arms with a quiet groan. His lips sought hers in a hot devouring kiss that made her body ache for more.

Reluctantly he pulled away and handed her a helmet.

"It's wet," he murmured, kissing her again as if he couldn't help himself.

"I don't care," she whispered, moving into his arms again and feeling his raspy beard against her skin. The feel of the light mist against their face and lips as they kissed lent an unbelievable eroticism to the moment.

"Put it on," he breathed against her mouth. "Let's go home."

Georgia was happy to have time to snuggle against Cord as they headed back to town. This time she let herself relax completely, hugging him tightly around the waist and placing her chin against his back.

The approaching storm moved quickly from the south, chasing them along the dark, almost deserted highway. And although the heaviest rain did not reach Farmington until Georgia and Cord pulled into her driveway, they were still soaking wet from the forerunning showers.

Georgia was shivering as they hurried into the house. She barely had time to reset the security alarm before Cord pulled her into his arms.

His hands moved quickly around her waist and he turned her around to face him, wrapping her in his embrace so tightly that she could hardly breathe.

Georgia clung to him, her fingers in his wet hair, her skin burning from the roughness of his beard as he kissed her.

Outside, the lightning flashed and thunder shook the house. The lights flickered, then went out, leaving them in a hot delicious darkness as they gave in to all the emotions they'd pushed aside these past few days.

"Cord," she whispered.

His hands pulled at her sweater, ripping it out from the waistband of her tight satin pants. In the darkness, Georgia could hear the rasp of his heavy breathing and beneath her hands, she felt the quiet thud of his heart.

"I want to love you," he murmured, groaning as his hands moved to her warm full breasts.

"Oh...I want you, too," she whispered, catching his face between her hands, wanting to taste all of him. Wanting so much that she felt desperate with the need.

His hands were rough and impatient as he pulled her sweater over her head and tossed it onto the kitchen floor. Georgia's hands, clumsy from being cold and wet, moved to the buttons of his damp shirt and she smiled when her actions brought a soft impatient groan from his lips.

His hands moved downward, quickly cupping her hips and pulling her tightly against him and letting her know how much he wanted her. Then just as suddenly, his arms moved beneath her knees and he picked her up, kissing her hungrily as he moved through the kitchen with only the flashes of lightning to guide him.

There were soft battery-powered emergency lights along the upstairs hallway and now they guided his way as he carried her up the steps. At her bedroom, he kicked open the door and moved toward the bed.

When Cord set her on her feet, she kicked off the stiletto heels, her small hands pushing his shirt away from his broad shoulders and down his arms.

He was big and muscular—no longer a boy but a man, every inch of him arousingly virile. Touching him, kissing him in the darkness, was erotic and exciting, but Georgia wished for a light. She had changed, too—she was no longer a shy young girl. She wanted to see all of him.

"Wait," she said, remembering the candles she always kept in a drawer by the bed. Quickly she took out a crystal holder and lit one of the candles, turning to him with anticipation glittering in her eyes.

When she moved her hands down his jean-covered hips, she could feel him holding his breath, waiting...wondering what she intended. With a smile, she slipped her fingers beneath the red bandanna that he had tied around his thigh. Then, sensually aware of the tense muscles beneath her hands, she deftly unfastened the knot.

That slow, seductive act made Cord groan and left both of them breathless. After that, the rest of their clothes were discarded quickly and they stood for a moment, neither of them able to believe that this moment had actually come.

Cord reached forward, touching her breasts and causing her to close her eyes as she sighed with pleasure. Her hands moved to his flat stomach as she reveled in his caresses and as she felt his hands move down the length of her body, over her hips and her thighs.

Georgia began to tremble as little groans of desire moved past her lips. Her knees were like jelly, even her very bones seemed weak and hot with her need for him to take her. Soon.

"Oh, Cord," she breathed. "Make love to me... please..."

Cord gasped with pleasure when Georgia's hand moved down to hold him. He had made himself forget this. Made himself push aside all the sweet, soft memories of her after a while. It had simply been too painful, remembering. And now all of it was back—the heat and desire that he had felt for no other woman. Every primitive instinct in him urged him to take her quickly and put an end to the long, torturous waiting.

He pushed her back onto the bed, looking down into her eyes before his mouth took hers in a hard, sensual kiss that left both of them gasping for air. Those liquid brown eyes, that sweet mouth, had haunted his dreams for ten long years. And now she was here. She was his—sweet and yielding, waiting. His for the taking.

Cord's big strong body shook with desire. And as he entered her, she cried out with some never-forgotten pleasure. It was an unforgettable moment for both of them as together, finally, they gave in to the passion they'd been denied for so long.

Georgia's arms moved up over her head, her hands grasping the scrolled ironwork of her bed. Her eyes were narrowed and languid with desire as she looked up at him, encouraging him and whispering out all her needs.

Cord's body was demanding and Georgia met him with pure, open giving, arching her body to meet his, matching his rhythm until he thought he might die from the pleasure of it.

Neither of them could hold back any longer. This moment had taken too long to reach, the tension between them bursting with a hot and desperate urgency.

Georgia gave a little cry, closing her eyes and clutching his shoulders. Cord took her mouth, capturing her quiet moans and savoring the sweetness of her surrender. When he felt her shuddering release, he moved with her—faster, harder, until his own fulfillment joined hers.

Still holding her tight, Cord opened his eyes and looked down at Georgia, and he was surprised to see the glisten of tears on her cheeks.

"Baby," he whispered, his fingers touching her damp face. "What is it? Did I hurt you? Did I—"

"No," she said, frowning and reaching up to kiss his mouth. "No, you would never hurt me."

"I wouldn't," he said with a little shake of his head. "Tell me what's wrong."

"Not wrong," she said, her lips trembling as she moved her head against the pillow. "It's just that nothing in my life could ever compare with this . . . with what we have when we're together. It's been such a long time and I was so afraid . . ."

"Shh," he said, taking her face in his big hands and wiping away her tears.

"You don't have to be afraid any longer. I'm here now. I'm here."

Georgia put her arms around him, holding him against her. He was still her rebel hero. The only man who could satisfy her so completely. A man of fierce pride and integrity—a man she could depend on to be brutally protective, if need be. The only man she had ever loved.

Would ever love.

They went to sleep in each other's arms, safe and secure from the world and the storm that raged through the trees outside and against the big old house. When Georgia stirred an hour later, the lights were back on and the candle beside her bed had melted in its glass holder into a pool of rose-scented wax.

She lay quietly for a moment, listening to the soft patter of rain on the rooftop as she watched Cord sleeping. She didn't want to wake him. She was glad for the moment of quiet and peace, and to be able to look at him.

With his eyes closed and his black hair rumpled against the pillow, he looked younger, more vulnerable than when those blue eyes riveted their full power on her. She reached to touch his rough, unshaven face and was rewarded with the lifting of his dark eyelashes. His eyes in the dimly-lit bedroom had a sleepy, smoky look.

Then he smiled.

"Hey," he whispered, taking her fingers and bringing them to his mouth. "Are you all right?"

"All right?" she asked, her look one of awe and wonder as she gazed into his eyes. "I'm more than all right. I'm wonderful…marvelous…out of my mind with happiness…" She sighed and snuggled against him, letting her hand trail down his naked chest to rest atop his flat stomach.

Cord frowned, taking her hand and moving it upward. Those were the words he might use to describe how he was feeling right now, too. Along with an amazement that it had been so good…so right. And yet the word *forbidden* always seemed to creep into his subconscious where Georgia was concerned. Not to mention the guilt he felt for taking advantage of tonight. The smoky, primitive atmosphere at Queenie's had set the mood, the seductive pounding rhythm of the music…the sensual pleasure of their ride home in the rain. All of it had brought their desire to one wild, irresistible conclusion.

And here she was, in his arms, sweeter and softer—more voluptuous and desirable—than even he remembered. Words were not even adequate to describe how he felt about what had happened between them.

Whoever said you could never go home again hadn't known Georgia Blake Ashley.

He closed his eyes when he felt her body move against his, when he felt his own body responding to her touch and the whisper of her breath against his neck.

He wanted her. God, he wanted her again, just as hotly, just as urgently as he had before. And all he had to do was turn to her, take her in his arms and make love to her.

And then what? Would making love to her again change the inevitable? Change who she was in Farmington or the kind of life she obviously preferred? All he had to do was look at this bedroom, this house, to see what she had grown accustomed to. Certainly more than his salary could afford.

But his mind was no worthy opponent. Not when his body craved hers so strongly that he thought he would die rather than relinquish the pleasure of making love to her again.

With a soft protesting groan, he turned over on his side so that he and Georgia were facing each other. She reached up to meet his mouth as he pulled her tightly against the length of his body.

Their lovemaking this time was not as urgent, but just as sweetly, just as hotly anticipated as before.

Georgia thought she had never been so happy as she was that night, lying next to Cord, listening to the sound of the rain on the roof. Hearing his steady heartbeat beneath her ear as she lay against his chest.

They talked for a while about insignificant things. About people they'd known, about how their lives had changed.

"What will we do now, Cord?" she asked. "About the two men we saw tonight?"

"I'll call my partner in Atlanta, have him run their names through the computer, check their records at Leavenworth. See exactly what they were in for and if there are any significant names from Farmington in their court documents."

"That reminds me of something else I thought about tonight."

"What's that?" he asked. Cord propped up on his elbow, his look warm and tender as he gazed down at her. He ran one finger across her collarbone and down between her breasts.

Georgia shivered, and a quiet smile moved across Cord's features. When he bent his head toward her breasts, she closed her eyes and caught his hair in her fingers.

"How can I tell you...ohh...when you...keep doing that?"

He laughed softly and lay back against the pillows, cradling her in his arm and pulling her close again.

"Tell me," he murmured.

"Bob used to keep a lot of personal information in his computer at the office. He could be pretty secretive about money sometimes, even with me."

"Do you think you can get into his files? Do you have access?"

"To some of them, yes. And we might even find files I don't know about."

"When can we do it?"

"I think it would be better to do it at night, after the real-estate office is closed. Mrs. Ramsey is sweet and harmless, but she is a bit of a gossip. Everyone in town would know what we're doing."

"Tomorrow night then," he said. "In the meantime, I'll have my partner work on information about the two red-necks-for-hire." He stretched and looked at the watch on his wrist. "Do you know what time it is?"

"I don't care," she whispered, nuzzling against him.

Cord reached out and turned off the bedside lamp. His fingers caressed her hair as he placed a kiss against her forehead.

"Go to sleep," he said, his voice a quiet rumble. "Tomorrow will be a long day."

"Cord?" she whispered after a few moments.

"Hmm?"

"I'm glad you're here. I'm glad you came back to Farmington."

He said nothing, pulling her closer. But long after he heard the sound of her quiet breathing and knew she was asleep, he lay awake in the dark.

He heard the sound of the rain and wind, and the distant familiar sound of a train whistle. They'd lived near the tracks when he was a kid and sometimes that sound soothed him in the night, comforted him and blotted out the other sounds in the house. The sound of raucous, drunken laughter...the sound of slamming doors and his mother's voice as men came and went in the house in a steady stream, sometimes all through the night.

Was it any wonder that poor Sheila had turned out the way she had?

Cord gritted his teeth, thinking again of his determination to find out why she had died. And as he held Georgia, he thought of other things, as well.

About what would happen between them now. What she would say...how those brown eyes would look when he left to go back to Atlanta.

He couldn't stay here. God help him, this town...even this house, as beautiful as it was, was stifling to him. And it held all the reminders of where he came from. That was one thing about a small southern town—no one ever let you forget your roots—good or bad.

All that held him here was Georgia. This soft, sweet, vulnerable woman in his arms that he'd sworn to avoid. The scent of her, the feel of her even now, made him close his eyes in the darkness and grit his teeth against the pleasure and the pain.

He growled softly in his throat, then lay very still when Georgia moved and murmured something in her sleep.

Why had he done it? Why had he given in tonight to all that he'd been feeling about her? Had it been the music? The bourbon? The look of sweet surrender on her face when they danced?

Hell, why couldn't he have waited a few more days—kept pushing her away? It wouldn't have been so hard then to leave. And he wouldn't have these new, disturbingly erotic memories of Georgia's lips and hands, her warm accepting body, to take back with him.

With a shake of his head, he sighed and closed his eyes to sleep.

It was still early the next morning when the doorbell rang. Georgia had showered hurriedly, but she was still in her robe, trying desperately to pull herself together and make it to work on time, despite the tiredness she felt.

She glanced up the stairs, knowing Cord would not want her to go to the door alone. But he was in the shower and she needed to hurry.

Georgia peeked through the curtains and groaned, then opened the front door. The air that swirled in past her carried the scent of rain and wet leaves. It was colder this morning and for a moment she shivered as she stood staring into her mother's eyes.

"Mother," Georgia said, frowning slightly. "What are you doing here this time of morning?"

"I came to try to talk some sense into you. You're always too busy at work so... Georgia, for heaven's sake, have you lost all sense of decency? Do you have any idea what everyone in town is saying about you?"

"No, Mother, what are they saying?" Georgia asked with a sigh.

She knew it was a mistake as soon as she said it. She stood for a moment staring at the petite gray-haired woman who, even at this hour of the morning, was immaculately dressed. Not one strand of hair was out of place, despite the rather brisk wind that rustled through the trees outside. Her makeup was perfectly applied and Georgia caught the scent of her mother's favorite, very expensive perfume.

Her mother pushed her way past her, her eyes scanning the entire house. Looking for Cord, no doubt, Georgia thought.

"Would you like some coffee?" she asked her mother, moving ahead of her into the kitchen.

"Where is he?" her mother asked. "Is he here? Has he actually moved in the way everyone says? Dear Lord, it wasn't bad enough that I'm the only one in my canasta group who doesn't have a grandchild. Now I have a daughter who is living in sin. And with a man of Cord Jamison's reputation." Her mother was fairly huffing with displeasure as she spoke.

"Mother, you're talking about the past. Cord Jamison has changed. He's a respected agent with the Georgia Bu-

reau of Investigation now. His reputation, as you call it, is
something you and Daddy dreamed up ten years ago.''

"He wasn't good enough for you then and he isn't good
enough for you now.''

"Well, for God's sake, Mother, who is?'' she asked,
whirling around from the coffeepot to glare at her mother.
"Bob Ashley? Did his wealth and position make him treat
me with any more respect? Was I any less humiliated by his
infidelities because of it?''

"You know who Cord Jamison's mother was,'' her
mother whispered, her eyes wide with disapproval. "*What*
she was. What kind of man can he be . . . raised in such an
atmosphere?''

Before Georgia could answer, Cord walked into the
kitchen. Georgia knew he had heard every word. This
morning he was clean-shaven and his blue eyes were wary
and cool. She thought he had deliberately left his blue denim
shirt unbuttoned just to taunt her mother.

"Good morning,'' he said.

Georgia held her breath as she looked from him to Regina Blake. Her mother's cheeks were flushed and as she
turned to meet Georgia's eyes, there was a look of disapproval, a look that said I told you so.

"You remember Cord Jamison, don't you, Mother?''

"Yes, indeed,'' her mother snapped. "I remember him all
too well.''

Cord's mouth moved to one side as he stepped to the
coffeepot to pour himself a cup of coffee. In the kitchen,
between the two women, he looked big and daunting. The
lights gleamed against his dark skin and as he lifted the coffeepot, the muscles in his chest rippled.

"Don't let me interrupt,'' he said blithely, staring at
Georgia with a wry, cool look. "After all, I believe I was the
topic of conversation.''

"Mr. Jamison," her mother huffed, "any decent, respectable man would not have eavesdropped and he certainly wouldn't have mentioned it if he had."

"Well," he said with a dismissive laugh, "that's just the point you were making, wasn't it? I'm neither decent, nor respectable. Isn't that right?" He meant the question for Mrs. Blake, yet his blue eyes met Georgia's as if he asked the same question of her.

"Cord," Georgia began, troubled by the look in his eye. "I..."

"Say it, Georgia," he said, his voice a rough whisper. "Say that it doesn't matter who my mother was or where I came from."

Suddenly the room was very quiet. And it seemed to Georgia that she and Cord were the only two people in the world as she stared into his troubled eyes.

"You know how I feel," she whispered, pleading. This was too personal, too dear to be discussing in front of anyone else, especially her mother. "You know none of that means anything—"

"No, I don't know—I guess that's one of the things we never got around to discussing last night."

Georgia could feel her face growing hot, could hear her mother's scandalized gasp.

"How *do* you feel?" he asked pointedly, challenging her. "Tell me. And set your mother's mind at ease."

"Cord, this is not the time...don't do this," she said quietly.

"Don't do what? Don't tell your mother that I'm good in bed, but hardly husband material. Not in Farmington, anyway. That she has no more to worry about now than she did ten years ago?"

Georgia closed her eyes. She could feel her heart trembling. Yet all she wanted to do was reach out for him. Move into his arms and tell him that she loved him. That she had always loved him and nothing her mother or anyone else said would ever change that.

But how could she when there was such a look of quiet disdain in those stormy blue eyes?

"Well, I've heard quite enough," Regina Blake huffed. "Enough to know that you're just as coarse and unrefined as we always thought." She turned to Georgia, her dark eyes troubled as she stared into her daughter's face. "I only hope that my daughter has enough sense to do what is right this time. I'll talk to you later, Georgia," she added, moving quickly through the kitchen and toward the front hallway.

When the front door slammed, Georgia turned to Cord, intending to explain, wanting to comfort him somehow.

"Cord," she whispered, putting her hand on his arm.

Cord pulled away and began to button his shirt. His blue eyes were cold and clear and there was a forced smile on his lips.

"Let it go, Georgia," he said. "You don't have to explain. I've been there before . . . remember?"

"Damn you, why do you do this? What is there to explain?" she said, her eyes pleading. "I'm not my mother. I don't feel the way she does. You know that. Didn't last night—"

"Last night?" he asked. He stepped forward, reaching now to touch her cheek. "Last night was good, baby. I never denied that sex was always great between us. But we're not kids anymore. We both know that a relationship has to be based on more than sex."

"Cord, don't do this," she whispered, unable to believe that after what they'd shared last night, he could even think of pulling away from her again. "Don't say things that can never be taken back."

"You seem to have to keep telling everyone here how I've changed, Georgia. How respectable I am now as opposed to whatever I was back then. You keep defending me and I wonder why you find that necessary."

"I—"

"I haven't changed," he said, his eyes hard and cold. "I'm still the same man I was before. Still a rebel at heart. Still distrustful and hard to get to know. Still blunt and stubborn . . . coarse, as your mother so aptly put it."

"You're not—"

He smiled then and there was a hint of regret in his eyes.

"Georgie," he said with a sad shake of his head. "The past is gone and too much has happened. We can never bring it back."

"But last night—"

"Last night was good, dammit," he said, his voice growing hoarse as he stepped closer. "Better than good. I don't deny wanting you and I don't deny how good we are together. But I haven't changed, and I don't intend changing. Not to suit this prudish little town, not to suit your parents . . . not even to suit you, baby. After this is over, I don't intend coming back to Farmington, or ever again living my life beneath the scrutiny of people like the Blakes and Stones and Goodwins. It sickens me what these people did to my sister and me. And it sickens me every time I hear you trying to defend me to them."

Georgia thought nothing could compare to the pain in her heart at that moment. All those years ago, when Cord had left . . . it had been agony. But it was nothing compared to this. It was like having a fortune at your fingertips, then suddenly seeing it all go up in flames.

Her eyes were tortured as she stared at him.

Couldn't he see that she was the one who had changed? That he no longer had to worry about fitting into Farmington's small, restricted world? She would do anything for him . . . go anywhere to be with him. Didn't he know that?

But she knew it was over. Last night had meant nothing to him except good sex, while for her it had been everything. For Georgia, it had been a promise—a sweet bright glimpse into a future that held every happiness she'd ever dreamed of. And now it was gone.

Chapter 11

Cord grabbed his leather jacket and started toward the door.

"Is that always your answer?" Georgia cried, her voice bitter with anguish. "Running away? How are we ever going to settle this between us Cord if—"

"I'm not running from anything," he said, stopping at the door. "I'll be back." His eyes when he looked at her were steady and cool. He had the look of a man determined to go his own way, a man who could not be moved nor persuaded by a woman's tears. "I've decided to go to Atlanta myself, find the files I need ... run my theories by some of the other guys. But I should be back before dark. We'll check your husband's office then—if we're lucky, I'll find what I need. Who knows?" he said with a wry grimace. "Maybe by this time next week, it will all be over and I'll be out of your hair. You'll be able to go back to your friends ... and your own life."

"You know that's not what I want."

"I'll see you tonight," he said, ignoring her words, ignoring the sadness in her brown eyes.

Outside, Cord started the motorcycle, not looking back at the house. All he wanted was to ride, as hard and fast as the sleek low-end torque engine would carry him. He wanted to forget brown eyes and soft arms, pale skin that shimmered in candlelight and seemed made for the touch of a man's hands.

It was almost more than he could do to leave her this way, with tears in her beautiful eyes. But her mother's visit this morning had brought everything back into perspective for him.

The proper and elegant Regina Blake had reminded Cord all too well that he had never fit into Georgia's world and never would. Even if he wanted it—they would never accept him. And he knew that he would not be doing Georgia a favor by pretending otherwise, no matter how much he might want her, no matter how much he might be willing to sacrifice to be with her.

Every nerve in him cried out to do just the opposite. Every instinct he had told him to stay, to pull Georgia into his arms and make love to her. To kiss her until she was breathless and begging for more.

He could ask her to leave Farmington. To put aside the life she'd known here—the only way she'd ever lived—and come to Atlanta with him. She would have to start over in a big city, a place as foreign and unwelcoming as the moon for someone like her. Luxuries would be few—the most he had to offer was maybe a modest house in the suburbs, three kids and a dog, a station wagon. Dinner and movies on a Friday night, perhaps a two-week vacation on the beach every summer.

Hardly the life-style anyone would suspect Cord Jamison of wanting. In the old days, no one guessed just how badly he longed to fit in—to perhaps one day be able to offer Georgia everything. Wouldn't they laugh if they knew that the quiet simple life sounded pretty good to bad-boy Cord Jamison right now?

But it was too late. Too much had happened. Too much had changed . . . and not enough had changed.

Georgia dressed and went to work, her mind in a fog as she drove. Judge Stone remarked to her more than once about her distraction.

"What is it, Georgia?" he asked just before noon. "Tell the old judge all about it," he added with a grin meant to tease and soothe. "That Jamison boy's not making trouble for you, now, is he?"

Georgia sighed and shook her head.

"He's not a boy, Judge Stone. And no, he isn't making trouble for me. I don't know why everyone in this town keeps asking me that."

"You're kind of special in this town, hon. We just want you to be happy," he said. He had taken off his black robe to go to lunch and now he came and sat on the edge of her desk. "Your daddy's worried about you."

"Daddy worries too much."

"He's afraid you're in love with the man."

Georgia bit her lips, trying to hold back the tears that threatened to spring to her eyes every time she thought of Cord and the look in his eyes this morning before he rode away on that black monster of a motorcycle.

"I just don't understand why Daddy...and everyone else, can't see that Cord is..." Remembering Cord's quiet reprimand about her defending him, she vowed not to say he had changed.

"He's good and decent and he always was," she said softly. "He's intelligent...and the most honorable man I've

ever met. He believes in doing what's right. Can you tell me
what's so wrong with that?" she asked, gazing up at the
judge, who was smiling benevolently at her. "Can you tell
me where the sin is in being born poor and single-handedly
pulling yourself out of poverty to become a man who fights
against the wrongs in our society? Who won't back down
from what he believes because of someone's money or position?"

"Well," Judge Stone said softly, "I believe you just answered my question. I don't think I've ever heard you defend anyone quite so vehemently... or so eloquently, my
dear."

After the judge left for lunch, Georgia sat at her desk,
staring out the window and watching the last of the autumn leaves drift to the ground.

She *did* love him. She'd always known that. And now she
wanted Cord to know it and believe it. She wanted the whole
world to know it.

When Mike Goodwin's wife, Brenda, came by at noon,
Georgia decided it was time she stopped avoiding her and
everyone else.

"Lunch?" she said. "Sure. But on one condition."

Brenda was a tall, willowy brunette who could sometimes have a hard edge in her dark eyes. But today, she
looked surprised and a little concerned by Georgia's quick
acquiescence.

"What condition?"

"That I don't have to spend the entire hour defending
Cord Jamison. Or the fact that he's staying at my house."

"Hey," Brenda said with a quick smile. "You've got it,
girl. Although I can't promise that I won't ask personal
questions."

"And I can't promise that I'll answer," Georgia said, returning Brenda's good-natured banter. It had been a long

time since she'd been out with Brenda, or any of her friends, for that matter. And she found she was looking forward to it.

Now that she had come to terms with her feelings for Cord, she felt better—peaceful almost. She did love him. She couldn't make him stay. And she couldn't make him love her back. But she was going to do her best to try.

It was almost time to go home that afternoon when the phone on Georgia's desk rang.

"Judge Stone's office," she said.

"Georgia?" The woman's voice on the other end of the line sounded breathless and panicky. And although it sounded familiar, it took a few moments for Georgia to realize it was one of her neighbors.

"Yes. Janie... is that you?" she asked. "What is it? Is anything wrong?"

"Your alarm system went off a few minutes ago and—"

"Oh," Georgia said, clutching at her chest in relief. "Is that all? Was there a power surge? It's probably just messed up again. You know it does that sometimes—"

"No. I saw a man running from your house just a few seconds later. I've called the police, but I think you'd better come home, Georgia. I really think someone's broken into your house this time."

"I'll be right there," Georgia said, putting the phone down and reaching for her purse. Judge Stone was in court so she left him a message on his desk and hurried out of the office.

By the time she got home, the police were already there, including Mike Goodwin. But she wasn't surprised. Even though he was a county officer, Farmington was such a small town that none of them paid much attention to whose jurisdiction they were in. Besides, Mike would come, being a friend of the family.

The front door was standing open and for a moment Georgia felt a wave of panic wash over her. She left her car in the driveway and ran to the front of the house. Mike was just inside the hallway.

"Mike?" she said, her eyes darting to the interior of her house. Nothing seemed disturbed. "Was it a false alarm? Did someone—"

"I think there was definitely someone here," he said with a disturbed little frown. "Probably someone who knows you're a widow and that you live alone. Everyone in town knows you're at work during the day."

"What did they take?" she asked, stepping farther into the hall.

"Well," Mike said, running his hand over his chin. "That's the problem. The study's a mess—looks as if someone spent a great deal of time rummaging around in there. But there were no obvious missing items. I'll need you to tell me if anything's gone. Jewelry perhaps. And didn't Bob keep a collection of gold coins?"

"Yes, he did," she said, going quickly to the study.

But Georgia wasn't concerned about any items that might be missing, not even Bob's priceless coin collection. She was worried about the bank statements and other papers she and Cord had locked into the bottom drawer of the big rolltop desk.

The first thing she saw was the open drawers of the desk. Including the locked one. There was evidence in the wood of something being inserted to pry open the drawer. Splinters stood out like spikes around the small locking mechanism.

Georgia dropped to her knees, pulling the drawer out and looking inside. Everything was gone. Bob's bank statements as well as Sheila's. All the comparison charts that Cord had made. Everything.

"Oh, no," she whispered, sitting back on her heels.

"What is it?" Mike asked. "The coins?"

"No," Georgia said, glancing at him distractedly. "No, it was just some...some important papers."

Mike sighed and reached down to take her elbow, pulling her to her feet.

"Are you all right?" He glanced around the room for a second. "Where's Jamison? Is he still here? Do you want one of the men to stay here at the house tonight? Or better yet, why don't you come home and stay with us."

"I don't know," she said, feeling lost and confused. "He...he had to go...somewhere today." She glanced at Mike, wishing she could trust him and yet after today, wondering if she'd ever be able to trust anyone again. "He'll be back. There's really no need for anyone to stay here. I'll lock everything up..."

"What I want you to do is make a list of everything you think is missing. Give me serial numbers and descriptions if you can. I'm going to call your dad and tell him what's happened."

Georgia didn't protest. Instead, she sat in a chair, looking at the chaos of what was once her orderly study. Suddenly, knowing that someone had actually been in her house, she felt more afraid than she ever had in her life.

She was still sitting there when Cord came in.

"Georgia," he said, coming immediately to her and pulling her up and into his arms. "God, I saw the police outside and I—"

Nothing had ever felt so good as the strength of his arms around her. Georgia clung to him, not caring that the policemen, who were still there, walked by and grinned at them. She didn't care about anything except that he was here.

"What happened?" he asked, the earlier anger and distrust gone now from his blue eyes.

"My neighbor called me at work to tell me the alarm system had gone off. Oh, Cord," she said, whispering. "They broke open the locked drawer. They took the statements, the charts you made . . . everything." She was trembling.

"Shh," he said, touching his fingers to her lips. "It's all right. It's almost over," he said, glancing around as Mike Goodwin came into the room.

"Jamison," he said with a curt nod.

Georgia felt Cord pulling away, but she put her arm around his waist, refusing to let go. She looked at Mike rather defiantly as she clung to the man beside her.

"I don't think Georgia should stay here in the house tonight," Mike said. "I've called her father and he said he'll be right over. He says he'll take Georgia home with him."

"I think that's a good idea," Cord said, his voice steady and quiet.

Georgia glanced up at him, startled at his easy agreement. But then she felt his arm tighten around her waist and she said nothing.

"I don't think there's anything else we can do here, Georgia," Mike said. "Until we get a list of what's missing. We've taken fingerprints and a few photos, but right now we have absolutely nothing to go on."

"Whoever did this was an amateur," Cord said, glancing around the room. "A professional would never have set off the alarm system. Whoever broke in here is small-time— a flunkie for someone else."

"Yeah, well, I guess you big-time law enforcement officers have to look at things that way," Mike said with a sneer. "Personally, I think it's just a small-time burglary, plain and simple."

"There's nothing plain or simple about any of this," Cord said, his voice deadly with some unspoken warning.

"Have it your way," Mike said.

Georgia could hardly wait until Mike and the others had gone. Then she turned to face Cord.

"What do you mean you think it's a good idea if I go to my parents' house? I'm staying with you, Cord. I have no intention of going home with my father or—"

"Listen to me, angel," he said, running his knuckles across her chin. "I think whoever did this knows we're getting closer to finding out what happened to Bob and Sheila. I'd be willing to bet that the man your neighbor saw was either our friend Soames or Watson. And I'm not about to take a chance on your being here if they decide to come back."

"I won't be afraid if you're here."

"Georgie," he whispered, shaking his head. His eyes were troubled and dark. "I would defend you with my last breath—you know that. But what if I can't protect you? What if something happened to me and you were left alone to—"

"Don't say that," she said, cupping her hand over his mouth. "Don't..." Her eyes were wide with fear.

He took her hand and turned it over, placing a kiss in the palm, then leaning his forehead against hers.

"We have to face reality. Whoever's behind this has already committed murder and arson. Whatever the stakes are here, evidently they're high enough that two more deaths wouldn't matter. And I don't intend to let anything happen to you. Do you hear me? Not ever."

"It won't matter if you're not here," she said, looking deeply into his eyes.

"It does matter," he said, taking her by the shoulders and holding her tightly. "God, it does matter." He pulled her into his arms then, holding her hard, as if he might never relinquish her to anything or anyone.

"I want to be with you," she said, her voice muffled against his chest. "Whatever happens, I just want to be with you."

"God, Georgie," he said, leaning his head back and sighing aloud. "Why do you make this so difficult?"

They heard the sound of a car door slam outside and she looked up into his eyes.

"It's Daddy," she said. "But I'm not going with him."

"All right," he said, shaking her for her stubbornness, but smiling slowly as he gazed into her big brown eyes. "This is what we'll do. You go home with him, pretend you're perfectly willing to stay there. I have a cabin in the mountains that I've been intending to renovate—it's rough, but livable. Tonight I'll come for you and we'll go to the cabin. We can't gamble now on anyone knowing where we are or what we're doing."

"Georgia?" they heard her father calling from the front door.

"You promise you'll come," she asked, her hands clasping the sleeves of his jacket.

"Georgia!" Her father sounded frightened now.

"In here, Mr. Blake," Cord shouted over Georgia's head.

"Promise me," she said, her words urgent as they hissed past her clenched teeth.

"All right...I promise," he said, almost smiling. "God, if I don't, you'll probably track me down like a dog."

"I would," she whispered just as her father stepped into the study.

"What in hell's going on here?" he said, looking quickly around the disheveled study.

"Someone broke into the house, Daddy. One of the neighbors saw a man running away."

"Well, my God... what did he take?"

Georgia felt Cord's hand touch the back of her arm.

"Nothing," she said. "I... I think the alarm frightened him away before he could steal anything."

Horace Blake gritted his teeth, his gaze swinging to focus on Cord.

"I blame you for this, Jamison."

"Yeah, well, what else is new?" Cord murmured.

Cord turned away and began looking through the papers on the desk, hoping to find even the smallest clue.

"If you hadn't come back here... if you hadn't convinced Georgia to become involved with you in this crazy scheme—"

"Look, Mr. Blake," Cord said, turning to face the man. He was a good six inches taller than Georgia's father. "Regardless of what you and your rich cronies think, I have as much right to be in this town as anyone. My sister was murdered here and I intend to find out who did it and why. Then... and only then do I plan on leaving." Cord stood straight and tall, staring into Horace's eyes.

Georgia thought Cord was the only man she'd ever known who could stand up to her father. He wasn't intimidated one iota by Horace Blake's overbearing ways and imperious manner. Her father might have been an insignificant insect for all Cord's appearance indicated. A mere nuisance. She realized as she stared at the two that Cord's restraint where her father was concerned was for her peace of mind as much as anything. Still, she wished it could be different between Cord and her father.

"Please," she said to her father. "I don't want to talk about this anymore. I'd like to go home with you, Daddy, if you don't mind."

Horace's eyes changed. They reflected surprise and a genuine joy.

"Mind?" he whispered. "Of course I don't mind. And your mother will be delighted—she's been worried sick about you." Only briefly did his gaze swing back to Cord. "I'll be waiting for you in the car."

Georgia stood watching as her father left the house, then she turned to Cord, placing her hands on his chest.

"You won't forget me," she whispered.

How could he ever forget her? How could any man forget once he'd held her in his arms, kissed those soft lips, gazed into brown eyes that were as trusting as a fawn's.

"I won't forget," he said. "Midnight—bring a change of clothes, only what you can carry easily." He took her arm and pulled her close, touching his finger to her nose with his other hand as if to warn her. "But for no reason are you to step foot outside that house until you hear me. Wait until you see me stop beneath the streetlight on the corner north of your father's house."

"Maple and First," she said.

"That's right. If something happens and you can't come, I'll wait five minutes. Five," he said, holding up his hand and spreading his fingers.

"I'll be there," she said fiercely. "Don't you dare leave without me. I'll be there."

"All right. Once we get to the cabin, we'll decide what we're going to do next. Now go. Your father's waiting."

Quickly Georgia moved forward, standing on tiptoe and throwing her arms around his neck. At first, Cord seemed surprised by her almost desperate kiss. Then slowly his arms went around her and with a groan, he pulled her tightly against him, almost swinging her off the floor in the process. He raked his fingers into her golden hair, pulling her head back, tasting her sweetness and kissing her as if it might be his last chance.

Then he pulled away, feeling her soft gasps against his chin, his mouth hovering just inches from hers.

"We're going to fight this together, Georgie. You and me," he whispered.

She nodded, not trusting herself to say anything. Then, still looking into his eyes, she backed away, finally turning at the door and running outside to her father's car.

It was a long evening. Georgia was nervous and distracted, and even though she sensed that her parents were trying to temper their comments about Cord Jamison and the situation they felt he had put her in, Georgia still found herself growing impatient and angry.

Finally, unable to stand another moment of conversation, she excused herself.

"I'm really tired," she said.

She planned on leaving her mother a note, not telling where she was but reassuring her that she was all right. No matter how angry she became with her parents or how much she wished they wouldn't interfere, Georgia loved them. She didn't want to worry them any more than was necessary.

Georgia was ready long before midnight. The house had grown quiet an hour ago and now Georgia sat before the window gazing down at the streetlight on the corner of Maple and First.

She heard the sound of the motorcycle engine . . . felt it, even, vibrating through her body like a charge of electricity. She jumped up, staring out the window to make sure it was Cord. When she saw the motorcycle and the glimmer of light against a black helmet, she grabbed the small canvas backpack that held her clothes and slung it over her shoulders.

Slipping quietly out of the house, she ran across the yard and toward the man waiting on the motorcycle. She didn't hesitate, but leaped onto the back of the bike and clasped her arms around him. The engine purred quietly, but still they didn't move.

"Jeez, Georgie," she heard. Then quietly muttered curses.

"What?" she asked, looking around his shoulder as he pulled off his helmet.

Cord raked his hands through his black hair and turned to stare at her over his shoulder.

"Don't you think it would have been a good idea to make sure it was me before you hopped onto the back of the bike?" His voice was rough with impatience.

"I knew it was you. Let's go," she said, poking him in the back and feeling exuberant that he had come for her as he'd promised. "Let's get out of here."

"How did you know?"

Georgia thought about those muscular legs, stretched out, supporting the bike while he waited. She ran her hands over the leather jacket that encased his unmistakable broad shoulders. She was smiling when she hugged him around the chest and lay her head against his back.

"I knew," she murmured.

"You should be more careful."

She could sense him shaking his head before he clamped the helmet back on. His actions as he swung the motorcycle away from the curb seemed a little impatient and irritable.

She laughed aloud, but the wind snatched the sound away and tossed it into the darkness behind them.

She was beginning to like this big, black, powerful motorcycle.

Georgia paid little attention to where they were going. She didn't care, as long as it was away from Farmington. She trusted Cord to do what was best for them, trusted him with her very life.

She knew they were going up the mountain, and after a while she could see the lights from town in the valley off to the right of the winding road. Far below they twinkled like stars—small yellow lights clustered together, then spreading farther and farther apart out toward the farms to the south.

She threw her head back and looked up at the stars that lay across the black skies above the mountain.

"Beautiful," she murmured.

Cord couldn't hear her, but she could sense him turning his head slightly, trying to capture her words.

"We're almost there," he shouted back to her.

The cabin lay at the end of a long winding road, a good distance from the main highway. Cord slowed the motorcycle, but still Georgia had to cling to him to keep from being thrown off onto the rocky ground.

She couldn't make out the cabin very well in the darkness, just that it was wood with a wide front porch that sat well up off the ground.

Cord unlocked the door and pushed it open and Georgia scurried inside, shivering in the cold mountain air.

"It's freezing," she whispered, wrapping her arms around her body.

"There's no heat, I haven't had the electricity turned on since I didn't think I'd be staying here. But there is a fireplace. You sit here and try to stay warm. I'll have a fire going in a minute."

Georgia stumbled in the darkness to a wicker settee in front of the fireplace. She watched while Cord went around the room, lighting kerosene lamps. In the dim, flickering light, she could see that there was one large room downstairs, the kitchen and dining area separated from the living area by a bar, and upstairs was a railing that overlooked the room below.

The place smelled musty and old and the hint of wood smoke still lingered in the stale air. On the floor against one wall lay pieces of wood and some carpenter's tools.

Her eyes moved back to Cord as she watched him start a fire. She wondered if the tools belonged to him, if he had hidden talents she didn't know about. Knowing him and his fierce independence, she thought he probably intended on doing all the work here himself.

"Is there anything I can do to help?" she asked, watching him.

"No," he said.

The fire lit the room now as it began to crackle and pop in the large stone fireplace. Its flickering light made Georgia feel warmer in a way that went beyond the physical.

Cord went to a tall cabinet across the room and pulled out a quilt. He came to Georgia and placed it across her lap before sitting on the other end of the settee. In the light, Georgia saw now that it was an antique wicker piece with plaid cushions.

Cord turned, focusing those silvery blue eyes on her for the first time.

"This is not what you're used to..."

"I love it," she said, shaking her head and wondering why he always said such things. "It's beautiful, Cord. It's going to be magnificent when you're finished."

He didn't answer her. They sat for a long time with only the quiet whisper of wind in the pine trees outside and the crackle of the fire in the fireplace.

The memory of last night's lovemaking lay between them in the still room like a tangible object. Georgia could feel Cord's reluctance to discuss it and yet neither of them could deny how that memory affected them now that they were alone. When one look, one touch would be all it took to start it all over again.

Georgia longed for that look, that special touch. She longed to feel his body against hers, to have him hold her and take her to bed the way he had last night. There had been magic between them—sweet hot magic that had pushed its way past the barriers that Cord had erected between them. And once they were past that, it had been so easy...so good. Just like old times, only better and even more exciting.

But at the same time, she wanted Cord to come to her of his own will and need. To realize that she was not the same impressionable girl she had been ten years ago. That she loved him now more than she ever thought it possible to love anyone. And that she would follow him to the ends of the earth if he asked it.

"Did you find out anything today about the two men we saw at Queenie's?" she asked. Her instincts told her to give him space and time.

"Yeah," he said. He seemed relieved to be talking about something besides the tension that sizzled between them. "It took a while to dig through all the paperwork. Our friends Soames and Watson both have extensive arrest records." He pulled a piece of paper out of his pocket and handed it to her. "Have you ever heard of a corporation called Tri-Co?"

She saw the name scribbled across the piece of paper.

"No," she said, shaking her head and handing the paper back.

"A lawyer named Curtis Mims defended the two in an arson case about a year ago—worked out a plea agreement with the state."

"I know him," Georgia said, her eyes wide with surprise. "He's a very upscale, high-priced lawyer—hardly the kind of man those two could afford. And I can't imagine him taking on gratis cases."

"That's where Tri-Co comes in," Cord said. "Mims does a lot of work for this corporation and it seems that in the Soames and Watson case, Tri-Co paid all of Mims's fees."

Georgia frowned and shook her head.

"And you think if we can find out who runs Tri-Co..."

"It might be a false trail, but then again, who knows?"

Georgia sat for a long time staring into the fire. She'd seen Curtis Mims several times at the courthouse. He'd been to see Judge Stone a time or two. He was the kind of man who flaunted his Patek Philippe watch and Louis Vuitton briefcase. She hadn't liked his slick appearance the first time she'd seen him—from his alligator shoes to the five-hundred-dollar suits and silk ties. Something about the man rang little alarm bells in her head.

"What is it?" Cord asked quietly. He had been watching her all along and he had seen the troubled look on her face. "Something's bothering you."

Georgia shook her head, turning to look into his eyes.

"I don't know. I guess . . . I'm afraid."

With a low murmur, Cord moved across the settee and pulled her toward him. His arms moved quickly, protectively, around her.

"I don't want you to be afraid," he whispered against her hair. "I never wanted that. I shouldn't have involved you in all this."

"Don't feel guilty about me," she said, pushing her face against his leather jacket. "I wanted to help and I know now that something had bothered me about Bob's and Sheila's deaths all along. It was my choice to get involved. Like you said today, we're going to do this together, Cord," she whispered almost shyly.

She liked the tangy scent of the leather mingled with his cologne. And the feel of his warm solid body beneath the leather made her feel secure, made her wish they could stay here in the cabin together, safe and sound for the rest of their lives.

She moved her head back and found him looking down at her. For once, his eyes were unguarded, filled with no resentments, no barriers. The tenderness she saw there simply took her breath away.

"You are so sweet," he murmured. "So... sweet."

"Cord," she whispered, lifting her mouth toward his.

Chapter 12

Somehow, as always, there was no need for words between them. Cord pushed her jacket off her shoulders, then removed his own and tossed it aside. There was no time now for either of them to discuss the way he had left that morning, or why there was still such a touch of bittersweetness in his kiss and his look.

He pulled her down onto the floor between the settee and the fireplace and pushed the quilt beneath her.

Between kisses, he murmured to her.

"Today... in Atlanta, I wasn't able to think of anything except you... except this." His hands impatiently pushed aside her blouse. "I need you," he whispered.

Those three words sent a thrill racing through Georgia's body. Nothing mattered except this, except their being together, not the lumpy quilt under her or the rock-hard floor. Nothing mattered except the way he moved, the way his mouth went quickly down over her lacy bra, trailing kisses until he reached impatiently beneath her and unfastened the snaps and pushed the undergarment out of the way.

Cord hesitated above her, letting his eyes take in all of her in the shimmering firelight. Slowly he lowered his head, the touch of his tongue on her skin sending delicious shivers through Georgia's body.

She felt hot and breathless, completely out of control as her fingers fumbled with the buttons of his shirt. She watched impatiently when he pulled the shirt off and lowered himself against her, letting his muscled chest rub against her naked breasts.

A soft groan moved up from his chest and into his throat.

"Woman," he muttered, his mouth against hers, "you're driving me crazy. Do you know that?"

"Am I?" she whispered, moving her hands up and tangling her fingers in his black hair. "Make love to me," she gasped, arching against him. Wanting him. Dying for him. How could she not know, when he did the same thing to her?

"Soon," he whispered, his mouth hot against her throat. "Soon, baby."

He undressed her quickly, then kicked off his jeans and lay against her again. His hands moved quickly over her body, his fingers teasing, coaxing until Georgia thought she would scream from the sweet, sweet torture.

His mouth, his deep hungry kisses, were just as sweet, just as torturous. Until finally Georgia was at a fever pitch, responding to every touch. She could feel the heat consuming her, feel the power of his body urging her on until she cried out for him to help her.

"Please," she groaned, pushing her fingers through his shining black hair.

Cord looked down into her face, seeing the hunger that transformed her. Seeing the heat turn her brown eyes liquescent. He felt a satisfied triumph race through his body, knowing that the woman he wanted most in the world wanted him just as hotly, just as passionately.

That thought made him know that he could wait no longer.

Quickly he moved to take her.

Georgia cried out at the pleasure of his lovemaking. Finally... finally. His teasing mouth, his experienced hands, had left her so ready that every inch of her body tingled with sensitivity and life.

"Baby...baby," he whispered, his voice hoarse and soft.

Cord couldn't think...couldn't speak for his need of her. Nothing mattered now except the two of them... the pleasure of this intimacy as they moved together with a hard, powerful urgency. Both of them moving toward fulfillment, toward the last shattering ecstasy.

Georgia's body shook violently with wild, unbridled desire. And when she heard Cord's hoarse cry mingling with her own, she thought she had never felt such joy, such absolute euphoria.

Slowly the room came back into focus. The fire had died down to red embers that cast a warm, flickering light against their naked skin. Cord pulled the quilt over Georgia's shoulders as he cradled her in his arms and kissed her softly on the mouth.

Georgia murmured against his mouth, whispering soft love words to him. He was her man, her strong, fiercely independent man who knew how to take care of himself in the world. And yet now he lay against her, holding her tenderly, his powerful body weak and shaken.

At that moment, she loved him more than she had ever loved anyone or anything in her life.

The cabin had never grown completely warm and now as the fire died down, Georgia shivered.

"I think I'd better take you up to bed," Cord said, leaning on one elbow and looking down at her. His fingers pushed a strand of hair away from her eyes, then trailed down the side of her face to her swollen lips.

"Mmm," she said, smiling up into his eyes. "I like the sound of that."

"To sleep," he said with a wry grin.

Georgia reached up to nibble at his chin, then his lower lip.

Cord felt his body stirring to life again and he grinned, feeling surprised and a bit bemused that this petite woman had such power over him.

"Well," he muttered, scooping her up in his arms. "Maybe not."

It was early morning before they finally lay still, quietly laughing with exhaustion and wonder. It was cold in the bedroom and Cord had piled so many quilts on top of them that they could barely move.

But Georgia didn't care. She sighed contently and snuggled against Cord, listening to the low rumble of his voice as he talked.

"Tomorrow . . . today," he corrected with a grunt, "we'll ride across the mountain and buy some groceries. Grocery shopping is one of the times when riding a motorcycle is a distinct disadvantage."

"We'll manage," Georgia said. She looked up at him, able to make out more than the silhouette of his face in the darkness. "We won't be here that long, will we?"

"We shouldn't be," he said. He didn't say anything for a while and Georgia thought she could almost feel his mind working.

"I don't know how all this is going to end," he said, touching her hair. "A lot depends on what we find in Bob's computer. If we find nothing, I guess I'll have to go another route—concentrate on the Tri-Co connection, learn who the officers are and why they'd be interested in defending two small-time punks."

Georgia felt closer to him than ever. There, in the isolation of the cabin, snuggled together in the cold room, she felt that she was a part of him, spiritually connected, as if it were the two of them against the world. And suddenly she wanted to make her peace with him, once and for all.

"Cord," she whispered, turning in his arms to try to see his face. "When you left Farmington...when my father offered you money and told you those lies about what I wanted..."

She could feel the muscles in Cord's chest tense beneath her hands. But he moved toward her, holding her and waiting for her to say what she had to say.

"I wanted to tell you that I'm sorry," she said softly. "I'm so sorry that it happened and that he made you feel so...so—"

"Worthless?" he said quietly.

"If I could go back and change it, I would. If I could take away what my father did..." Georgia's voice cracked and she had to take a deep breath before she could continue. "God, Cord, it kills me, even now, thinking of how you must have felt, what you must have thought about me."

"Shh," he said, finding her mouth in the darkness. "It's over and done. You weren't to blame for how I felt. I should have come to you and demanded an explanation. Maybe I would have if I'd felt more secure about myself...about us. I should have insisted on the truth. But I didn't, Georgie. I ran, just like you said this morning—making up my mind without even giving you a chance to tell me what had happened. It's what I've done all my life. At the first sign of trouble, the first sign of pain, I just shut down...close everyone out. I shouldn't have done that with you, Georgie. Not with you."

"Forgive me," she whispered through trembling lips.

"There's nothing to forgive."

"For... for Bob," she added. "For not trusting you enough to come after you and demand the truth, too. For turning to a man I didn't love."

"I won't lie to you, baby. Your marriage—living with him... making love with him." He seemed not even able to say Bob's name aloud. "That's something I'm not sure I'll ever be able to come to terms with."

Georgia gasped and closed her eyes against the quick pain that attacked her heart.

"But I'm trying," he said gently, feeling her withdrawal. Then, as if to ease the effect of his words, he pulled her closer against him. "I am trying," he said. "Maybe you need to try, too... to forgive yourself."

She didn't say anything. She couldn't. All she wanted at that moment was to feel his arms around her and to enjoy the closeness that they shared. Neither of them knew what tomorrow would bring. And in her heart, even with Cord's sweet, generous words, she wasn't sure how long he would let her stay close this way.

They spent the next day as if it would be their last, as if there had been no murders, no investigation. No separation even. Cord reverted to the playful young man of her youth, teasing her, flirting outrageously with her. He held back nothing that day and neither did she.

That evening before it grew dark enough to venture back down the mountain and into Farmington, they enjoyed a quiet meal before the fireplace. The cabin was warm now and cozy and a little more orderly. They had managed to carry enough food on the motorcycle to make dinner. Cord even produced a dusty bottle of wine from one of the cupboards in the kitchen.

"I wish we didn't have to go... I wish we could stay here forever," Georgia said, sighing as she leaned back against him on the floor in front of the fireplace.

"What?" he said, his voice teasing. "With no curling irons or makeup? No electricity, no water?" He ran his fingers through her tousled hair that was still damp from her recent bath before the fireplace.

His reminder made her heart beat just a bit faster. Earlier, they had heated water in an old iron kettle and poured it into an antique copper tub in front of the fire for a bath. Cord had offered to wash her back and before long both of them had been soaking wet and laughing.

Even now, Georgia felt a little weak as she remembered his joining her and how the water had felt against their naked skins, slick and warm, the way his lips had slid down her neck to her breasts. The way he had pulled her out of the water, wet and gleaming in the firelight and made love to her with an unbridled passion that had left her gasping for breath and wild with pleasure.

"Just you," she whispered, answering him finally. "I don't need anything else except this... and you."

Cord said nothing. But as they sat before the fire, waiting for darkness, she could sense his thoughts and his apprehension about what they were about to do.

Did he want it to be over so that he could go back to Atlanta? Away from Farmington and all the people who had hurt him and his sister?

Georgia couldn't blame him for feeling that way. She understood his rage, felt her own rage at what her father had done to both of them. But God, she thought she would die if Cord left her again.

They waited until nine o'clock, until all the stores and offices in town would be closed and everyone had gone home. Outside, Cord helped Georgia with her coat, pulling her close and wrapping a scarf around her neck and tucking it into her jacket. He took the lapels in his hands and pulled her against him.

"Are you afraid?"

"A little," she said quietly, looking up into his face. She placed her hands on his where he held her jacket.

"Someone might be waiting for us," he warned. "Since finding the bank statements at your house, they know what we're doing now and I don't think they're just going to let it slide."

"I know."

"I just wish I could leave you here, safe and sound and—"

"Cord," she whispered, touching his face. "Don't. Whatever happens, this is what I want. Besides, I'd die, sitting here alone, waiting for you to come back."

"If someone finds us," he said, his voice growing hoarse with warning and with the thought of what could happen, "if I sense the slightest possibility of a confrontation, I'm turning this big black hog around and coming straight back up here. I don't intend taking any chances where you're concerned. So be prepared to hang on tight."

"Don't worry about me," she said. But in her heart, his tender protectiveness touched and moved her as nothing ever had.

He stepped away from her and handed her a helmet. Then she saw him reach inside his leather jacket to adjust the shoulder holster he was wearing. She shivered, praying silently that he wouldn't have to use it.

There was time to think on the ride down the mountain. Time for Georgia to plan in her mind exactly where they would park, which door they would enter, how long it would take them.

By the time they reached the city limits, she could feel her insides quivering nervously and her legs trembling where she had held them so tightly against the seat of the motorcycle.

Cord saw the county patrol cars before she did. They were sitting, one on each side of the highway, just past the city-limit signs. Their headlights were off and if it hadn't been for the orange glow of the streetlights glimmering on the tan cars, she and Cord might have passed by without noticing.

"Hold on," she heard Cord say.

"It's the law, Cord," she shouted. "They aren't waiting for us . . . are they?"

"We'll see," he yelled.

She felt his muscles tensing beneath her hands as he turned the motorcycle around in the middle of the highway and headed back out of town. Georgia wrapped her arms tightly around him and closed her eyes.

When she opened them again, she saw that Cord had turned off his headlight. Everything around them was pitch-black. Georgia glanced over her shoulder and her heart skittered when she saw the patrol cars turn on their lights and pull out onto the highway. By then, Cord had turned onto a narrow dirt road.

Georgia thought her heart would actually stop as they raced headlong into the night with no lights to guide them. Even though she realized that Cord was in his element—challenging the darkness, challenging the patrolmen behind them, she was still numb with terror.

He had seen the police in time and realized that they were waiting for him. And because of his foresight, they were now beyond the reach of the patrol headlights. The officers couldn't see them as Cord pulled off onto a narrow side road that was almost overgrown with brush and pine trees.

As they pulled farther into the brush beneath towering pine and hemlock, Cord turned the motorcycle around, facing the highway. Georgia couldn't imagine how he found the place, how he saw well enough in the dark to turn off the road. But she knew him well enough to know that he was unpredictable and daring and very skilled when he rode. The thought occurred to her that he might even have hidden here before, sometime in the past when he had a reputation for outrunning the law and for being the talk of the town the next day.

"You all right?" he murmured, turning his head toward her.

"I'm fine," she said, still hugging him tightly.

Car lights flashed past them and they could hear the low roar of the police cars' high-speed engines, moving farther away. And a few moments later they saw the distant glare of headlights again as the deputies realized they'd lost them and turned to move slowly back toward the main highway.

Georgia held her breath when she saw the brilliant glare of a spotlight moving from one side of the road to the other. They sat quietly, neither of them moving as the cars passed on the road, not more than a hundred feet away from where they sat hidden by the trees and low-hanging evergreen boughs. As soon as the cars had passed, she felt Cord lean forward, heard the quiet hum of the engine and felt the kick of the motorcycle beneath her as he slowly, without lights, turned around and continued through the woods away from the highway.

She sensed that they were headed back in the direction of town, but it was so dark, she had no idea exactly where they were. Within a few minutes she began to see streetlights and the glimmer of lights from houses and she realized that they had entered town from another side. She knew where they were. Even though the area seemed rural, they were probably no more than four blocks from the courthouse and Bob's real-estate office.

Cord stopped and helped her off the motorcycle. Georgia could hear her heart pounding, could feel it pulsing through her veins with excitement. She was so nervous that she was afraid her legs might not hold her.

Cord parked the motorcycle behind a huge old tree on a vacant lot, then, breaking pine boughs from a nearby tree, he covered it and turned to take her hand.

"Are you still with me?" he asked.

"Barely," she whispered.

He laughed softly in the darkness and squeezed her hand.

"You're doing great. Come on. We're going to sneak through backyards and alleys till we work our way around to the real-estate office."

Georgia could hardly believe it when they did just that— despite several moments of sheer panic and a couple of barking dogs that sounded big and vicious enough to swallow both of them.

The alleyway behind the office was dark but Georgia managed to unlock the door and get them inside.

She pulled the blinds in Bob's old office and Cord stood by the window, peeking out toward the street as she went quickly to the computer and turned it on.

The blue light from the screen seemed glaring in the darkness and for a moment Georgia glanced toward Cord with concern.

He motioned for her to continue.

She quickly scanned the file list, selecting one that said "Personal."

"More bank statements," she whispered. "Looks like the ones we've already seen. Do we need another copy?"

"Yeah," he said. "Go ahead."

The high-pitched whirring sound of the printer seemed loud enough to wake the entire town, and it seemed to go on forever.

"Come on, come on," Georgia whispered impatiently.

When the printer stopped, Georgia didn't hesitate, but went quickly back to the file list, selecting several more and coming up with nothing.

She smiled when she saw one of the file names.

"The 'Three Amigos'," she muttered, remembering how much Bob had liked the silly movie. Then she frowned and pushed a key to recall the file.

The screen blinked "Please enter password."

"Password," she muttered. "I should have known I'd have to have a password," she said to Cord in growing desperation.

"Try his birth date, his social security number," Cord said, still gazing through the small opening in the blinds.

"No," she said, shaking her fingers nervously. "Too mundane," she murmured. "Bob liked to think of himself as clever where these things were concerned."

Without saying anything to Cord, she typed in the word *Sheila,* but that, too, was denied.

"Damn," she murmured, feeling the desperation build inside her.

"Relax," Cord murmured. "We have time." She saw his look of encouragement and she felt her mind clear.

"Three Amigos," he reminded her. "Who were his three best friends?"

Quickly Georgia entered the name Mike and when it was denied, she entered two more names. Neither of them worked.

"Dammit, what can it be?" she muttered. "What word would he use?"

"Think of his personality," Cord suggested. "What did he like? What did he pride himself on most?"

"Money," she said with a sarcastic twist to her lips. "And he prided himself on all the clever ways he had of making it," she added.

"Greenbacks," she said suddenly, her eyes wide with hope. "It was kind of a catchword for him and his friends when they were working on a deal."

"Try it."

When she typed in the word and heard the clicking whir of the computer's insides, she felt her heart jump and clasped her hands together thankfully.

"Oh, Lord," she murmured, unable to believe it. "That's it. Cord, that's it!"

He moved away from the window, glancing briefly at the screen before going back to keep watch.

"Anything?" he asked.

Georgia's eyes moved quickly down the page.

"The safe-deposit box," she whispered, awestruck. "He's listed the contents of the safe-deposit box." She pushed a button and waited impatiently as the printer buzzed again, then she went to the next item.

Seeing the next name on the screen, Georgia gasped and her gaze flew toward Cord.

"Tri-Co," she whispered. "There's a list of land acquisitions that went through Bob's company for Tri-Co Corporation. Condemnations," she said, her voice filled with horror as she read on. "Cord, they've condemned land west of town. Houses, lots, parcels, farmlands," she whispered in disbelief as she read the list.

She pushed the print button and looked up to meet Cord's eyes. She saw triumph there, and anger, too. It was the area where Cord and his family once lived. The poorest section of Farmington. A place where Sheila would know everyone and might be able to influence them to sell their property at a cheap price to a big powerful corporation like Tri-Co.

"Oh, Cord," she said, shaking her head.

"This is it, baby," he whispered through clenched teeth. "You did it—this is it. Is there anything else?"

"No, that's all in the Amigo file. Shall I look through some of the others?"

"No time," he muttered, pushing the blinds closed. "One of the patrol cars just went by. Let's don't push our luck. We'll take what we have back to the cabin. Just print it— we'll read it later."

Her hands were shaking as she ripped the sheets from the printer and stuffed them inside her jacket. Then she turned off the computer and took Cord's hand. He gave her a quick kiss before she slipped out the back door into the alley.

"Good work," he said, his voice filled with approval.

As they scurried through the darkened yards and alleys, they had to stop twice when they saw more patrol cars cruising through the neighborhoods.

Georgia prayed that the motorcycle was still intact and that no one lay hidden in the bushes, waiting for them. She knew Cord had thought of it, too, and as they drew nearer, he held her back as he took one slow step at a time. He stopped for long moments, listening . . . waiting. Then he hurriedly stripped away the pine boughs and handed Georgia her helmet.

"We'll have to take the back roads again," he said. "It'll be slow and rough. Then we'll head south across the farmlands until we're far enough away from town to avoid any more roadblocks." He helped her onto the motorcycle and turned with a wry grin. "You think you can manage to hold on to me and those papers at the same time?"

She patted her jacket and smiled, whispering toward him in the dark. "I'll take care of the papers—you just watch for cows."

They both laughed before Cord put his hand over her mouth.

"Shh," he said. But she could feel him shaking with relieved laughter, too.

He removed his hand and pulled her to him, taking her mouth in the darkness in a quick, hot kiss that made her feel warm and tingly all over.

The ride seemed to take forever. Georgia's behind felt numb from sitting so long and she was certain she'd have bruises from the bumps after riding through rough pastures and along pothole-filled back roads.

At least once they were away from the main highway, Cord could turn on the headlight. She was just thankful that he knew his way around the county so well. When they finally pulled back onto the main highway well past town, she had no idea where they were.

She sighed with relief as the motorcycle purred along on the smooth highway. And without further sightings of the law, they took the road leading to the mountains and away from Farmington.

When Cord parked the motorcycle behind the cabin, Georgia thought she'd never been so relieved in her life. Both of them hurried inside, anxious to get warm and to look at the papers she carried.

She could hardly believe it. After all their suspicions, after all this time of searching, she still couldn't believe that Bob actually had played a part in something illegal. But she knew that this land scheme, whatever it was, was certainly that. It was big and it involved some very influential people, not just in Farmington, but in the entire state of Georgia.

But something <u>had</u> gone wrong . . . terribly wrong. What on earth had happened to make someone in the organization turn against Bob and Sheila—murder them? At this point, she realized that she was dreading the moment they found out who was involved.

Chapter 13

Cord pulled a table toward the fireplace and impatiently raked the magazines that lay atop it off and onto the floor. As Georgia placed the papers from her jacket on the table, Cord poked at the logs in the fireplace until the fire came to life. Then he brought a lamp and sat it on the table so they could study the printouts from Bob's computer.

"Here are the bank statements," Georgia said. "You might have to ask for more copies of Sheila's and duplicate your comparison charts again."

"Good," he said, shoving those papers aside. "Show me the Tri-Co papers."

Georgia shuffled through the bundle of papers and spread the ones he asked for out on the table.

Quickly Cord flipped through the pages before stopping and tapping his forefinger against a column.

"What is it?" she asked breathlessly, looking over his shoulder.

"It's a list of the Tri-Co partners. Looks like Bob was one of them and it seems we've just found the other two. Thus the file name 'Three Amigos,' which is no big surprise."

Georgia held her breath as she looked more closely and read the names.

Her gasp filled the room and mingled with the quiet whisper of the fire.

"Reginald Logan," she read. "He's the county assessor of property. And my God—William T. Stone—Judge Stone." She turned and looked into Cord's blue eyes. "I can't believe this. I simply can't believe it."

"Believe it," Cord said tersely. "It's all here in black and white."

Frowning, Georgia looked at the papers again, her gaze scanning the page as she made note of all the land acquisitions in that one area west of town.

"Why do you think they wanted this land so desperately?" she asked. "And why was it done in secrecy?"

"There's a reason—you can depend on that." He turned around, raking his hand through his hair before slamming his fist down on the table. "Damn, I wish I had a phone. I'd bet my last dime that there's a big state or federal construction project coming to Farmington and it's going to be situated on the west end of town. All I need is a list of projects."

"I was thinking earlier, when we were at the real-estate office...it's obvious now what Bob's role was in all this. They ran everything through his real-estate office. But what about Sheila? Do you think it's possible that she used her old connections on the west side to get people to sell their property?"

"I think you're right," he said. "That and whatever information she could get out of her high-powered men friends." Cord studied the papers again, tapping his fingers against the next page.

"Look here," he said, whistling between his teeth. "Payouts. Look at the ones to Bob and Sheila—I'd be willing to bet these dates match the ones on their bank statement deposit sheets. Damn, no wonder they burned Sheila's house and then ransacked yours. This list could ruin a lot of people."

For a moment, Georgia didn't want to look at the list. She was afraid of what she might see. All these men were friends of her father's. The county tax assessor was a frequent visitor to her parents' home, as were some of the high-rolling state politicians she saw listed.

Suddenly she felt Cord's arm around her shoulders, felt his gaze on her. She looked down at the next page where the list of payouts continued and saw where his finger pointed.

"Mike Goodwin," she gasped. She closed her eyes, feeling nausea grip her stomach, feeling her legs begin to tremble. She felt betrayed.

"I'm sorry," he whispered, holding her steady. "I know you didn't want to believe this about him. Are you all right? Do you want—"

"I'm fine," she said, shaking away the pain and disbelief. Then she glanced up into his concerned blue eyes. "Oh, Cord," she whispered. "This scares me to death. It's so big...so many people are involved. And Mike...you suspected him all along, didn't you?"

"I think you did, too," he said softly. "Deep down inside, I think you knew that some of the things he was telling you didn't quite add up. Withholding the autopsy report—not being able to come up with the contents of the safe-deposit box. And tonight when the county patrol cars were waiting. He had to be involved."

She nodded, not trusting herself to speak.

"What about my father? You think he's involved, too."
It was not a question, but a soft, sad statement.

"Yes," he said, not bothering to hedge his words. "I
think your father is involved."

"His name isn't on this list," she said, gritting her teeth
together.

Cord ran his finger down the page to the end of the list.
There, instead of a name, was a code number.

"This man is the payee," Cord muttered. "The man in
charge. He's taken all the precautions against being found
out—even using a coded number instead of his own name.
We have no way of knowing who he is." He hesitated as he
looked down into her eyes. "Not yet, anyway."

"But you think it's my father."

Cord nodded, his gaze steady and serious.

"No, Cord, you're wrong," she said. "My father might
be a lot of things. He's overbearing and manipulative when
he wants something. I'll admit he's controlling and powerful enough to do this...but he's no thief, and he's certainly no murderer. Do you really think he would have
played a part in having my husband killed? In making his
only daughter a widow?"

Cord didn't reply, but his look said it all.

"You *do* believe it," she whispered.

"Maybe we should wait and see," he said, making an effort to hold his comments.

"I know you hate him," she said. "And I can't blame you
for that after what he did to you . . . after what he did to us.
But Cord, you can't believe this. You can't—"

"I do believe it," he said. His jaw tightened, and his eyes
turned to that quicksilver color that signaled danger. "And
I have to tell you honestly...if I'm right, then I'll be the one
to arrest him."

Tears came suddenly to Georgia's eyes. She backed away from him, away from the accusation in his clear blue eyes.

"Georgia," he said, reaching his hand out toward her. "Come here."

"No," she gasped. "You're enjoying this. You're actually hoping that he is involved, just so you can arrest him. So you can finally have your revenge."

"That's not true," he said, taking a step nearer.

"Don't," she said. "Just don't, Cord. Don't you see? Don't you know what this will do to me . . . to us if—"

"It won't," he said. He shook his head and put his hands at his hips, swearing beneath his breath as he stared at the floor and tried to remain calm.

It took all his strength to meet her wounded accusing eyes. "I won't let that happen, Georgia. Trust me, I won't let it happen."

"It already has," she said, frowning at him, unable to believe he didn't understand what his position meant for them. "Can't you see that—it already has."

She turned from him and ran up the stairs.

Cord watched Georgia race up the stairs and every part of his mind and body urged him to go after her. To grab her and shake some sense into her, to hold her and make her understand, make her see that he would cut off his right arm before he'd hurt her.

But he'd been an agent for a long time now. The bureau had helped him find his confidence, his niche in society. He felt he was contributing something to a world that had never looked upon him with great favor. He liked his job, dammit. For a long time, it had been all he had, his defining characteristic. He had an instinct for it. He knew when he was right, and this time he was right.

Then why did he feel that nagging little ache in his heart? And why did every part of him urge him to go upstairs and tell Georgia that he would turn the case over to someone else, someone more objective, if it was what she wanted. Hell, he'd offer to quit the damned job if that was what she wanted.

Cord grunted and shook his head, turning back to the fireplace and leaning his hand against the mantel. His vision blurred as he gazed into the dancing flames. He saw Georgia's face, her brown eyes, the pain he had put there.

But he couldn't quit. Not now and certainly not because the father of someone he was close to might be involved.

Close to hardly described what he felt for Georgia. Holding her again, making love to her here before the fire, made him think that this was all he'd ever wanted in life. Not money or position. Just Georgia.

How could he lose her again? How could he deliberately let her think that he was putting his job before her feelings or that he was out to get her father?

Because he wasn't, dammit. He was doing what was right. And he knew that if he didn't do that, he would never be able to look into those brown eyes again with any shred of self-respect. That was what he wanted her to know and to understand.

If he was ever lucky enough to have a son, it was the one thing he wanted to be able to tell him. To do what's right, no matter how hard or how dangerous, no matter how many people tell you it's impossible.

Cord clenched his teeth and glanced toward the stairs one last time. Then he pulled on his jacket and went out to the motorcycle. He wanted to call Hagan Cantrell in Atlanta and tell him to start the ball rolling on this case. The sooner it was settled, the better, as far as Cord was concerned. They would need an investigative team, a mobile communications unit and a lawyer here as soon as Hagan could put everything together. Cord knew that his GBI partner and best friend, would be just the one to wield the whip.

For all the scoundrel's charm and good looks and his playboy image, Hagan Cantrell was hard as nails when it came to his work. And he was the best when it came to getting things done in a hurry.

Upstairs, Georgia heard the roar of the motorcycle engine and stepped to the window in time to see the shadow of the machine and rider as they moved around the cabin and out to the narrow road.

Her heart ached as she watched the taillights disappear into the darkness.

"Oh, Cord," she whispered. She placed her fingers against the cold glass of the windowpane, then leaned her forehead wearily against it.

She loved him and wanted him. Needed him more than she'd ever needed anyone in her life. She had hoped he would come up those stairs and take her in his arms, tell her that he would not pursue her father as a suspect. She had even fantasized about them going away together, forgetting everything that had happened in Farmington.

She smiled weakly, knowing that Cord would never do that. He had too much honor and integrity to run from anything. She knew Cord well enough to know that he would never deliberately turn away from doing what was right, no matter who was involved.

She didn't want her father to be involved. Couldn't believe that he actually was. And yet everything they'd learned, every name on that list, had some connection to Horace Blake.

"He's a banker," she whispered fiercely, pulling away from the window. "Of course everyone in town knows him. But that doesn't mean he's guilty." Georgia walked across the room to the large bed with the down-filled mattress. She sank onto the bright coverlet and pulled her knees up to her chest, huddling there alone like a small child.

Her father couldn't have had anything to do with the horrible way that Bob and Sheila had died. Please God, he just couldn't.

Georgia fell asleep whispering those prayers, still curled into a small protective ball.

Later, when Cord came back to the cabin, he glanced toward the settee, hoping to see Georgia waiting there. But she wasn't. The fire was out and he thought she hadn't come back downstairs at all.

Efficiently Cord set to work, stirring up the fire and turning on the small gas camp stove that they used to cook their meals. Quickly he poured water into the teakettle and let it heat while he placed sugar and cream and a small plate of cookies on a tray.

When the tea was brewed and the pleasant aroma filled the air, Cord placed a cup on the tray, then took a deep breath and squared his shoulders before heading for the stairs.

He knocked at the bedroom door, but there was no answer.

"Georgia?" he asked softly, kicking open the door with the toe of his boot.

He saw her then, curled on the bed, her blond curls feathered around her face. Her cheeks were flushed with sleep and for a moment all he could do was stare at her.

She was so beautiful. Even more beautiful than when she was younger. She still had that fresh clear complexion, born of warm southern nights and humid days.

Even now, he felt his fingers tingle with their need to touch her.

Instead, he set the tray on a table and moved to the bed. When he sat down and leaned over her, she stirred and her eyelashes fluttered, then opened.

"Cord," she whispered, frowning as she saw him staring down at her. "Is anything wrong? Is—"

"No, no," he said, giving in to his need to touch her. His fingers brushed her hair away from her face and he let his knuckles linger against her cheek. "Aren't you cold? There's a kerosene heater downstairs if—"

"I'm fine," she said, pushing herself up in bed and away from him. Away from those riveting blue eyes and that look of regret she saw in their depths. "What time is it?"

"Past midnight," he said. "You didn't eat much dinner—I thought you might like some tea," he said quietly, his eyes never leaving her face.

Georgia frowned and she felt tears stinging her eyes. Her gaze flew to the tray beside the bed, then to Cord.

Why did he have to be so sweet to her? And why did he have to look at her that way, as if she had somehow betrayed him by defending her father?

"Thank you," she whispered.

She was hungry and if the truth were known, she was cold. She longed for his arms around her, his big warm body next to hers in the feather bed. And for a moment, she wished both of them could go downstairs and sit in front of the fire, have their tea there, then cuddle together on the settee the way they had before.

Cord stood up, his look solemn as he gazed at her.

"I spoke to my buddy, Hagan, in Atlanta. The team will be here sometime tomorrow ... today, actually. They'll use the cabin as their headquarters until we have all the indictments worked out."

Georgia nodded. She knew he had to do it. It was what she'd wanted, what he had come to Farmington for. It had taken both of them to accomplish it and she felt proud of her part and she knew Cord was pleased, too.

"Well," he said. "I'll let you drink your tea."

He turned to go. Georgia thought he seemed sad and uncomfortable. It was the first time in her life she'd ever seen him that way. He was usually so confident, so sure of himself. For a moment, she actually started to call out to him, beg him to stay, reach out her arms for him and welcome him into the bed they had shared with such passion.

He stopped at the door and turned to her, staring directly into her eyes. His voice was soft and husky when he spoke.

"I'll sleep in the bedroom next door."

The door closed with hardly a sound and for a moment Georgia sat there on the bed, feeling stunned. She felt lost and wounded and worst of all, she felt as if she'd done something wrong.

Stubbornly she swung her legs off the bed and pulled the table containing the tray toward her.

The hot tea did help warm her and the aroma and taste of it soothed her. But when she'd finished, she stood up and walked impatiently to the window, then to the door.

With a sigh, she turned down the bed. But she felt awake now and too restless to sleep. She paced the floor for what seemed like hours. And moments later when she heard Cord's footsteps on the stairs, she froze, hardly breathing, her eyes riveted to the door. She heard him walk past her room, heard the door next to her room open and close softly, heard him moving around inside.

Georgia walked to the wall that separated them and placed her hand on the smooth, finished logs. As if he might feel her there, as if he would know that she was reaching out to him in her confusion and anguish.

No sounds came from the other side.

Suddenly Georgia swung away from the wall, clasping her hands together against her breasts and pacing the floor.

Finally, growing cold, she pulled off her jeans and slid into bed, lying very still until she became warm.

What did he expect her to do? How did he expect her to feel, knowing that the man she loved wanted to arrest her father?

Cord was right—he was still a rebel. He resented the established order in Farmington and he resented Horace Blake more than anyone in his life.

But he was honorable and decent. Honest to a fault.

Georgia could almost see him now, as if the wall standing between them was invisible. He was probably lying there in that cold room, staring at the ceiling. Feeling alone. Feeling like an outcast, the way he'd always felt in Farmington.

How many times that summer had he told her she was the only one who accepted him the way he was ... the one person who believed in him and cared about him, despite his upbringing, despite his reputation?

Her father, with his lies and his high-handed ways, had taken even that away from Cord.

Georgia made a quiet little noise in her throat. She closed her eyes, feeling the pain in her heart, feeling the longing begin to build inside her.

She loved Cord with all her heart. And this time, she was not going to lose him. If it were in her power, she wasn't going to let anything or anyone take him away from her again.

Without conscious thought, she pushed the heavy covers away and slid out of bed, padding softly to the door.

The fire in the living room below burned brightly, throwing its light into the rafters and against the upstairs walls.

Georgia took a deep breath and walked to Cord's door. Slowly she turned the knob and pushed the door open. The room was black except for the dim shaft of light from the doorway where she stood.

Cord woke suddenly, not sure what had wakened him. He sat up, his hand moving automatically to the weapon beside his bed.

And then he saw her, silhouetted in his doorway, the flickering light from the fire behind her, outlining her slender legs and rounded hips and making a soft halo of her fair hair.

"What's wrong?" he asked, pushing the quilts away but making no attempt to leave his bed.

In the dim light, Georgia saw his naked chest, the outline of his broad shoulders against the paler sheets and pillows.

What if he didn't want her? What if he intended it to be over and she had made a mistake coming to him now?

She didn't move from the doorway.

"I'm sorry," she whispered.

Cord threw the covers away from him and came quickly out of the bed. As he walked slowly toward her, Georgia saw that he still wore his jeans.

He stopped just in front of her, making no attempt to touch her. His blue eyes reflected the glittering light from the fire as he stared down at her.

"I'm sorry for doubting you," she said, her voice soft and apologetic. "I know you, Cord Jamison, better than anyone else in the world. And I know you would never use your job to help gain revenge on anyone. Not even my father. And God knows, he probably deserves it."

Cord's expression changed, his eyes grew warm and tender. But still he said nothing as he continued to stare at her. He couldn't see her face in the shadows with the light

behind her, but he could feel the anguish in her voice and he
knew the price she'd had to pay for coming to him this way.

"I'm sorry," she breathed. "I...I just don't want to lose
you again. And if—"

"Baby," he whispered. "Come here." He held out his
arms to her.

Georgia stepped into his embrace with a sigh. His touch,
his warmth, his easy acceptance, was like coming home.

Cord's hands moved to the nape of her neck as he bent to
kiss her. His arms held her tightly against him and she could
feel the steady beat of his heart against her. His mouth, at
first sweet and patient, soon changed. He groaned as his kiss
deepened and Georgia opened her mouth, accepting, seeking, wanting all of him.

They were both trembling when Cord pulled away. From
the cold, from the emotion that surged through them both.
From what this night meant for both of them.

"Whatever happens," she said breathlessly, clinging to
him, "I'm here."

"Don't say it if you don't mean it," he said softly, staring into her warm brown eyes. "I won't lie to you angel, I
don't know what's going to happen, or whether or not your
father is actually involved. But it's not going to be easy. And
if I know your dad, it's not going to be pleasant. Horace
Blake is the kind of man whose motto is, 'If you're not with
me, you're against me.'"

"I know," she whispered. "And if he hates me for that,
if he turns me away, then I'll regret it with all my heart. I
won't lie to you, either, Cord—I'll probably regret it for the
rest of my life. He's my father. He was once my hero. But if
he had anything to do with Bob's death, with your sister's..."

She could see the clenching of his strong jaw as he looked
into her eyes and waited for her to finish.

"But it's his choice. I don't intend to let him separate us ever again," she said with a defiant little lift of her chin. "No matter what happens, I won't lose you. I can't."

There was a catch in her voice when she said those last words. But the words were sincere, Cord had no doubt about that when he looked into her eyes and saw the tears.

Quickly he picked her up in his arms, cradling her against him as he walked to the other bedroom—their bedroom. He kicked open the door and walked to the bed, lying her gently on the fluffy feather mattress, then crawling in beside her.

He pulled her against him and put his arms around her, holding her until her soft body stopped trembling and the effects of their bodies together warmed the entire bed.

Cord wanted to make love to her then more than he'd ever wanted anything. His body ached for her, for the fulfillment that she alone could give.

He knew in his heart that tonight might be their last time together like this. That tomorrow or the next day, when the case was solved and the perpetrators were in jail, Georgia might change her mind. No matter how great was her desire to be with him, no matter how sincere was her wish to be at his side and stand against her own father, he knew that in the light of day, things might look different.

That thought alone was more than enough reason to make love to her one last, sweet time, his mind whispered. One time to remember for always. One time to hold in his memory and in his heart, in case the worst happened and Georgia couldn't live up to her vow.

Cord sighed and touched her face in the darkness. He could feel her tremble, could feel her waiting.

"Go to sleep, sweetheart," he whispered against her hair. "Tomorrow is going to be a big day for both of us."

Chapter 14

Georgia thought nothing in the world could compare to the feeling she had waking up in Cord's arms. She felt safe and loved and she wished it could be this way forever.

But, despite her feeling, she could still sense the distance between them that morning. When Cord got out of bed with a muttered excuse that Hagan and the GBI team would be there soon, she knew it was just another way of separating himself from her.

They'd finished breakfast and Cord was looking over the papers from Bob's computer again when they heard the first car pull up in front of the cabin.

They came out of the cars and a van like quietly efficient storm troopers set on a mission—two men with a gas-powered generator, another with a computer, one to connect a phone system. Georgia could see them swarming outside like bees, going about their business quickly and completely.

But it was Cord's friend, Hagan, who captured her attention immediately. He had that same heady masculine appeal as Cord, although they were quite different in appearance. Hagan was more slender, with the wiry, muscular frame of a football running back. His brown hair had golden sunstreaks and his eyes, black as midnight, sparkled with mischief. When he looked at her and Cord with that little knowing glint in those black eyes, Georgia felt as if this was a man who never intended to be close to any woman, except perhaps in a physical way.

Yet there was something about him that reminded her so much of Cord that it made her heart beat a little faster. It was that hint of danger and quiet recklessness, that sense of a man who won at all costs, who went his own way no matter who might stand in his path.

"Georgia, this is Hagan Cantrell, my partner at the Bureau. Stay away from him," he added with a wry grin.

"Hey," Hagan said in a soft Georgian drawl. He took Georgia's hand and looked into her eyes.

Georgia recognized mischief and a quiet attempt at flirtation in his eyes. And she thought Cord was right. This probably was a man that most women should steer clear of.

"Well," Hagan said, gazing around the cabin. "A cozy little setup you've got here, Cord, old buddy."

"It would be more cozy in summer," Cord said with a quiet laugh.

It was evident immediately how much the two men liked each other. Cord had an easiness when he talked to Hagan that wasn't there with Georgia.

"We'll fix that," Hagan said, grinning. "Soon as Junior there gets the generator going, we'll have lights and heat. I talked the boss into paying per diem, so the truck's loaded with food. Hell, we can probably live really good here for a week or so."

"I hope it won't take that long," Cord said, growing serious again.

"I hope not, either," Hagan said with a meaningful grin. "I've finally convinced the boss's new secretary to fly to Mexico with me."

"Mexico?" Cord grunted humorously. "What's in Mexico?"

"Sand and sun," Hagan said, faking a punch toward his partner. "Warm Mexican nights and music beautiful enough to charm the birds out of a tree."

Cord grinned and shook his head and the two of them went to the table to study the papers.

Georgia watched them for a moment and listened to their murmured conversation. She liked seeing Cord this way—relaxed and easy. And she was glad he felt that way with Hagan. But as for that one, she thought he had more in mind in Mexico than 'charming birds out of trees.'

Georgia smiled faintly and went to check the coffee.

It was a hectic day, spent with GBI lawyers and agents, explaining their ideas about what had happened, going over the papers and making their case. Altogether there were at least a dozen men running in and out, eating, drinking coffee, smoking cigarettes and filling the small cabin with stifling smoke until Georgia would be forced to go outside to relieve her scratchy throat and watery eyes.

It was late in the afternoon and the pale autumn sun had already fallen past the tree line, although its rays could still be seen in the tops of trees and against the steep roof of the cabin.

Georgia stood on the front porch, breathing in the cold mountain air and wondering if she'd ever have a chance to be alone with Cord again. She heard the front door open and turned to see Hagan Cantrell step out onto the porch behind her.

"Beautiful sunset," he said quietly, coming to stand beside her.

"Yes, it is."

She caught the scent of some sexy, expensive cologne. From the corner of her eye she noted the elegant cut of the sport jacket he wore, and if she wasn't mistaken, his candy-striped silk shirt and Turnbull & Asser tie were exclusively Neiman Marcus.

He was very different from Cord and yet his obviously expensive taste did nothing to detract from his undeniable masculine sex appeal.

"Cord's told me a lot about you." He stood with his hands in his pockets, obviously at ease, gazing at her with what Georgia could only describe as a devastating southern charm.

"Has he? Then I suppose you know that Bob Ashley was my husband?"

"And that Horace Blake is your father."

Georgia met his dark gaze, then turned away to look at the sun-tinted treetops.

"Have you managed to break the name code?" she asked, almost holding her breath.

"No." He shifted his weight and leaned one shoulder against one of the porch supports. "Look, Georgia... whatever happens, whatever we learn when we go into Farmington to deliver the warrants, I hope you know that this is not personal."

"I know," she said, biting her lower lip.

"Then why do I get the feeling that there's a little friction between you and Cord?"

Georgia glanced back to the house, as if she might find Cord standing there behind them.

"Cord is..." She stopped and sighed, feeling tears choking her throat. "Cord has every right to be hurt and

wary," she managed to say. "My father did an unforgiv-
able thing to him years ago... in fact, not very many people in Farmington were nice to Cord in those days."

"Except you," he said quietly.

"I loved him," she whispered, not looking at Hagan.

"Ah," he said softly. "And do you still?"

She turned her head, looking into his eyes just as the last
rays of sun faded from the treetops.

"Yes," she whispered. "With all my heart. More now
than before, if that's possible."

"Does he know that?"

Georgia shrugged her slender shoulders and shivered. She
wrapped her arms around her body, frowning into the
gathering darkness.

"He should," she said.

"Tell him," he said.

She was surprised at the intensity in his voice. And when
she glanced up to meet his eyes, she was surprised to see the
mischief completely gone.

"Don't let him leave Farmington again without telling
him," he said. He nodded down at her and smiled faintly.
"Personally I think it's all he's waiting for and I'm not sure
even he knows that."

"Do you really think...?"

He nodded again, grinning at her this time.

"I think," he said. "Come on, let's go back in. Artie's
making his famous steak dinner tonight and believe me, you
don't want to miss it."

He turned to open the door.

"Hagan," Georgia said, hesitating a moment. "I'm glad
you came and I'm happy Cord has a friend like you."

"Hey, he's a lucky man... what can I say?"

Georgia laughed, seeing the devilry sparkle in his black
eyes again.

That evening, after their delicious supper, they all sat around the fire, the presence of the action-oriented men making the cabin seem small and insignificant.

There was a quiet camaraderie that evening. The teasing and mischief was gone and there seemed to be an air of expectancy about the men, as if they were anxious to get to the heart of the matter and begin the operation.

Georgia found Cord's gaze on her every time she glanced up and she wished for the peace and quiet of their other nights here, for one last night to be alone with him.

The man they called Artie was talking about the case.

"I'd feel a lot better about everything if we knew who the man with the code name is before we go in."

"I think Sheriff Goodwin is the key," Hagan said, moving forward in his seat. "He's the one who received the most payoffs... obviously he's the runner, the lieutenant for the corporation. I'd say he knows the entire operation, from top to bottom."

"We can set up a surveillance, tap Goodwin's office and home."

"That could take weeks... months," Cord said impatiently.

"Got any other suggestions?" Artie asked.

Cord stood up, pacing restlessly from the stairs to the fireplace.

"I have a suggestion," Georgia said quietly.

She had remained quiet most of the evening and now the room suddenly grew silent as the men all turned to stare at her.

Cord stopped pacing and came to lean an elbow against the fireplace mantel as he gazed down at her. There was encouragement in his eyes, and a quiet admiration.

It was all Georgia needed to continue.

"What if I go back to Farmington...go to Mike and tell him that Cord and I found something in Bob's files. What if I pretend to be concerned about the magnitude of what we found and about who might be implicated?"

"No," Cord said, shaking his head and looking at Georgia with warning in his blue eyes. "No way. It's too dangerous."

But Hagan leaned toward Georgia, his black eyes glittering with interest.

"You're thinking that Goodwin would go straight to the main man and warn him," he said, his look one of approval and understanding. "That would tie the case up in a neat little package," he said, glancing at Cord.

"Knowing Mike, I think that's exactly what he'd do," Georgia said.

"I said no," Cord said.

"He trusts her, Cord," Hagan said. "She's the perfect choice."

"Dammit, aren't you listening?" Cord's fist slammed down against the mantel. "Having the case tied up neatly is not my top priority. We can get the final connection with a little more work and without involving Georgia."

"And a few more weeks," Artie said, nodding toward Georgia with his obvious approval.

"Cord," Georgia said, looking at him pleadingly. "You're being stubborn. You know we're right. Besides, don't you think it's a little late to be worrying about my involvement?"

"You know whose name it might be, who Mike might go to warn," he said, his voice soft with caution.

"I know."

"Isn't that enough to make you back away from this?"

"I thought we settled this last night," Georgia said, her voice low.

The room grew deathly quiet and Georgia could see the uneasy glances of the men seated around the room. But at that moment, there seemed to be no one else in the world for her. Just Cord and the power of his silvery gaze.

"Uh, would you two like to have a few minutes alone?" Artie asked, moving as if to stand up.

"No," Georgia said quickly, holding her hand out to stop him. "I'm going to do this. It's the best way to end everything quickly. And that's what you want, isn't it, Cord? To end it and go back to Atlanta...back to your own life?" With a steady look, she challenged him.

She could see the clenching of his jaw as he gritted his teeth. His fists were clenched at his sides and his eyes were as furious as she'd ever seen them.

"Then it's settled," Hagan said, standing up and seeming to break the tension. He went to refill his coffee cup. "Coffee?" he asked, looking directly at Cord. "Something a little stronger?"

Cord's gaze had not left Georgia's face. But now he turned, banging his coffee cup down and grabbing his leather jacket off the back of a chair.

When he slammed the front door behind him, the entire cabin shook. Georgia stood up, frowning at the door and taking a step in that direction.

"Let him go," Hagan said quietly. "He just needs a few minutes to cool off that hot temper of his. And to adjust himself to the fact that we're right."

"Well," Artie said. "Looks like it's time to get our bedrolls out and turn in."

"Before you do that, Art, I want you to get everything ready for tomorrow. I want Georgia to wear a wire when she goes to Goodwin, and I want everything in working order and ready to go early tomorrow morning."

"You got it," Artie said, nodding to Hagan.

After the others went outside to bring in their sleeping bags, Hagan and Georgia stood before the fireplace.

"I want to help him, Hagan," she said. "And I don't know how."

"You're doing fine, believe me, you are," he said, smiling at her. "He has a lot of pride...too much pride, but Cord's a damned lucky man, if you ask me."

Her smile was weak and she shook her head, willing herself not to cry. She hated crying and yet since Cord's return, it seemed that was all she ever did. She bit her lips and blinked, vowing that from now on, that much at least, was going to be different.

"You go on up to bed," he said. "And I don't want you to worry too much about tomorrow. We've got the best damned team in the South here in this cabin. And believe me, we're not going to let anything go wrong."

Long after the house grew quiet, Georgia lay awake, staring at the ceiling in the upstairs bedroom. The cabin was warm now and there were lights, but she had turned hers out more than an hour ago as she lay waiting for Cord.

She wasn't sure what time it was when she heard the faint creak of the door. A shaft of light spilled into the room and across the bed. Georgia held her breath as she turned her head and saw Cord silhouetted in the doorway. But she said nothing.

Cord closed the door, casting the room into darkness again. There was enough light so that she could see him moving around the room, pulling off his clothes and tossing them on a chair.

When he turned toward the bed, Georgia moved slightly and pulled the heavy covers back, out of the way.

He came to her quickly and easily, all the distance and misunderstanding of before seemingly vanished. Now, there was just the two of them and the silence of the mountain night.

She wished she could see his eyes, watch the way they moved over her, as powerful and erotic as the hands of a lover. She had waited for this moment all day, for this one moment when he would come to her and hold her, kiss her and touch her in that way that no one else ever had.

Cord bent his head to her neck, breathing deeply of her sweet woman's scent. He wanted her more than he'd ever wanted any woman. And yet each time was like the first. He couldn't seem to get enough and he wasn't sure now that it was a physical longing so much as a spiritual one. As always, he wanted her with desperation, with some quick, powerful longing that he didn't quite understand himself.

Holding her, kissing her, was like some old bittersweet addiction. Always there. Always ready to be awakened.

And this night was like none other would ever be. Neither of them knew what tomorrow held. Or if there would be anything for the two of them past tomorrow. It all depended on what they learned from Mike Goodwin, and how that information affected Georgia and her feelings about Cord.

Cord felt her sweet surrender as soon as he came into bed. She had moved into his arms easily, as if no distance had ever existed between them, as if no harsh words had ever been spoken. And he knew that if he could see her face, he would see her hunger, her complete surrender and adoration. That waiting look in her eyes.

He lowered his head and covered her mouth with his, lost in the feel and the taste of her. He felt her welcome, felt her lips nipping at his, felt her tongue meeting his until he was not sure who was the conqueror and who was the conquered.

His muscles shook with desire as he lay slanted across her. He felt her bury her face against his neck and he groaned. Felt her small, soft hands moving over him, urging him on as her mouth and teeth nipped at his neck.

"Baby, I want you so much," he whispered. One last time, he thought. One last, unforgettable time.

"I know," she gasped, her body trembling beneath his. She ran the palms of her hands up his slender hips, across his flat stomach. Feeling the hardness of him, savoring every muscular inch, implanting the memory of him in her mind forever.

Quickly he pushed her soft T-shirt up and out of the way; she wore nothing underneath.

The pleasure of their lovemaking was intense, almost unbearable for both of them. There was an urgency born of the unknown, a poignancy that had not been present before. It was as if a lifetime of longing and wanting had come together into this one unforgettable night.

Their loving was quick and hot, a melding together into one heart-pounding journey toward fulfillment. Georgia cried out, not caring if anyone heard, not caring about anything or anyone except this moment and the man loving her.

"I love you, Cord," she cried against his throat. "I love you."

Her sweet words, her trust and surrender sent Cord spiraling out of control. She had been his dream longer than he could remember, the one person he could trust and turn to. How odd that she was also the woman he desired so deeply that he couldn't believe it, the woman who drove him crazy as no one else ever could.

He didn't want to lose her. Lose this.

Long moments after his body cooled, he still held her tightly against him, refusing to let the moment end. He felt her soft breath against his throat and he bent his head to kiss the corner of her mouth.

"Whatever happens," he murmured against her ear, "we have this. In case you've ever had any doubts, Georgie, I did love you that summer, more than life. I've wished a million times since then that I hadn't left you without saying good-bye."

Georgia frowned into the darkness, unsure of what he meant. He *loved her*—past tense? Was he saying goodbye tonight—apologizing for the past? But before she could ask, she heard his steady breathing and knew that he was asleep, and before long, exhausted, she followed.

She wasn't aware of when he left her the next morning. She came awake to find him sitting beside the bed watching her, his look a mixture of tenderness and concern.

She sat up in bed, pushing her shirt back down and self-consciously running her fingers through her tousled curls.

"Is it time?" she asked, her voice still raspy with sleep.

"As soon as you've had breakfast," he said.

"I couldn't," she whispered, feeling her stomach tighten with nervousness. "Just a shower and a cup of coffee."

He nodded, his gaze not leaving her face.

"I'll bring the coffee while you shower," he said.

She watched him leave, thinking how much he had changed since last night. He seemed to have adjusted to their plan, just as Hagan promised he would. But there were so many things she wanted to ask, so many things she wanted to say to him. And she didn't know if he would let her.

When she came out of the shower, he handed her a steaming cup of coffee. He had a small transmitter and wires spread across the bed. He picked up a roll of tape and glanced at her.

"You . . . you're going to put the wire on me?" she said.

Slowly he pulled the towel away from her fingers, letting it fall to the floor. His gaze raked down her naked body and a glint of pleasure appeared in his blue eyes when she made no effort to cover herself.

"You don't think I'd trust any of those yahoos downstairs to do it, do you?"

She laughed then, feeling pleased beyond any reasonable measure that he was joking, smiling at her in that boyish way.

"Shouldn't I at least put on my underwear?" she asked.

"Not yet," he said, his eyes growing dark, his voice taking on a soft, husky quality.

"Cord," she protested with a quiet self-conscious laugh.

"Don't worry," he said, placing the wires against her skin and pulling a piece of tape free from the roll. "The boys are waiting downstairs. Or else, ma'am—" he feigned a slow southern drawl "—I'd be sorely tempted to ravish you right here in broad daylight."

She smiled at him, trusting him, knowing that she would do anything he asked.

"Are you all right with this now?" she asked, glancing down at the wires that he continued taping to her body.

"I guess I'll have to be," he muttered, not looking at her face.

"I'll be all right, Cord," she whispered. She lifted her hand and touched his black shining hair.

He took a deep breath and looked into her eyes.

"I won't let anything happen to you," he said. "We'll be right outside in the van, listening to every word." He patted the last wire in place and motioned her toward her clothes.

He helped her pull a heavy white sweater over her head, pulling it smoothly down over her hips before putting his arms lightly around her.

"Baby... if there's the least bit of trouble, if you feel uncomfortable or in danger, I want you to turn around and get out of there. Run like hell. Do you hear me?"

"I hear you," she said, grinning at him.

"And Georgie," he said, his look growing soft and tender. "Just in case you don't already know—I hope I'm wrong about your dad. I hope it isn't him."

She smiled up at him and touched his face.

"I hope not, too."

There was a light knock on the door.

"You two going to stay in there all day?"

"Come in, Hagan," Cord said, laughing as he stepped away from Georgia.

"She wired?" he asked, pushing the door open and stepping into the bedroom.

"She is," Cord said.

Hagan walked toward Georgia, his black eyes assessing, running over her snug-fitting jeans and the soft white sweater that enveloped her curves.

"Shall I check it out?" Hagan asked mischievously.

"If you want to lose a hand," Cord said, his voice just as light, yet with a note of warning.

"Old buddy," Hagan said with feigned anguish, "you wound me." Then he laughed, showing even white teeth and a smile that Georgia thought was undoubtedly one of the reasons women couldn't seem to resist him.

"You ready?" Hagan asked, turning serious as he looked at Georgia.

"Whew," she said. "I think so."

"I'll be right outside the jail, waiting," Cord told her. "I'll hear every word that's said. If you get in trouble, just say my name. You can do this, angel." Cord's voice was so low and intimate that it caused his friend, Hagan, to stare at him with a hint of disbelief.

Old Cord was in love, Hagan thought to himself. By damn, it had finally happened. By God, the ironman himself was in love.

Chapter 15

Georgia and Cord rode in the back of the van with Artie driving and Hagan sitting in the passenger seat. Her transmitter had been checked and rechecked and as they approached Farmington, Cord reached over to take her hand.

"We're going to let you out at your house to avoid anyone downtown seeing you get out of the van. You drive your car; we'll be close behind. After your conversation with Mike Goodwin, come back outside, get in your car and drive back to your house."

"No," she said, looking Cord straight in the eye.

"Georgia..."

"Cord, you know very well I'm not going to go to my house and sit and wait to hear what's happened. I'm going to be there when you follow Mike and I'm going to find out firsthand who he goes to see."

Hagan grinned back at Cord.

"I think the lady's made up her mind," he said.

"Dammit, Georgia..." Cord sighed and shook his head. "All right. But you'll have to sit in your own car and wait. We can't take a chance on Mike seeing you get into a strange van. It could blow everything."

Later, when Georgia walked into the police station, she was so nervous that she could actually feel her insides quivering. She tried taking long slow breaths of air, but still her heart pounded and her knees felt weak. She smoothed down her sweater and went to Mike's office, breathing a quiet sigh of relief when she saw through the glass door that he was alone. She stared at him for a moment, unable to believe that this man, whom she had known most of her life, was actually involved in a land scheme that had resulted in the deaths of two people.

She tapped her knuckles against the door.

Mike frowned when he looked up from his desk, then stood up, pushing his chair away and taking three long steps to the door.

"Georgia. My God, where have you been? Your parents have been worried sick about you. Not to mention me and Brenda and just about everyone else in town."

"I'm all right," she said, not having to feign nervousness as she glanced around. "May I speak to you alone? It's important."

"Of course," he said, reaching out to take her arm. "Come in."

Georgia felt her skin crawl at his touch, and not just because she was afraid he might somehow detect the wires beneath her sweater.

"What is it?" Mike asked. "You seem upset."

"Mike...I...I didn't know who else to come to."

"You can tell me anything. Does it have to do with why you left and didn't tell anyone where you were going?"

"Yes," she said, sinking onto a wooden chair with a heavy sigh of relief. "I'm really worried about some of the things Cord has said."

"Like what?" Mike said, his eyes narrowing suspiciously.

"He thinks Bob and Sheila were involved in some kind of conspiracy, a land-buying deal because of a multimillion-dollar state project planned on the west side of town. I'm afraid, Mike. From what I've heard, the operation is huge and it could involve several people in Farmington. I...I don't know what's going to happen or where it's all going to lead."

Mike had sat down behind his desk and now he leaned forward, his elbows resting on the wooden surface.

"That's ridiculous," he said with a forced smile.

"He says he has proof," she said.

"Proof?" Mike said, turning in his revolving chair and placing his booted feet on the desk. "What kind of proof?" His pose was one of nonchalance, but Georgia could see the apprehension in his eyes. For a split second, she almost felt sorry for him...until she remembered that he had known all along about Bob's death...might even have had it done.

"I'm not sure," she lied. "He's been very secretive about the entire thing. But I do know that when he has a case, he intends calling in the GBI as well as the FBI."

Mike stared at her for a moment, his eyes wary and suspicious. Then he swung his legs away from the desk.

"Why are you telling me this?"

"Because I'm afraid," she said. "I know I shouldn't have come here. Cord will be furious if he finds out, but..."

"I thought maybe you liked Jamison," he said, his look still wary. "Thought maybe you might even fancy yourself in love with him again."

"I might have . . . once." God, she hoped Cord knew she was lying when he heard that over the transmitter. "But you know how he feels about Daddy. What if he tries to implicate him somehow. What if—"

Georgia knew she had him when she saw the smile move slowly across his boyishly handsome face. His eyes changed, too, became more confident.

"He can't touch your daddy," Mike said. Then with a quiet sigh, he stood up and walked over to where she sat and stood looking down at her. "I knew you wouldn't turn against your friends or the people in this town," Mike said.

"Mike," she whispered. "Is it true? Is there a project coming to Farmington? Was that why Bob and Sheila died?"

"There is a new four-lane coming through," he said quietly. "I don't reckon there's anything illegal in folks buying land beforehand. And I'd heard rumors that Bob's real-estate office might be handling some of the acquisitions. But . . ."

"Mike," Georgia said, feeling desperate. "You owe it to me to tell me what you know about Bob's death."

He looked at her through narrowed, suspicious eyes.

Outside in the van, Cord whispered beneath his breath.

"Don't push it, baby," he murmured. "Take it nice and easy."

"We've been friends for a long time, Georgia," Mike said cautiously. "And I wouldn't ever say this to anybody but you. Bob was a friend of mine, but sometimes he could be a sorry lowdown bastard. He was greedy and sometimes he wasn't too smart about who he crossed."

Little tingles of apprehension raced along Georgia's arms and the back of her neck. The look in Mike's eyes was frightening.

"He didn't deserve a woman like you," he continued, his voice hard and intense. "And just because he was the local football hero and born into money didn't make him any better than any of the rest of us. Some people in this town didn't like his uppity ways very much. And they didn't like the way he treated you. I would think you'd be grateful for that."

Georgia frowned, seeing an ugly ruthlessness in Mike she'd never seen before. She shivered.

"But... he didn't deserve to die... to be murdered."

"That's all I'm sayin'," he said, glancing through the window of his office door. "Don't ever ask me about this again, Georgia. We'll have to talk later...somewhere else."

"But..."

He walked to the door and opened it.

"You did the right thing, coming to tell me. I'll take care of everything—don't you worry." He seemed restless and his eyes darted from her to the hallway.

Georgia sensed the finality of his words and she knew she'd gotten all the information she was going to get. She felt she'd failed, for Mike had confessed nothing.

She walked outside, glancing at the van across the street before going to her car and sliding into the leather seat.

She didn't have to wait long until Mike Goodwin stepped out the door of the police station. He didn't see her, didn't even look around, but began walking quickly down the sidewalk without hesitation.

Georgia's heart sank when she saw him going in the direction of her father's bank. She waited until Mike was almost to the bank, then she got out of the car just in time to see Cord and Hagan coming across the street toward her.

Cord took her arm, holding her close as she was propelled between them down the walkway.

"You did great," Cord murmured as they walked.

"But I didn't get him to confess."

"It's enough," he said. "We already have the evidence against him. What we want now is the man in charge. I'm sorry, sweetheart."

His words and his eyes said it all. He'd seen Mike go into her father's bank, too.

Georgia's heart was pounding when they stepped through the door and into the bank. She looked immediately toward her father's office and saw him sitting at his desk . . . alone.

She frowned and glanced toward Cord but he and Hagan were both focused elsewhere . . . on Mike Goodwin's retreating back as he went into another office across the lobby of the bank.

"Uncle Henry," Georgia whispered. "It's not Dad, it's Uncle Henry."

They stood for a moment, watching through the glass windows of Henry Jarvis's office as Mike Goodwin went in and approached the man behind the desk. Henry stood up, clearly disturbed by Mike's presence. Mike was agitated, waving his arms and pacing in front of the desk, his body hunched forward aggressively.

Henry seemed angry and nervous and when he glanced up and saw Georgia and Cord and Hagan, there was the strangest expression on his face.

Georgia knew then. She knew as well as she knew anything that Henry Jarvis was the man at the top. She should have felt relief that her father wasn't the one and yet she couldn't. All she felt was unbelievable pain and betrayal. This man was like a second father to her and she thought she couldn't have felt much worse if it had been her father that Mike went to.

"Let's go," Hagan said, marching toward the door.

Cord pushed Georgia behind him and she saw him reach beneath his jacket to the shoulder holster he wore, and she saw Hagan's hand beneath his sport jacket.

Georgia looked into Henry Jarvis's eyes, saw his gaze dart nervously away from her. That look confirmed it all for her. They still didn't know why Bob and Sheila had been murdered, but now she knew in her own heart who had been responsible.

Mike Goodwin was obviously stunned. Still, his first instinct was to reach for the police revolver that he wore at his side.

"Don't do it, Goodwin," Cord said, pulling his own gun and pointing it at Mike.

"What the hell..." Mike's incredulous gaze swung toward Georgia and suddenly his eyes became bright with fury.

"Hagan Cantrell, Georgia Bureau of Investigation," Hagan said, flashing his badge and reaching with the other hand toward Mike. "Hand over your weapon, Officer."

"You did this," Mike said, his gaze swinging toward Georgia. "You were wearing a wire when you came to the office, weren't you?" His voice was filled with rage and disbelief. "Why, you little bitch..."

Suddenly Mike moved the barrel of the pistol upward, pointing it straight at Georgia. "You'll have to shoot me, Jamison," he growled. "But she'll be the first to go."

"Mike," she gasped.

"Shut up," he snapped. "Just shut up."

Georgia could see his body trembling, could see the barrel of the gun waver just the slightest bit. He was as scared as she was, but the difference was, she knew Mike was capable of murder and that he was furious enough at her betrayal to actually pull the trigger.

Her eyes darted toward Cord. She saw his anger and his frustration and for a moment, she managed a weak smile, wanting to reassure him. Whatever happened, she never wanted him to feel guilty or to blame himself.

"Put the gun down, Goodwin," Cord growled.

"She's goin' with me."

"You don't want to do this," Hagan said, his manner cooler than Cord's.

Georgia could feel her knees trembling as she stared down the barrel of the gun.

"Mike, listen to them," Henry Jarvis said finally. "They don't have any hard evidence against you. It's all speculation—you told me so yourself."

"Why, you old fool. Of course they do. You might have furnished the money and the know-how, but you don't know a damned thing about the law. That's why you wanted me in on it—remember? Why do you think they're here? The GBI doesn't send its agents in unless they have a solid case. And if you think I'm going to go to jail for you and the rest of your cronies..." His hand trembled as he continued aiming the gun at Georgia.

"At this point, I'm not concerned about myself," Henry said. "Georgia is like a daughter to me. Please, Mike, put the gun down. I'll see that you have the best lawyers available."

Georgia saw her father step to the door and for a moment she wanted to scream for him to go away. The very thought of him standing where he might be shot was almost more than she could bear.

"Mike," Horace Blake said, his voice steady and hard. "If you harm a hair on her head, I'll kill you myself. Don't be a fool, son. Think of Brenda... your kids. This man is not going to let you out of here alive if you hurt Georgia."

For once, his glance toward Cord held a hint of respect and admiration.

Mike wavered then. Georgia could see the hesitation in his eyes as he glanced from one of them to the other.

"I can't go to jail," Mike whispered, his voice wavering. "Do you know what they do to police officers in jail?"

"We'll work out a deal," Hagan said, his dark eyes focused on Mike. "Just hand me the gun, grip first and we'll get you a lawyer in here. After you give us a statement, we'll see what kind of deal we can work out."

Mike chewed at his lips nervously, his eyes darting from Hagan to Cord.

"You better not be lyin'," Mike said.

"Me?" Hagan said innocently. "Lie? Why, son, I'm a respected agent with the Georgia Bureau of Investigation."

Georgia might have laughed if she hadn't been so scared.

But suddenly Mike lowered the gun, turning the butt of it toward Hagan with a muttered curse. His shoulders slumped in defeat.

Georgia's knees almost buckled, and she had to force herself to remain standing.

"What kind of deal can I get?" Mike asked as Hagan placed the handcuffs on his wrists.

"Deal?" Hagan asked, frowning. "Did I say something about a deal?"

"Damn you," Mike sputtered. "You promised me. You said—"

"Well, son, I'll swear," Hagan drawled. "For a good old Georgia cracker, you ain't too smart, are you? Don't you know you can't trust someone like me? Why, just ask Cord there. I've been reprimanded more times than I can count for lyin'." He shrugged his broad shoulders and grinned. "It's a habit I can't seem to break."

Georgia watched as Hagan pulled Mike out into the bank lobby. Artie and the others were there now, and with Hagan, they escorted the sheriff outside. There was no one left in the office except her and Cord, her father and Henry Jarvis.

"How could you?" Georgia asked, her eyes focused on her Uncle Henry. "How could you have done such a thing?"

"Money," her father said, his voice angry and bitter. "I've seen you do some pretty rotten things for money, Hank, but this is unbelievable. But then, there never was enough money in this town to satisfy you, was there?"

"We'll need to take your statement, Mr. Jarvis," Cord said. "Perhaps you'll want to call your lawyer and ask him to meet us at the sheriff's office?"

The life seemed to have drained out of Henry and he looked old and completely defeated as he sank into his chair.

"You tell me now, Hank," Horace demanded, staring at his longtime friend and partner. "Tell me how you could do it. How you could kill two people and put Georgia and Mr. Jamison through such hell. Would you have killed them, too, to keep them quiet?" He growled and started toward the man in the chair, but Cord stopped him.

Henry shook his head. He didn't look up, as if he were too ashamed to meet Horace's eyes, and Georgia's.

"I'm sorry," he muttered. "I never meant for it to go so far, or for anyone to get hurt. Other people were involved—powerful people who would stop at nothing to—"

"Perhaps you'd better save any statements you might have until your lawyer is present, Mr. Jarvis," Cord said.

In a moment, Hagan was back. He handcuffed the man behind the desk and led him from the office as Horace stood dumbfounded, gazing from the man he trusted like a brother, then back to his own daughter.

Cord hadn't moved from Georgia's side and she could feel him squeezing her tightly around the waist. Quickly he explained to Horace about the land-buying deal they had uncovered and how Bob and Sheila might have been involved.

"We'll want a statement from you, too, Mr. Blake," Cord said. "Since you are the bank owner and since most of the acquisitions were funneled through this bank."

"You came here expecting to arrest me, too, didn't you?" he said, his look incredulous.

"I fully expected that, yes, sir," Cord said.

"Why, you arrogant son of a—"

"Daddy," Georgia said. "Did you know about any of this? Did you know all along about the state highway project and that Bob's and Sheila's deaths weren't really a murder/suicide?"

Horace Blake looked old as he stared into his daughter's eyes.

"How can you ask me that?"

"Did you, Daddy?" she said, pulling away from Cord. "I know about the money you offered Cord to leave Farmington. And I know about all the lies you told, how you manipulated Bob and his family and everyone else to get what you wanted. It's not beyond anyone's imagination to think that Horace Blake would stoop to anything to get what he wants, is it? Why wouldn't I ask it?"

"I knew about the project," he said, unable to meet her eyes. "But that was all. I swear I had no idea that any of this was going on."

"I hope you're telling the truth," Georgia whispered. "For your sake and for Mother's."

"How can you doubt...?" Horace clenched his jaws and stared hard at Georgia, returning to his old tactics to try to convince her. "I warn you, daughter...your doubts are putting a wedge between us that can never be removed," he said, his voice low with warning.

"No, Daddy," she whispered. "You did that a long time ago when you tried to run my life for me. When you almost ruined the best chance at happiness I ever had." She was crying now, tears running unchecked down her cheeks. "I loved Cord, Daddy. He's a good, decent man—the kind of man I'd think a father would like to see his daughter fall in love with and marry. But not you, not the almighty Horace Blake," she whispered. "For you, the defining criteria for a husband has always been money and power."

"These are words you can never take back," he said warningly.

"I should have said them long ago," she said, her voice soft and choked with tears.

"You're not thinking straight," her father said, his voice carrying a pleading tone now as he realized that she meant every word. "Once this is all over and settled, you'll feel differently. You have obligations here, Georgia, honey. Do you really think you'll be happy settled down in a trite little suburb somewhere . . . married to a man who's never been your social equal?"

"Don't you say that!" she lashed out. "Don't you ever say that to me again."

"Georgia," he said, trying a more pleading tone. "You are my only daughter. The family fortune will be all yours one day and with that comes responsibility—"

"I don't want it," she shouted. "Don't you understand anything I'm trying to say? I will never feel differently and I don't give a damn about my responsibilities toward the family fortune. I'm going to think about myself now, Daddy. For once in my life, I'm looking out for Georgia Ashley and what makes her happy. And Cord is the man who makes me happy. I love him," she said, crying. "I've always loved him and no matter what you say or how you feel, he's the one man I will love for the rest of my life.''

Her father's expression was one of disbelief as she turned in Cord's arms and looked up at him. He was so still and quiet.

"Can we go back to the cabin?" she whispered, her words muffled against Cord's chest.

Cord didn't say anything, but wordlessly led Georgia from the office. He didn't glance back and he didn't make any explanations to Hagan. Georgia was still crying when they walked back to her car, and if everyone in the street looked at them with odd, curious expressions, she didn't notice. All she wanted was to get out of this town, away from the looks and the comments, away from the dirtiness of what had happened here and away from the look on her father's face when she had walked out.

She didn't have to say anything. Cord got in on the driver's side and she handed him the keys. His look was tender and understanding as he started the car and pulled quickly away from the curb and headed out of town.

Georgia was lost in her thoughts. And yet she couldn't help being fully aware of Cord beside her. Or the fact that she had proclaimed her love for him to her father. Neither of them had spoken of that, but she could feel the tension between them now, the need to have all the emotion, all their feelings, out in the open. And yet, she sensed that Cord, like herself, wanted to wait until they reached the cabin.

It was quiet on the mountain and a light breeze stirred the tops of the pine trees. As they got out of the car, a formation of cranes flew above them, singing out their garbled calls, and looking more like geese than long-legged cranes. Normally, Georgia would have stopped to watch, would have been delighted at such a show of nature.

But now she turned to Cord and reached out her hand toward him.

Instead of going inside the cabin, Cord pulled her toward the stand of trees and they walked along a narrow trail that led through the piney woods. When they came to the edge of the mountain and the Georgia farmlands lay below them, Georgia murmured her quiet approval and turned to find Cord watching her, his gaze intense and questioning.

"I was wrong about your father," he said. She could see how hard it was for him to admit it. "But I'm glad I was wrong and that he wasn't the man."

"I don't want to talk about him now. I want to talk about us, Cord. You and me. You and I have been tiptoeing around this subject ever since you came back."

"Did you mean what you said back there?" he asked, his voice quiet.

"About loving you?" She smiled at him, her heart in her eyes. "With all my heart."

He pulled her into his arms then, sighing as he rested his chin against her hair. He gazed off into the distance as he spoke.

"I think today was the first time I truly believed it in both my heart and mind."

"That I would love you?" she asked, pulling away so she could see into his blue eyes.

"I've pushed you away. Since coming back to Farmington, I know I've done everything in my power to convince you that it couldn't work between us again."

Georgia waited, holding her breath as she watched the expression on his handsome face.

"It can," she whispered.

Cord nodded.

"But I meant what I said before. That I haven't changed much. I'm still stubborn and overbearing sometimes. When

I know I'm right, sometimes I go headlong into destroying whatever barriers are in the way."

"I love that about you," she said. "Cord Jamison, if you're trying to discourage me, I might as well tell you, you'll never succeed. I love everything about you—your stubbornness, your honesty, even your bossiness when I know you're trying to take care of me." She hesitated and smiled up at him as she continued. "The way you make love," she whispered, loving it when she made him groan with desire.

He turned her toward him, touching her face with his fingers and looking straight into her eyes. "Even if I intend taking you away from Farmington for good? Even if I will never live here and will never accept anything from your father?"

"What was it you told me not so long ago? Never say never?" she teased. "You know, you and my father are more alike than either of you know. You might both change your mind when our first son is born."

Cord closed his eyes and groaned again, but there was a smile on his face.

"Damn, woman, you sure know how to get to me, don't you?"

"I hope so," she murmured. "I truly hope so. And I don't care about leaving Farmington. Wherever you go, that's where I want to go."

He frowned and his teeth chewed at his lower lip.

"Atlanta?" he asked as if he still couldn't believe it. "A small house in a middle-class suburb. No memberships to the country club, no credit cards to exclusive salons or boutiques."

"I don't care," she said again.

"My profession is dangerous, hon. And I'll be gone a lot of the time—sometimes when you need me the most."

"Cord," she scolded. "I love you and I'd die if anything happened to you. But after what we've just been through, do you really think I would turn away from you, from what we have, because I'm afraid? Do you?"

"No," he whispered. "Not anymore. When I came back this time, I could see how strong you were, how courageous. I could see it in your eyes, hear it in your voice when you talked. But you seemed so sad . . . so alone, and I didn't want to add to that."

Georgia couldn't help the tears that filled her eyes. His look was so tender, so concerned. And it was all for her.

"I thought it was because of all that had happened," he said. "Your unhappy marriage . . ."

"It was . . . partly," she said, her voice husky. "But I realized after you came back that I've never been truly happy since the day you left, ten years ago. Then you stormed back into my life and forced me to see every day what I was missing. And I couldn't hide from that fact any longer—not with you here every day to remind me."

His mouth stopped her words and when he pulled away, both of them were breathless, clinging to each other as they stood facing the wind that swept across the mountain.

"God, I love you," he whispered.

"Oh, Cord . . . I thought you would never say it. I've waited so long to hear those words."

"I've always loved you," he said, kissing her mouth, her eyes, and letting his lips trail down to her ear. "But I was just so afraid of losing you again. This time it's forever, baby."

"Amen," she said, sighing.

"We're starting over. Right here . . . right now," he whispered.

"It's what I want . . . more than anything in the world. You're what I want."

"Let's go back to the cabin," Cord said, his look intense and impatient. "And if one damned GBI vehicle comes up that road, I'm going to shoot the tires out."

"Gimme a gun," she said, laughing. "I'll help you."

They were still laughing as they hurried back toward the cabin.

Cord stopped for a moment, pointing to the sleek black motorcycle parked beside the little red sports car.

"No wonder your parents worried about you," he said, shaking his head with amusement. "That's not exactly a white steed. And I'm hardly a knight in shining armor."

"You are to me," she said. "You always were and you always will be."

He pulled her against him, kissing her thoroughly before swinging her up into his arms and carrying her up the steps.

* * * * *

MILLION DOLLAR SWEEPSTAKES (III)

No purchase necessary. To enter, follow the directions published. Method of entry may vary. For eligibility, entries must be received no later than March 31, 1996. No liability is assumed for printing errors, lost, late or misdirected entries. Odds of winning are determined by the number of eligible entries distributed and received. Prizewinners will be determined no later than June 30, 1996.

Sweepstakes open to residents of the U.S. (except Puerto Rico), Canada, Europe and Taiwan who are 18 years of age or older. All applicable laws and regulations apply. Sweepstakes offer void wherever prohibited by law. Values of all prizes are in U.S. currency. This sweepstakes is presented by Torstar Corp., its subsidiaries and affiliates, in conjunction with book, merchandise and/or product offerings. For a copy of the Official Rules governing this sweepstakes offer, send a self-addressed, stamped envelope (WA residents need not affix return postage) to: MILLION DOLLAR SWEEPSTAKES (III) Rules, P.O. Box 4573, Blair, NE 68009, USA.

SWP-S1294

Maura Seger's
BELLE HAVEN

Four books. Four generations. Four indomitable females.

You met the Belle Haven women who started it all in Harlequin Historicals. Now meet descendant Nora Delaney in the emotional contemporary conclusion to the Belle Haven saga:

THE SURRENDER OF NORA

When Nora's inheritance brings her home to Belle Haven, she finds more than she bargained for. Deadly accidents prove someone wants her out of town—fast. But the real problem is the prime suspect—handsome Hamilton Fletcher. His quiet smile awakens the passion all Belle Haven women are famous for. But does he want her heart...or her life?

Don't miss THE SURRENDER OF NORA
Silhouette Intimate Moments #617
Available in January!

HUSBAND: SOME ASSEMBLY REQUIRED
Marie Ferrarella
(SE #931, January)

Murphy Pendleton's act of bravery landed him in the hospital—and right back in Shawna Saunders's life. She'd lost her heart to him before—and now this dashing real-life hero was just too tempting to resist. He could be the Mr. Right Shawna was waiting for....

Don't miss
HUSBAND: SOME ASSEMBLY REQUIRED,
by Marie Ferrarella,
available in January!

She's friend, wife, mother—she's you! And beside each Special Woman stands a wonderfully *special* man. It's a celebration of our heroines— and the men who become part of their lives.

EXTRA! EXTRA! READ ALL ABOUT...
MORE ROMANCE
MORE SUSPENSE
MORE INTIMATE MOMENTS

Join us in February 1995 when Silhouette Intimate Moments introduces the first title in a whole new program: INTIMATE MOMENTS EXTRA. These breakthrough, innovative novels by your favorite category writers will come out every few months, beginning with Karen Leabo's *Into Thin Air*, IM #619.

Pregnant teenagers had been disappearing without a trace, and Detectives Caroline Triece and Austin Lomax were called in for heavy-duty damage control...because now the missing girls were turning up dead.

In May, Merline Lovelace offers *Night of the Jaguar*, and other INTIMATE MOMENTS EXTRA novels will follow throughout 1995, only in—

INTIMATE MOMENTS®
™ Silhouette®

Blood *is* thicker than water....

A FAMILY CIRCLE—
a new Silhouette Intimate Moments
miniseries by

Dallas Schulze

They had a bond so strong, *nothing* could tear
them apart!

Read the first book in December 1994:
A VERY CONVENIENT MARRIAGE,
Intimate Moments #608

Nikki Beauvisage desperately needed her inheritance money to keep her day-care center
open—but she had to be married to get it.
And Sam Walker needed money for his niece's
surgery. So Nikki and Sam struck a deal. And as
the sparks flew, these two got a whole lot more
than they bargained for!

Don't miss the next installment of
A FAMILY CIRCLE
coming in the summer of 1995—
only from Silhouette Intimate Moments.

Silhouette® ...where passion lives.

SILHOUETTE... Where Passion Lives

Don't miss these Silhouette favorites by some of our most
distinguished authors! And now you can receive a discount by
ordering two or more titles!

SD#05786	QUICKSAND by Jennifer Greene	$2.89	☐
SD#05795	DEREK by Leslie Guccione	$2.99	☐
SD#05818	NOT JUST ANOTHER PERFECT WIFE by Robin Elliott	$2.99	☐
IM#07505	HELL ON WHEELS by Naomi Horton	$3.50	☐
IM#07514	FIRE ON THE MOUNTAIN by Marion Smith Collins	$3.50	☐
IM#07559	KEEPER by Patricia Gardner Evans	$3.50	☐
SSE#09879	LOVING AND GIVING by Gina Ferris	$3.50	☐
SSE#09892	BABY IN THE MIDDLE by Marie Ferrarella	$3.50 U.S. $3.99 CAN.	☐ ☐
SSE#09902	SEDUCED BY INNOCENCE by Lucy Gordon	$3.50 U.S. $3.99 CAN.	☐ ☐
SR#08952	INSTANT FATHER by Lucy Gordon	$2.75	☐
SR#08984	AUNT CONNIE'S WEDDING by Marie Ferrarella	$2.75	☐
SR#08990	JILTED by Joleen Daniels	$2.75	☐

(limited quantities available on certain titles)

AMOUNT	$_____
DEDUCT: 10% DISCOUNT FOR 2+ BOOKS	$_____
POSTAGE & HANDLING ($1.00 for one book, 50¢ for each additional)	$_____
APPLICABLE TAXES*	$_____
TOTAL PAYABLE (check or money order—please do not send cash)	$_____

To order, complete this form and send it, along with a check or money order
for the total above, payable to Silhouette Books, to: **In the U.S.:** 3010 Walden
Avenue, P.O. Box 9077, Buffalo, NY 14269-9077; **In Canada:** P.O. Box 636,
Fort Erie, Ontario, L2A 5X3.

Name:_____

Address:_____City:_____

State/Prov.:_____ Zip/Postal Code:_____

*New York residents remit applicable sales taxes.
Canadian residents remit applicable GST and provincial taxes.   SBACK-DF

Silhouette®
TM